I0785218

CYNTHIA HICKEY

ii

High Stakes

Cynthia Hickey

The Sheriff of Misty Hollow, Book 7

Copyright © 2025 Cynthia Hickey
Published by: Winged Publications

This book is a work of fiction. Names, characters, places, and incidents are the product of the author's imagination and are used fictitiously. Any resemblance to actual events, locales, or persons, living or dead, is coincidental.

No part of this book may be copied or distributed without the author's consent.

No AI Training: Without in any way limiting the author's [and publisher's] exclusive rights under copyright, any use of this publication to "train" generative artificial intelligence (AI) technologies to generate text is expressly prohibited.

All rights reserved.

ISBN-13:978-1-968792-45-9

To my readers who want to stay in Misty Hollow. I appreciate you.

Chapter One

A pounding on her front door jerked Sheriff Shea Callahan from the first deep sleep she'd had in what felt like months. The sound was urgent, desperate, completely unlike the typical middle-of-the-night emergencies she'd grown accustomed to handling. Her hand fumbled across the nightstand in the darkness, fingers closing around her Glock's familiar grip as thunder rumbled in the distance. The digital clock glowed an accusatory 4:00 AM. Nothing good came of someone knocking at that time of the morning.

Her German Shepherd, Heidi, growled low in her throat and bounded from the bed where she'd been sleeping peacefully at Shea's feet just moments before. The dog's hackles rose as another round of frantic pounding echoed through the small house, accompanied by the sound of rain hammering against the roof with spring storm intensity.

"Shea!" Someone screamed her name with raw

panic that made her pulse spike. "Shea, please open the door."

Recognition flooded through her even before she reached the entryway. "Becky?"

Shea rushed to the front door and yanked it open, her gun hand hanging ready at her side despite knowing the voice belonged to someone she trusted. The sight that greeted her was alarming. Becky Miller, her best friend since their college days at the University of Arkansas, stood on the porch, absolutely drenched from the downpour. Her typically styled blonde hair hung in wet strings around a face gone pale with fear and exhaustion. Dark circles under her eyes suggested she hadn't slept in days, and her hands trembled as she clutched a leather oversized bag against her soaked jacket. A small overnight bag sat at her feet.

Becky shoved her way into the house without waiting for an invitation, bringing with her the smell of rain. "I need your help." Her voice broke on the last word. She swiped wet hair out of her face with shaking fingers. "Can I have a towel, please? I'm dripping all over your floor."

"Oh, yes, of course." Shea set her weapon carefully on the hall table and rushed to the linen closet down the hallway, her mind already racing through possibilities for what could have driven Becky to make the three-hour drive from Little Rock to Misty Hollow in the middle of a thunderstorm. She returned with two fluffy towels and thrust them into her friend's trembling hands. "Let me make some coffee. You look frozen."

"No, I'll make it," Becky insisted, following Shea into the modest kitchen while attempting to towel-dry her hair with one hand. A puddle formed on the tile floor beneath her, but neither woman seemed to notice or care. "You can practically walk on that motor oil you call coffee."

Despite the tension crackling through the room, Shea grinned at the familiar joke that dated back to their freshman dorm days. "And you can barely call what you make coffee. It's more like flavored hot water with delusions of grandeur."

Becky managed a weak laugh that didn't quite reach her eyes. "Let's make our own then. Deal?"

"Deal." Shea pulled two mugs from the cabinet while Becky located the coffee maker. "Nice cabin. Very modern."

"Thanks. I've renovated since I bought the place."

They worked in companionable silence for a few minutes, moving around each other with the practiced coordination of old friends who'd once shared a cramped apartment and later, a terrifying experience in an isolated cabin that none of them talked about much anymore.

The coffee maker gurgled and hissed, filling the kitchen with its rich aroma. Rain continued to pound against the windows, punctuated by occasional thunder that made Heidi's ears flatten against her head. The dog had positioned herself between the two women, her intelligent eyes tracking every movement as if sensing the emotional undercurrent flowing through the room.

"I've heard about all the trouble this town has been having." Becky broke the silence as she watched coffee slowly drip into the pot. "The Christmas fires made national news. I'd hoped that after everything we went through together in that cabin...well, that things would be easier for you. That you'd found some peace here."

Shea busied herself pulling cream and sugar from the refrigerator, using the mundane task to avoid meeting Becky's concerned gaze. "I've got a great deputy to watch my back, and my Heidi girl here keeps me company on the quiet nights. I'm doing okay, really."

"Liar." Becky's voice carried affection mixed with exasperation. "I know you, Shea Callahan. I bet you've collected new scars since we last saw each other, haven't you? Both the kind that show and the kind that don't."

The observation cut closer to the truth than Shea wanted to acknowledge. Her right palm still carried the angry red mark from smothering Gary Richardson's match, and her dreams still occasionally featured burning buildings and trapped children. But discussing her own trauma wasn't why Becky had driven through a storm in the middle of the night.

"How is everyone from our group?" Shea deflected, carrying her steaming mug to the kitchen table. "I feel like I've lost touch with too many people lately."

Becky followed with her own coffee, which she'd doctored with so much cream it resembled café au lait more than actual coffee. She settled into the chair across from Shea with a heavy sigh. "Everyone's moving forward with their lives, I suppose. Getting married, having babies, climbing career ladders. We don't talk as much as we should—life gets in the way. I've been wanting to plan another girls' weekend, something like we used to do every year, but..." She trailed off, staring into her mug as if it held answers to unspoken questions.

"But what?"

"I'm not sure they'd come. Not after what happened during the last one. That cabin, everything that went wrong...I think some of them would rather pretend it never happened."

"They'd come if you planned it," Shea said with more confidence than she felt. They'd all made a pact during their senior year of college to take annual trips together and to be there for each other during major life events. Marriage, babies, job changes—they'd promised to show up. But life had a way of eroding even the most sincere intentions, and that particular girls' weekend two years ago had tested friendships in ways none of them had anticipated.

The silence stretched between them, comfortable despite the underlying tension. Outside, the storm showed no signs of abating, rain driving against the windows in waves that sounded like handfuls of gravel being thrown at the glass.

Finally, Becky looked up from her coffee, and Shea could see tears well in her friend's eyes. "I guess you know that my divorce from Bill is final now. Has been for about six months."

Shea nodded, reaching across the scarred wooden table to place her hand over Becky's cold fingers. "It was already in process when I visited last year. I'm so sorry. I know how hard you tried to make it work." She squeezed gently. "What's wrong, Becky? What's really going on?"

The dam broke. Tears spilled down Becky's cheeks as her carefully maintained composure crumbled. "Bill and Ryan spent last weekend together. It was Bill's scheduled visitation, nothing unusual. He picked Ryan up from baseball practice on Friday afternoon like he was supposed to." Her voice cracked, and she took a shuddering breath before continuing. "Shea, I haven't heard from either one of them since. It's been four days. Four days of calling, texting, driving to his apartment, calling hospitals, calling his work—nothing. They've just vanished."

Shea felt her law enforcement instincts kick in immediately, pushing aside the friend and embracing the sheriff. "Have you been to his house? His apartment in Memphis?"

"Of course I have. Multiple times." Becky's voice

carried a edge of frustration. "Everything looked normal, at least from what I could see through the windows. At first I thought..." She paused, shame coloring her features. "I thought maybe he was trying to get back at me for threatening to withhold his parental visits. I know, I know—" She raised her free hand before Shea could speak. "I know I can't legally do that because of the court orders. But he makes me so angry sometimes with his irresponsibility, and I say things I don't mean."

"What did he do that made you threaten that?" Shea kept her voice neutral, professional, even as her mind began cataloging possibilities and courses of action.

Becky's fingers tightened around her coffee mug until her knuckles went white. "Ryan told me that sometimes when he stays with his father, Bill leaves him alone for hours at a time. Just...disappears without explanation. Ryan is ten years old, Shea. He shouldn't be left alone in an apartment complex in Memphis for hours while his father does God knows what."

"What about Jaime?" Shea asked, referring to Becky's younger son, who was seven.

"He's with my parents in Little Rock, thank God. Bill tries to spend individual time with each boy once a month—one-on-one bonding or whatever the family therapist recommended. It usually works out fine, but this time..." Her voice rose with barely controlled panic. "Something has happened, Shea! I know it in my bones.

This isn't Bill being petty or irresponsible. Something is wrong."

Shea leaned back in her chair, forcing herself to think through the situation logically rather than react emotionally to her friend's distress. What did she know about Bill Miller? Disturbingly little. During her visits to Little Rock over the years, he'd rarely been around. Becky had always made excuses—working late, out with friends, running errands—but now those absences have taken on potentially darker significance.

"Maybe they went on an impromptu trip?" she suggested, though the explanation felt weak even as she offered it. "Fishing or camping? Trying to reconnect without the usual distractions?"

Becky gave a short, bitter laugh that held no humor. "Bill isn't the outdoorsy type, trust me. The man considers it roughing it if the hotel doesn't have room service. And he'd never, ever go camping voluntarily."

"Then what do you think happened?"

"Since you're my boys' godmother, I came to you instead of going to the Memphis police," Becky said, dodging the question as she studied Shea's face intently. "I need someone I can trust completely."

Shea tilted her head, confused by the logic. "Why me specifically? The Memphis PD has resources I don't have, jurisdiction I don't have. Why not start with them?"

"Because I found this." Becky jumped up abruptly, nearly knocking over her chair in her haste.

She grabbed her leather bag from where she'd dropped it by the door and pulled out a sheaf of papers that had been protected in a plastic folder. Returning to the table, she spread them out in front of Shea with trembling hands. "Bank statements for an account I had no idea Bill maintained. When I couldn't reach him, when his phone kept going straight to voicemail, and I didn't find either of them at his apartment, I let myself in with the emergency key he'd given me for Ryan's sake."

"You went through his personal files?" Shea asked carefully, already anticipating the legal complications that might arise.

"His office filing cabinet was unlocked, almost like he wanted someone to find this." Becky pointed at the bank statements with a shaking finger. "I wasn't snooping, Shea. I was terrified. And when I found these..." She took a deep, shuddering breath, visibly trying to compose herself. "Bill used to have a gambling problem. A serious one. We almost lost our house because of it before Ryan was born. He swore he'd stopped, went to Gamblers Anonymous meetings religiously for two years. I thought the meetings were working, that he'd beaten the addiction." Her voice dropped to barely above a whisper. "But now I doubt he ever went to those meetings at all. I think he's been gambling this whole time, and I think he's gotten himself into serious trouble and dragged my son right along with him."

Shea studied the bank statements, noting the pattern of large deposits followed by even larger withdrawals. The account showed a balance of negative twelve thousand dollars. Overdraft fees had been piling up for months. "Becky, there could be any number of explanations for—"

"He left his car keys and wallet, Shea." Becky's features hardened. "Both were sitting on his kitchen counter. His car is still in the garage. His wallet had his driver's license, credit cards, everything. What kind of explanation covers that? Why don't you believe me?"

"I do believe you." Shea stood and moved to the sink with her empty mug. She needed a moment to think, to process what she was hearing through both the filter of friendship and professional law enforcement training. "I'm a sheriff, Becky. We ask questions, even uncomfortable ones. It's how we gather information and build a complete picture of what might have happened."

She turned to face her friend, leaning against the counter and crossing her arms. "Will you help me find out what happened to them? To my son and his father?"

"Yes." The answer came without hesitation, despite the voice in the back of Shea's mind warning her about jurisdiction issues and the complications of investigating outside Misty Hollow. "I've got some vacation time I can take. We'll find Bill and Ryan, I promise. But I need you to be completely honest with me about everything, starting now. Where did Bill usually gamble?"

Becky's shoulders slumped with relief so profoundly she looked like she might collapse. "I don't know exactly. When I started suspecting he'd relapsed, I asked him directly several times. He always denied it, got angry at me for not trusting him, turned it around so I felt guilty for doubting his recovery." She wrapped her arms around herself. "God, I should have pushed harder. I should have demanded proof, followed him, something."

"Don't do that to yourself," Shea said gently. "Addiction makes people excellent liars, especially to the people they love. This isn't your fault."

Becky's eyes filled with tears again. "My coffee's gone cold while we've been talking."

"Want another cup?"

"No, I couldn't stomach this one anyway. Too much nervous energy. I'll warm it up in the microwave."

"Actually, I'm supposed to meet Deputy Bolton at Lucy's Diner in about an hour," Shea said, glancing at the clock and realizing dawn would be breaking soon. "It's something we do most mornings before our shift officially starts. You can get genuinely good coffee there, plus some of Lucy's famous biscuits and gravy. Give me fifteen minutes to shower and get dressed. If you want to change into dry clothes, there's another bathroom down the hall, and I can loan you something from my closet."

Shea quickly moved to feed Heidi, measuring out

the dog's breakfast with mechanical precision while her mind raced through what needed to happen next. She opened the back door to let Heidi out into the fenced yard despite the rain, knowing the German Shepherd needed her morning routine regardless of the weather or human drama unfolding inside.

"Is there something between you and this deputy?" Becky asked with the ghost of a smile, her first genuine expression of anything other than fear since arriving. "The way you said his name...there's history there."

Heat rose in her cheeks despite her best efforts at maintaining a neutral expression. "It's...complicated."

"That's what people say when they're in a relationship but don't want to admit it yet," Becky had been Shea's friend long enough to read between the lines. "Does he know it's complicated, or does he think it's simple?"

"I'm going to take that shower now." Shea headed toward the master bathroom. "Help yourself to anything in the kitchen. There are clean towels in the linen closet, and you can borrow clothes from my room. The second drawer has jeans and sweaters."

As hot water cascaded over her in the shower minutes later, Shea allowed herself a moment to process everything Becky had revealed. A missing child and his potentially troubled father. Gambling debts that could be connected to dangerous people. Her best friend was desperate for help and willing to drive three hours through a storm to ask for it. No way would Shea not help her.

And underneath it all, the uncomfortable truth that she was about to involve Trevor Bolton in an investigation that would take them far outside their jurisdiction and potentially into dangerous territory neither of them had experience navigating. Once Trevor found out where Shea planned on going, how she would spend her vacation, he'd insist on coming with her.

But Ryan was her godson. Becky was family in all the ways that mattered. And if Shea had learned anything from the Christmas arson case, it was that sometimes doing the right thing meant bending the rules.

She just hoped that this time, bending wouldn't turn into breaking.

Chapter Two

Deputy Trevor Bolton sat in his usual booth when they entered Lucy's Diner, glancing up from the morning newspaper with obvious surprise. His coffee mug paused halfway to his lips as he took in the unexpected third member of their morning routine. "We've got company."

"Trevor Bolton, meet Becky Miller." Shea slid into the booth across from him and gestured for Becky to follow. The vinyl seat squeaked slightly under their weight, familiar and comfortable after countless morning meetings in this exact spot.

"It's nice to meet you." Trevor set down his mug and thrust out his hand. "I've heard quite a lot about you over the past few months."

"Probably about how bossy and opinionated I am." Becky managed a ghost of a smile as she returned his handshake, though the expression didn't quite reach her tired eyes. "Shea and I have known each other since college. She's had plenty of time to collect stories."

"Actually, she mostly talks about how you were the only person brave enough to tell her when she was being too stubborn for her own good," Trevor replied with an easy grin that earned him an eye roll from Shea.

"Are you here visiting Misty Hollow?" Trevor asked casually, though Shea could see the wheels already turning behind his observant gaze. He'd noticed Becky's exhausted appearance, the tension in her shoulders, the way her fingers gripped her leather bag like a lifeline. After working together through the arson case, they'd developed an almost telepathic ability to read each other's signals.

"No, I've come to—" Becky began.

"Let's have breakfast first, okay?" Shea interrupted, opening her menu with perhaps more force than necessary. She needed a few more minutes to figure out how to present this situation to Trevor. "They have the best biscuits and chocolate gravy here. Lucy makes them from her grandmother's recipe."

Trevor and Becky both shot her questioning looks—Trevor's tinged with knowing amusement, Becky's with confusion—before obediently turning their attention back to their menus. The morning crowd hummed around them with the comfortable noise of a small-town breakfast spot: silverware clinking against plates, quiet conversations punctuated by laughter, the hiss of the griddle from the kitchen.

Lucy, the diner's owner, appeared at their table, order pad in hand and her customary warm smile firmly in place despite the early hour. "Morning, Sheriff, Deputy. And who's this lovely lady?"

"Lucy, this is my friend Becky from Little Rock," Shea said. "Becky, Lucy owns this place and makes the best comfort food in three counties."

"Don't let her flatter you into giving her extra bacon," Lucy warned with a wink. "I don't do much cooking anymore. Haven't for years. We've got an excellent chef. What can I get you folks?"

"I'll have the breakfast special," Trevor said without looking at the menu. Two eggs over easy, two buttermilk pancakes, two slices of thick-cut bacon, and a mountain of perfectly seasoned hash browns.

Shea shook her head slightly, wondering where he possibly put all that food. The man ate like a teenager but maintained the physique of someone who took fitness seriously—which, she supposed, he did. One more thing to appreciate about Deputy Bolton, though she kept that thought to herself.

"I'll have the same as Shea," Becky said, closing her menu and placing a hand protectively over the leather bag positioned between them on the bench seat. "Whatever the sheriff orders is probably good."

"Biscuits and chocolate gravy," Shea confirmed. "And keep the coffee coming, Lucy. It's going to be that kind of morning."

"Isn't it always?" Lucy collected their menus with practiced efficiency and disappeared toward the kitchen, calling out their orders to the chef with the precision of someone who'd been doing it for thirty years.

The three of them made stilted small talk while waiting for their food to arrive, dancing carefully around the elephant in the room. Becky asked polite questions about Misty Hollow's size and character. Trevor answered some of the questions directed his way, describing his own journey from the Memphis Police Academy to a small-town deputy, but Shea could feel his curiosity growing with each passing minute.

Becky added more sugar to her coffee. "I'm always curious about workplace dynamics in law enforcement. It must be interesting being the only two officers in such a small department."

"We're not the only two," Shea corrected. "There's Deputy Butler, who works evenings, and Deputy Hudson, who covers nights with another deputy. Plus, we have a part-time dispatcher and administrative coordinator."

"But you two work together most closely," Becky pressed, a hint of her old teasing nature breaking through the anxiety. "Shea's told me about some of your cases together. The Christmas arson situation sounded terrifying."

Trevor's expression sobered at the memory. "It was intense. Sheriff Callahan saved a lot of lives during that investigation, including mine." His eyes met Shea's across the table, holding a warmth that made her stomach do an uncomfortable flip. "We make a good team."

"Just a good team?" Becky asked, eyebrows raised, clearly not satisfied with the diplomatic answer.

"Becky," Shea warned.

"What? I'm just asking about your working relationship," Becky said innocently, though her smile suggested she knew exactly what buttons she was pushing.

Lucy's arrival with their breakfast provided a merciful interruption. Plates laden with food were distributed with efficient grace, steam rising from the fresh biscuits and perfectly cooked eggs. The chocolate gravy, a Southern delicacy that Shea had introduced Trevor to months ago, looked rich and inviting.

They ate in relative silence for a few minutes, the tension easing slightly as hunger was satisfied. Shea noticed that Becky only picked at her food, pushing hash browns around her plate without eating much. The worry clearly ate at her more than any appetite could overcome.

Trevor cleaned his plate with impressive speed and pushed it aside, fixing Becky with the direct gaze that made him effective in interrogations. "Okay. Now tell me what's really going on. Shea doesn't usually bring friends to our morning meetings, which means something's wrong. And you've got the look of someone who hasn't slept properly in days."

Becky glanced at Shea, who nodded encouragement. Taking a deep breath, Becky launched into the same explanation she'd given Shea earlier that morning—the missed pickup, the days of silence, Bill's history with gambling, the discovered bank statements showing financial chaos.

Trevor listened without interrupting. His expression grew more serious as the story unfolded. When Becky finished, he was quiet for a long moment.

"What else?" he finally asked, his tone gentle but probing. "There has to be more evidence that leads you to believe something nefarious is happening. A guy being out of contact for four days, while concerning, doesn't necessarily indicate foul play. Especially with someone who has addiction issues. They might go on a bender, lose track of time."

"There is more." Becky reached into her leather bag and extracted a laptop, setting it carefully on the table and opening it to reveal a screen filled with browser history and saved documents. "Over the last few months, I've been noticing some concerning signs that Bill might still be actively involved in gambling. Phone calls where he'd abruptly leave the room when he came to pick up the boys for visitation. He'd become overly defensive when I asked simple questions about his day or his finances—way more reactive than the situation warranted. And at least three times in the past two months, he's asked to borrow money to 'tide him over until payday.'"

She pulled up a series of screenshots showing text message conversations. "Look at these. He's vague about where he's going and who he's seeing. And these search history entries from his laptop..." She scrolled through lists of gambling websites, online poker rooms, and sports betting forums. "This isn't the browser history of someone who's successfully maintaining recovery from gambling addiction."

Trevor leaned forward to study the screen, his brow furrowed in concentration. "This definitely points to active gambling, especially combined with his previous addiction history and the financial records you found. Where exactly does your ex-husband live?"

"Memphis, in an apartment complex near the university," Becky said, her eyes filling with unshed tears. "A decent neighborhood, nothing fancy but safe. I really thought he'd stopped gambling after the divorce. He swore on the boys' lives that he was done with it, that losing our family had been the wake-up call he needed." Her voice cracked. "I wanted so badly to believe him."

"Most people do," Trevor said kindly. "Addiction is complicated, and the people struggling with it become very skilled at hiding it from the people they care about."

He folded his hands on the table and looked directly at Shea. "When are we leaving?"

She tilted her head, though she wasn't surprised by his immediate offer of support. Trevor had proven time and again during the arson case that he was the kind of partner who showed up when things got difficult. "We?"

"Sure." He said it as if there were no question. "Deputy Butler can handle things here in Misty Hollow. The town's been quiet lately, knock on wood. And if something urgent does come up, I can head back right away. Memphis is only a few hours' drive."

"I'm going too." Becky squared her shoulders with determination that reminded Shea of their college days when Becky had faced down a predatory professor on behalf of a frightened freshman. "Jaime is safe and happy with my parents for a few more days. They're planning to take him to the zoo and the children's museum. He'll barely notice I'm gone."

"This could get dangerous, Becky." Shea's sheriff instincts kicked into overdrive. "If Bill really has gotten involved with serious gamblers, the kind of people who loan money at predatory rates, then we might be walking into a situation that requires more than just asking questions."

"I've been in danger before and came through just fine." Becky lifted her chin with stubborn pride. She glanced at Trevor. "Shea probably didn't tell you about the cabin incident from a few years ago. Let's just say that I'm not completely helpless when things go sideways."

"That was different—" Shea began.

"Besides, I'll be with the kick-ass sheriff of Misty Hollow and her trusty deputy," Becky interrupted, managing a thin-lipped smile. "Nothing bad can happen to me with that kind of protection, right?"

"That's what I've been saying for the past two years." Trevor laughed, though Shea caught the slight edge of concern in his voice. "Yes, she told me about the time in the cabin. Once Sheriff Callahan sets her mind to something or someone, the bad guy honestly doesn't stand a chance. She's like a dog with a bone."

"That's quite enough." Shea's face flushed. She was extremely aware of Becky watching their interaction with the knowing eyes of someone who'd been her best friend for over a decade.

Trevor had the audacity to wink at her, which only made the flush deepen and spread down her neck. He pulled out his wallet and tossed a couple of twenty-dollar bills on the table. "Breakfast is on me. When do we leave for Memphis?"

"First thing tomorrow morning." Shea's mind already spun through the logistics. "That gives me today to clear my schedule and brief Deputy Butler on covering for us."

She slid out of the booth, Becky following suit. "I need to take care of some administrative things at the office this morning. Becky, feel free to make yourself at home back at my place. I'll have Deputy Hudson drive you—he should be finishing up his night shift right about now."

"That sounds wonderful," Becky said, relief evident in her voice. "I'll take a proper nap since I drove straight through the night to get here. Will your dog be okay with me being there alone?"

"Heidi's as docile as a bunny unless I tell her otherwise," Shea assured her friend. "She'll probably sleep on the couch near you and snore loud enough to wake the dead. See you at dinner tonight?"

"Definitely. I'll even cook something if you have ingredients in that sparse refrigerator of yours."

"I grocery shop," Shea protested. "Sometimes."

"You have condiments and takeout containers," Becky countered with a knowing look. "That's not the same thing as having actual food. I'll make a list, and you can stop at the store on your way home."

After arranging for Deputy Hudson to drive Becky back to her house, Shea headed to the sheriff's office with Trevor following in his own vehicle. The morning sun burned off the last of the storm clouds, revealing a crisp spring day that would have been perfect for a quiet shift filled with paperwork and maybe a few traffic stops.

Instead, she was about to dive into an investigation that technically wasn't hers, in a city where she had no jurisdiction, looking for a man who might or might not be in serious danger. All to help her best friend and godson.

How long did it take to find out whether someone was involved in something over their head? A few days? A week? She had no way of knowing, but she'd have to prepare for the possibility that this could take a while.

At her desk, Shea worked through the tasks required to hand off her responsibilities. She reviewed daily reports from the previous week, looking for any patterns or concerns that Deputy Butler should be aware of. She met with the night-duty deputies before sending them home, briefing them on her upcoming absence and making sure they had her cell number for emergencies.

Thank God that, for a few weeks at least, Misty Hollow had returned to being the sleepy town she'd initially hoped for when accepting the sheriff position. No major crimes, no serial arsonists, just the usual small-town issues—noise complaints, minor traffic violations, the occasional domestic disturbance that got resolved with conversation rather than arrests.

She signed off on warrants for minor infractions: a teenager who'd been caught shoplifting at the hardware store, a driver who'd accumulated too many speeding tickets, and who needed to appear before a judge. She checked her email to see whether she was required to be in court within the next week. Thankfully, nothing pressing appeared on the docket.

The staff time sheets needed review and approval, payroll needed to be submitted, and there were budget reports that Mayor Ferguson had been requesting for the past two weeks. Shea lost herself in the administrative details, grateful for the mindless work that kept her from obsessing about all the ways this Memphis investigation could go wrong.

Trevor appeared in her doorway around noon, carrying two wrapped sandwiches from the deli down the street. "Figured you'd forget to eat lunch if someone didn't remind you."

"Thanks." She gratefully accepted the turkey club, realizing she was actually hungry despite the large breakfast. "I briefed Deputy Butler, but did you have a chance to speak to him, too?"

"Yep. Also called my buddy Jack, who's still with the Memphis PD. Gave him a heads-up that we'd be in his territory for a few days, asked if he could provide any unofficial assistance if we need it."

"That was smart thinking." Shea unwrapped her sandwich, appreciating once again how well Trevor anticipated needs before she even articulated them. "What did you tell him about why we're coming?"

"Just that it's a favor for a friend, a missing persons situation that might overlap with gambling debts. He said to call him directly if we need anything—records searches, local knowledge, whatever."

They ate in companionable silence for a few minutes before Trevor spoke again. "You okay with all this? Going outside our jurisdiction, potentially sticking our noses into something that could blow up?"

"Ryan is my godson," Shea said. "Becky is family. What else can I do?"

"You could have told her to go to Memphis PD, let them handle it through official channels."

"I could have," Shea acknowledged. "But she came to me for a reason. She trusts me to actually care about finding them, not just file a report and add it to a pile of other cases."

Trevor nodded slowly. "Just want to make sure you've thought through the implications. If this goes sideways, it could affect your position here. Mayor Ferguson already had concerns after the arson case about you operating outside normal protocols."

"I know." Shea met his eyes steadily. "I'm going anyway. But I won't ask you to risk your career, too, Trevor. You can stay here and—"

"I'm going," he interrupted firmly. "We're partners, Shea. That means something to me. If you're going to potentially get in trouble, I'm going to be right there getting in trouble with you."

The weight of his words settled between them, carrying implications that went far beyond professional partnership. Shea felt that familiar flutter in her stomach that appeared whenever Trevor looked at her that particular way.

"Okay then," she finally said. "Partners."

"Partners," he agreed with a smile that made her heart skip.

Tomorrow they'd drive to Memphis and dive into whatever mess Bill Miller had created. Tonight, she'd have dinner with her best friend and try to project confidence she didn't entirely feel.

But for this moment, sitting in her office with

half-eaten sandwiches and a partner who had her back no matter what, Shea felt like maybe, just maybe, they could pull this off.

Chapter Three

After the six-hour drive from Misty Hollow to Memphis, Shea wanted nothing more than a hot meal and an even hotter shower before tackling Bill Miller's apartment. The interstate had been surprisingly crowded for a weekday afternoon, and by the time they crossed into Tennessee, her shoulders ached from tension and her eyes felt gritty from staring at the highway.

Rather than attempt to take Heidi into a restaurant where the German Shepherd's presence would draw attention and questions, they checked into a modest motel on the outskirts of Memphis proper. The Riverside Inn wasn't fancy, but it was clean and affordable, with adjoining rooms that would work perfectly for their purposes.

"I'll order Chinese takeout." Trevor pulled out his phone to search for nearby restaurants. "There's a place about two miles from here that has excellent reviews. You want your usual—sweet and sour chicken with fried rice?"

"You know me too well," Shea replied with a tired smile. "Add some crab rangoon if they have it."

Becky excused herself to the room she'd be sharing with Shea, explaining she needed to call her parents and check on Jaime before they got started with the investigation. Shea and Trevor settled into his adjoining room to wait for the food delivery, the door between their rooms left open so they could hear if Becky needed anything.

The room was standard motel fare with two double beds with thin floral bedspreads, a television bolted to a dresser, and a small table with two chairs positioned by the window overlooking the parking lot. Heidi immediately claimed one of the beds, circling three times before settling with a contented sigh.

"What's going through your mind?" Trevor glanced up from his phone, where he'd been reviewing the food order one more time. He knew her well enough by now to recognize when she was processing rather than just being quiet.

Shea moved to the window and stared out at the parking lot where their three vehicles sat in a row—her truck, Trevor's SUV, and Becky's sedan. "I'm hoping that Bill and Ryan are both okay. That there's some reasonable explanation for all of this that doesn't involve danger." She turned to face him. "A ten-year-old child shouldn't have to suffer because of his father's bad decisions and poor impulse control."

"Kids rarely deserve what they get caught up in," Trevor agreed quietly. "But they end up paying the price anyway."

Shea glanced toward the open door connecting to the other room, lowering her voice. "Becky must be absolutely torn apart inside. Wanting to be with Jaime because he's safe and needs his mother, but needing to find Ryan because he might be in danger. I can't even imagine the fear of not knowing where your child is, whether they're hurt or scared or..." She couldn't finish the thought.

"We'll find him," Trevor said with conviction. "And we'll bring him home safe."

Before Shea could respond, Becky appeared in the doorway between their rooms. Her eyes were red-rimmed from crying, but her expression was determined. "I need to go back home to Little Rock after I let you into Bill's apartment tomorrow morning. Jaime is really missing me, and my parents are getting overwhelmed trying to keep him entertained and not asking too many questions about where his brother is."

"Go tonight if you need to." Shea stood from where she'd perched on the edge of the bed. "Trevor and I can handle the investigation here. We'll keep you updated on everything we find."

Becky shook her head firmly. "No. I know Bill's place better than either of you. I'll show you around the apartment, point out anything that seems unusual, then drive back home. That's why I insisted on bringing my own car rather than having all of us drive together. I figured it would come to you needing to stay here longer than I could."

A sharp knock on the door made all three of them jump. Trevor moved to peer through the security peephole before opening the door to accept their food delivery from a young man in a baseball cap. He paid cash, added a generous tip, then spread the array of white takeout boxes across the small table by the window.

The aroma of Chinese food filled the room—ginger, garlic, soy sauce, and the distinctive smell of hot oil. Despite her exhaustion and worry, Shea's stomach growled.

"Promise me that you'll give me daily reports," Becky said as she claimed one of the chairs and immediately grabbed the container of chow mein. "I want to know everything you're doing, everywhere you go, everything you find. No matter how insignificant it seems."

"I promise." Shea reached across the table to squeeze her friend's hand. "You trust me." It wasn't phrased as a question because she already knew the answer. She and her college friends had been through enough together to build trust that ran deeper than blood. Shea didn't trust anyone as much as she trusted those women, except Trevor.

"Of course I trust you," Becky said softly. "More than anyone else in the world right now. That's why I drove to Misty Hollow instead of going to the Memphis police." She picked at her noodles without eating much. "What if some of them are on the payroll of whatever organization Bill got involved with? What if reporting this officially just tips off the wrong people and puts Ryan in even more danger?" She gave a self-deprecating laugh. "I guess I watch too many crime dramas on television."

"Hey, corruption happens more often than people think," Trevor interjected. "It's not paranoid to be cautious about who you trust when serious money is involved. You were smart to come to someone you know personally."

They mainly ate in silence after that, each lost in their own thoughts about what tomorrow might bring. Shea noticed that Becky barely touched her food, pushing it around in her container rather than consuming it. The worry clearly ate at her more than any hunger could overcome.

~

The next morning dawned gray and humid, with the kind of oppressive heat that promised a miserable summer day ahead. They met in the parking lot at eight AM sharp, having agreed the night before to get an early start before Memphis traffic became too congested.

Shea and Trevor followed Becky's sedan through the city streets, navigating toward a middle-class apartment complex situated near the Missippi River.

The building was nicer than Shea had expected. A brick construction with well-maintained landscaping, covered parking, and a security entrance that required either a code or resident approval for entry.

Becky used her key fob to access the gate, and they followed her into the complex. She led them to a second-floor unit. The morning air already felt thick and heavy as they climbed the exterior stairs to Bill's apartment.

"This is it." Becky's hand trembled as she inserted a key into the deadbolt. "I've had an emergency key since the divorce was finalized. You know. In case something happened to Bill while the boys were here, and I needed to get inside quickly."

She pushed open the door, took one step inside, and gasped. Her hand flew to her mouth as she stumbled backward into Shea.

Shea immediately stepped in front of her friend, her hand automatically reaching for the Glock holstered at her hip. Trevor moved to her right, his own weapon drawn as they entered the apartment. Heidi growled low in her throat beside Shea, the dog's entire body tense and alert.

The apartment had been completely ransacked. It was immediately clear that this wasn't the scene of a simple burglary or random vandalism. This was the work of professionals searching for something specific. Sofa cushions had been slashed open, their stuffing pulled out and scattered across the floor like synthetic snow. Kitchen cabinets hung open, their contents dumped carelessly. Drawers had been yanked from dressers and emptied, leaving a debris field of clothing, papers, and personal items.

Books had been pulled from shelves and their pages ripped out. Pictures had been torn from walls, their frames smashed to check if anything had been hidden behind them. Even the air vents had been unscrewed and removed, lying on the floor with their filters exposed.

"It wasn't like this the last time I was here," Becky whispered from behind Shea, her voice shaking with shock. "It was neat, organized. Bill was always particular about keeping things tidy."

"Everyone, stay alert," Shea commanded. "Trevor, I'll check the bedroom and bathroom."

After confirming the apartment was clear of intruders, Shea holstered her weapon and pulled two sets of latex gloves from her jacket pocket. She handed one pair to Becky and kept the other for herself. Trevor produced his own gloves from his duty belt.

"Search carefully for any clues," Shea instructed. "Take photos of anything that seems out of place or potentially significant. Document everything before you touch it."

"The whole apartment seems out of place," Becky muttered, but she pulled out her cell phone and began photographing the destruction. Her hands shook as she captured images of her ex-husband's violated living space.

Shea headed toward the bedroom, leaving the front section of the apartment to Becky and Trevor. The bedroom showed the same pattern of destruction. The bedding lay in a tangled heap on the floor. Someone had taken a knife or similar blade to the mattress, slicing it open and pulling out handfuls of foam and springs in their search. The box spring had received similar treatment.

Dresser drawers were overturned, closet shelves emptied, and even the ceiling fan had been disassembled and left hanging precariously from its mount. This wasn't simple vandalism or the work of desperate junkies looking for quick cash to steal. This was a professional search conducted by people who knew how to be thorough.

She moved to the small bathroom, noting that the shower curtain had been torn down and the medicine cabinet emptied. Towels lay in wet heaps, suggesting someone had even checked the toilet tank for hidden items. But as she scanned the small space, one thing caught her attention.

The overhead exhaust vent remained untouched, its cover still secured with screws that showed no signs of tampering. In a search this thorough, that seemed like an odd oversight.

Unless it wasn't an oversight. Unless whoever ransacked this place had been interrupted before finishing their search.

Shea carefully stepped onto the closed toilet seat, using her pocketknife to remove the screws holding the vent cover in place. The metal grate came free with a faint grinding sound. She reached into the dark opening, her fingers encountering plastic.

Carefully, she extracted a plastic Ziplock baggie containing a cheap burner phone and a business card. The phone's screen was cracked but still functional. She pressed the power button and waited for it to boot up.

The last text message on the screen made her blood run cold: "Time's up. Settling the debt now."

The business card was printed on thick, expensive stock with gold foil lettering: "Lucky Dragon Casino Cruise - Where Fortune Smiles on the Bold."

"Found something," she called out, stepping down from the toilet and returning to the main living area.

"So did I," Trevor responded from near the demolished sofa.

Shea entered the front room to find Trevor holding up a small baseball glove. Child-sized, worn from use, with "Ryan M." written in permanent marker on the leather palm. In his other hand was a tiny scrap of blue fabric, no bigger than a postage stamp.

Becky stood frozen beside him, one hand pressed over her mouth as tears streamed down her cheeks.

"That's Ryan's glove," she managed to say, her words catching on a sob. "And that blue fabric is from his Little League uniform. The Riverside Ravens. He was so proud of making the team this year."

Trevor's expression was grim as he indicated the space behind the toppled sofa. "I think Bill tried to hide Ryan back here when trouble came to the door. There's a nail sticking out from the sofa frame. That's where I found this fabric caught. The glove was wedged between the wall and the couch." He met Shea's eyes. "This wasn't a surprise attack. Bill knew trouble was coming and tried to protect his son."

"Maybe one of the neighbors saw something." Shea's mind already raced through investigative next steps. "People in apartment complexes notice things—strange vehicles, unfamiliar faces, unusual activity."

She turned to Becky, who looked as if she might collapse under the emotional weight of seeing her son's possessions in this context. "I need you to stay here and keep looking around. See if you can tell what's missing—documents, valuables, anything that might explain what they were searching for. But don't go anywhere else in the building and keep your phone on. Trevor and I will canvas the neighbors."

Becky nodded and began the heartbreaking task of sorting through her ex-husband's destroyed belongings, trying to restore some semblance of order while determining what was absent.

The neighbor to the left of Bill's apartment didn't answer despite Shea knocking three times. Either they weren't home or were deliberately avoiding involvement.

When they knocked on the door to the right side

of Bill's unit, a middle-aged woman answered almost immediately. She was probably in her fifties, wearing reading glasses on a chain and holding a paperback romance novel with her finger marking her place.

"Yes? Can I help you?" Her tone was pleasant but cautious.

Shea pulled out her badge and introduced both herself and Trevor. "We're investigating a situation involving your neighbor, Bill Miller. Did you know him?"

The woman's expression shifted to concern. "A bit. Bill kept to himself mostly, very quiet and polite when we'd pass in the hallway. He'd come and go at odd hours sometimes. I'd hear his door opening late at night or very early in the morning. But he was never loud or disruptive. Is he in some kind of trouble?"

"We're trying to locate him." Shea didn't want to reveal too much. "Have you seen anyone suspicious lurking around the building? Maybe watching his apartment or asking questions about him?"

The woman nodded immediately, her eyes widening. "As a matter of fact, yes. I saw a dark SUV, black or maybe very dark blue, parked out front in the visitor lot for a couple of days last week. It just sat there with someone inside; I never saw anyone get out. They were just sitting and watching, like they were waiting for someone specific." She frowned. "I almost called the apartment office to report it, but then it was gone and I figured I was being paranoid."

"How many people were in the vehicle?" Trevor asked.

"At least two that I could see. A driver and passenger. Both men, I think, though it was hard to tell through the tinted windows. They were there during the day mostly, from mid-morning until early evening."

"When did you last see Bill?" Shea pulled out her notebook.

"Maybe a week ago? He was leaving with his sons. Cute kids. One always carried a baseball glove. They looked happy together." Her face fell. "Why all these questions? Has something happened to Bill and his boys?"

"He hasn't been home in several days," Shea said vaguely. "We're just doing a welfare check. If you think of anything else that might help us locate him, please call me directly." She handed over one of her business cards with the information for the Misty Hollow Sheriff's Department.

The woman accepted the card, studying it with apparent confusion. "You're from Arkansas? That's unusual for a welfare check in Tennessee."

"Bill has connections to our area," Shea improvised. "We're assisting with inquiries."

As they turned to head back to Bill's apartment, Heidi's sharp bark echoed through the corridor. The German Shepherd's alert bark—the one she used when she'd found something significant.

Shea and Trevor hurried back to find Heidi

standing rigid in the center of the living room, barking insistently at a specific spot on the floor near the demolished entertainment center. Becky knelt nearby, trying to pry up a floor tile with a butter knife.

"Let me." Trevor took the knife from Becky and examined the tile Heidi had identified. He used his own pocketknife to work around the edges, prying carefully until the ceramic tile came loose with a soft crack.

Shea leaned over his shoulder as Trevor removed the tile, revealing a hollow space in the concrete beneath. A shoe box sat nestled in the cavity, its lid slightly askew.

She glanced at Trevor, who nodded. He carefully lifted the box from its hiding place and set it on the cleared space of the coffee table. With deliberate slowness, he lifted the cardboard lid.

Inside were neat stacks of hundred-dollar bills, bound with rubber bands. Even from a quick visual estimate, Shea could tell there had to be at least thirty thousand dollars in cash.

"Sweet mercy," Becky breathed. "Where did Bill get that kind of money?"

That was the question Shea was wondering. Because people didn't hide that much cash under floor tiles unless it came from somewhere they couldn't explain. And based on the burner phone's message about "settling the debt" and the business card for a casino cruise, she was starting to get a terrible feeling about exactly what kind of trouble Bill Miller had gotten himself into. Something that now involved his ten-year-old son.

Chapter Four

Shea hung up her cell phone and turned from the motel window to face Trevor, who'd been patiently working on his laptop while she made a series of calls to contacts in various agencies. "My FBI contact—Agent Sarah Martinez—said they've had suspicions for over two years that the Lucky Dragon is operating as a front for a major gambling syndicate. But no one has been able to gather enough solid evidence to prove it yet. Every time they get close, something falls apart or a witness disappears."

"Sounds like they have protection at multiple levels." Trevor looked up from his computer screen. "Let's pay the Dragon a personal visit then. Sometimes you need boots on the ground rather than surveillance from a distance."

"That's going to be considerably harder than you might think." Shea moved to sit on the edge of the bed. "The boat moves constantly up and down the Mississippi River, never staying in one place long enough for law enforcement to establish proper jurisdiction or build a case. It's deliberately designed to exploit legal gray areas between states."

She drummed her fingers against her thigh. "There are also credible allegations of money laundering and loan-sharking operations being run through the casino. The syndicate uses gambling as a cover for its real business. Lending money at predatory rates to desperate gamblers and then collecting through whatever means necessary."

"Okay." Trevor closed his laptop and crossed his arms, his expression shifting into the focused intensity that appeared when he was formulating a plan. "So, we go undercover as wealthy tourists. Mr. and Mrs. Harrison. Successful business owners from Little Rock who are looking for entertainment and high-stakes gambling." He glanced at Heidi, dozed on the other bed. "Mrs. Harrison has a certified service dog for anxiety and personal protection. We'll rent one of their luxury staterooms. Does this ship have those, or is it more of a day cruise operation?"

"According to the website, they have several tiers of accommodations ranging from basic cabins to full suites," Shea confirmed, pulling up the information on her own phone. "The top-tier suites run about five thousand dollars per night and include private dining, concierge service, and access to exclusive high-stakes gaming rooms."

Trevor's eyebrows rose. "That's our target then.

The high rollers get access to areas regular gamblers never see. If Bill got involved with something serious, it would be in those private rooms where the real money changes hands."

"We'll need convincing identification," Shea pointed out. "Background stories, credit cards in our cover names, the right clothes and accessories. These people cater to genuinely wealthy clients. They'll spot fakes immediately."

"I can handle the documentation," Trevor assured her. "I still have contacts from my time with Memphis PD who specialize in undercover operations. They can create legends that will hold up under casual scrutiny—employment history, social media presence, credit reports, the whole package." He paused, then added with a slight grin, "I'll also handle booking our stateroom while you take care of whatever shopping you'll need to do."

His eyes held that particular warmth that always made her stomach flutter. "It'll be fun pretending to be married to the most beautiful woman in the state of Arkansas."

Heat flooded Shea's face, and she ducked her head to avoid his gaze. She'd never get used to the way his voice deepened slightly when he looked at her like that, or how his eyes seemed to darken with an emotion she wasn't quite ready to name. "Ready to go on a ship, Heidi?" she asked, deflecting her own reaction by addressing the dog.

Heidi huffed dramatically and rested her head on her paws without even opening her eyes.

Shea laughed despite her nervousness. "I'll take that as a definitive no."

The next two days passed in a blur of preparation. Trevor's contacts came through with impeccable documentation—driver's licenses, credit cards, even a fabricated social media history showing the Harrisons as successful real estate developers with properties across the South. Shea spent an uncomfortable afternoon shopping for the kind of clothes a wealthy woman would wear on a luxury casino cruise, spending more on a single outfit than she typically spent on clothes in six months.

~

Two days later, a sleek black limousine dropped them off at the Memphis dock where the Lucky Dragon was moored. The riverboat was far more impressive than Shea had anticipated. A massive three-deck vessel that gleamed white in the afternoon sun, its decorative paddle wheel slowly turning even while docked. Red and gold dragons were painted along the hull, their serpentine bodies coiling artistically around windows and railings.

Two young men in crisp white uniforms rushed forward to collect their expensive leather luggage— another prop purchased specifically for this operation. A woman in her mid-twenties wearing a burgundy blazer with the Lucky Dragon logo embroidered in gold thread bustled toward them with a professional smile.

"Welcome to the Lucky Dragon," she announced cheerfully. "We hope you enjoy your stay with us and find fortune smiling on your ventures." Her gaze dropped to Heidi, and her smile faltered slightly. "We don't really have anywhere designated for animals to... well, to relieve themselves. Our standard policy is—"

Shea channeled every wealthy, entitled woman she'd ever encountered during her years in law enforcement and lifted her chin with practiced arrogance. "I'm quite certain you have housekeeping staff who can handle any necessary cleanup. My service animal goes where I go." She brushed past the girl without waiting for a response, doing her best to project the kind of casual dismissiveness that came from never being told no. "Come along, Heidi."

The casino's reception area was breathtaking—all polished marble and brass fixtures, with crystal chandeliers casting prismatic light across plush carpeting. Everything screamed money and sophistication, clearly designed to make wealthy patrons feel comfortable parting with their cash.

The woman caught up quickly, her professional composure restored. "Of course, Mrs. Harrison. I apologize for any confusion. I'm Amy Barker, and I'm here to serve you in any capacity during your stay. Would you like a tour of the facilities? I can show you the restaurants, spa, gaming rooms, and other amenities."

Shea met Trevor's gaze briefly, recognizing this as an opportunity to reconnoiter without raising suspicion. "Yes, that would be lovely. Don't you think so, darling?"

"Absolutely," Trevor agreed smoothly, slipping naturally into the role of doting husband. "We'd like to get our bearings before diving into the evening's entertainment."

"Wonderful." Amy gestured elegantly toward a grand staircase. "Your luggage will be delivered to your suite while we tour, and you'll find everything prepared to your specifications. Here are your key cards." She handed each of them a sleek black card embossed with gold dragons. "These function not only as your room keys but also as charge cards. You can use them throughout the ship—spa services, dining, shopping, and of course, at the gaming tables. Everything will be billed to your account and settled when you disembark."

Shea gave what she hoped was an appropriately pleased smile and linked her arm through Trevor's as they followed Amy through the ship's impressive interior. She kept her expression interested but slightly bored, the way someone who'd seen many luxury venues might look, while her trained eyes catalogued security cameras, emergency exits, and potential points of vulnerability.

Amy guided them through multiple restaurants. A formal dining room with white tablecloths and a dress code, a casual buffet with international cuisine, and an exclusive chef's table that required reservations. They passed a spa that would rival any five-star resort, a small theater showing recent films, and eventually arrived at what Amy called "the nerve center" of the operation.

When they stepped through double doors into what appeared to be the captain's administrative offices, Shea's attention immediately focused on a wall covered with photographs. The display was labeled "Restricted Patrons" in discreet lettering.

While Amy chatted with Trevor about the ship's history and safety protocols, Shea drifted toward the wall, pretending casual interest. Her eyes scanned methodically across rows of photos showing individuals banned from the casino. Most were presumably caught cheating or causing disturbances.

Bill Miller's photograph appeared in the third position of the second row. The image showed a man in his late thirties with thinning brown hair and tired eyes, his expression somewhere between defiant and defeated. Shea's heart rate spiked with the confirmation that Bill had definitely been here, had been deeply involved enough to warrant a ban.

She continued scanning the other photos, committing faces to memory while maintaining her cover as someone merely browsing out of idle curiosity. Several faces showed the distinctive marks of serious gamblers—haunted eyes, hollow cheeks, the desperate look of addiction.

A door on the side of the office suddenly opened, and two men emerged in conversation. Both wore expensive suits that spoke of authority and money.

"Ah, Mr. and Mrs. Harrison!" Amy's voice took on added enthusiasm. "Perfect timing. This is Victor Swanson, our casino manager, and Marcus Wade, our head of security. You'll likely see them frequently during your stay."

Victor Swanson was perhaps fifty, with silver hair impeccably styled and a smile that didn't quite reach his calculating eyes. He moved with the smooth confidence of someone accustomed to reading people and exploiting their weaknesses.

Marcus Wade presented a stark contrast. Early forties, broad-shouldered and intimidating, with the alert posture of someone trained in tactical operations. His handshake was measured but firm, and his eyes performed a rapid assessment that Shea recognized from her own law enforcement training. This man had been military or police at some point.

Trevor stepped forward with the easy charm he'd perfected for this role, shaking each man's hand. "Pleasure to meet you both. Impressive operation you're running here. Is there a safe available where we can secure valuables? My wife brought some rather expensive jewelry for the formal dinners."

"Each suite is equipped with a personal safe," Marcus Wade replied, his voice carrying a faint

Southern accent. "You can program your own access code and clear it when you depart. We take security very seriously aboard the Lucky Dragon and strive to make every guest's experience as comfortable and worry-free as possible."

His gaze dropped to Heidi, and a small frown creased his forehead, but he said nothing about the dog's presence. Shea got the distinct impression that Marcus Wade noticed everything but chose his battles carefully.

"We pride ourselves on discretion and excellent service," Victor Swanson added smoothly. "If you need anything at all during your stay, special accommodations, private gaming arrangements, or restaurant reservations, please don't hesitate to contact me directly." He produced an embossed business card and presented it with a slight bow.

After several more minutes of polite conversation and completion of the tour, Amy escorted them to their suite on the top deck. The accommodations were stunning. Easily larger than Shea's entire house, with a living area, separate bedroom, marble bathroom with a soaking tub, and a private balcony overlooking the river.

Once Amy departed, promising to check on them later, Shea immediately kicked off the designer heels that had been pinching her feet for the past hour. "I am absolutely not cut out for high fashion," she groaned, wiggling her toes on the plush carpet. "Give me my boots and jeans any day."

"You look beautiful." Trevor hung up the suit jacket that had probably cost him several weeks' salary. He'd insisted on paying for his own clothes, refusing to let this operation deplete Becky's resources more than necessary. "But I understand the sentiment. Designer clothes look great but rarely prioritize comfort."

Shea padded barefoot to the bathroom and found a crystal bowl, which she filled with water for Heidi. The dog lapped gratefully before settling on the cool tile floor with a contented sigh.

"Rest for a bit." Trevor loosened his tie. "Then we'll make our first appearance at the poker tables this evening. Gambling is the primary reason people come on this ship, and we need to establish ourselves as legitimate high rollers before we can start asking questions."

"I'm a fairly competent hand at poker." Shea settled into an overstuffed armchair that probably cost more than her monthly salary. "My college friends and I used to have regular game nights. Becky usually won, but I held my own."

The mention of Becky brought a sobering reminder of why they were here. Her friend had insisted on providing fifty thousand dollars in cash for their gambling stake. Money from an inheritance that was supposed to fund her retirement. "I have no better use for this money than getting my son back safely," Becky had said firmly when Shea protested. "Find Ryan, and whatever you spend will be worth every penny."

After a short rest, Shea grimaced as she squeezed her feet back into the stylish black pumps. "I noticed an onboard boutique during our tour. Maybe I can find a better pair of shoes that won't leave me hobbling by the end of the evening."

"Wouldn't expensive sneakers be sufficient?" Trevor asked. "Plenty of wealthy people wear designer athletic shoes."

"Not to a formal casino." She shook her head. "It would look odd and potentially raise questions. But maybe some elegant flats that won't destroy my feet."

The boutique did indeed carry several options, and Shea purchased three pairs of designer flats in different colors—black, navy, and a deep burgundy. She wanted to throw the torture-device heels directly into the Mississippi River, but restrained herself. Despite Becky's insistence that money wasn't an issue, wasting resources felt wrong.

Several hours later, hand firmly gripping Heidi's leather leash, Shea entered the main casino floor at Trevor's side. The sensory assault was immediate. Flashing lights from hundreds of slot machines, the electronic symphony of bells and chimes, cheers and groans from winners and losers, and the underlying current of desperate hope that permeated all gambling establishments.

The air was thick with cigarette smoke despite supposed ventilation systems, mixed with expensive perfumes and the distinctive smell of money changing hands. Cocktail waitresses in short dresses circulated with trays of complimentary drinks, keeping the gamblers lubricated and their judgment impaired.

They located a poker table in the high-stakes section with two vacant seats. The minimum buy-in placard read $500. Shea motioned for Heidi to lie quietly at her feet, then extracted a substantial stack of chips from the designer clutch she carried. Another prop that had cost an absurd amount. She slid the chips forward to cover the five-hundred-dollar starting bid for the first hand and let her carefully practiced poker face slide into place.

The other players at the table were an interesting mix. An older gentleman in an expensive suit who reeked of old money, a younger tech-bro type wearing designer casual wear, and two middle-aged women who appeared to be sisters based on their similar features and constant whispered communication.

An hour later, Shea's pile of chips had grown to over one-hundred-thousand dollars. She'd played conservatively at first, establishing a pattern of careful betting before gradually becoming more aggressive as she read her opponents' tells. The older gentleman was predictable, the tech-bro overconfident, and the sisters too timid to capitalize on good hands.

Trevor had quit playing several hands ago, having lost about fifteen thousand in a deliberately mediocre performance. Now he stood behind her chair, playing the role of supportive husband content to let his talented wife dominate the table.

He leaned over in an intimate gesture, his lips close enough to her ear that his breath tickled her skin. "You're attracting serious attention," he murmured, his hand resting on her shoulder in what would look like affection but was actually a warning.

Shea raised her gaze from her cards and met the sharp, assessing stare of Marcus Wade, who stood near the bar with arms crossed and his attention focused entirely on their table. His expression was unreadable, but the intensity of his observation suggested he was calculating something—running probabilities, looking for patterns, determining if she was counting cards or cheating in some other way.

Her gaze slid past the security chief to a striking woman in a red dress who had positioned herself near one of the private gaming room entrances. The woman was perhaps thirty-five, with dark hair pulled into an elegant chignon and the kind of beauty that came from excellent bone structure and expensive maintenance. But it was her eyes that caught Shea's attention. Sharp, intelligent, and currently fixed on Shea with obvious interest.

Their gazes locked for a brief moment. The woman gave an almost imperceptible nod of acknowledgment, then turned and disappeared through a doorway marked "Private Gaming - By Invitation Only."

The message was clear: someone wanted to talk to Mrs. Harrison, and it wouldn't be a casual conversation about gambling strategy.

Chapter Five

One hundred and fifteen thousand dollars in chips now sat in front of Shea—more than twice her annual salary as sheriff. The other players at the table eyed her with a mixture of respect, resentment, and in one case, barely concealed suspicion.

"I think I'll take a break." She gathered the chips into the designer clutch that somehow managed to hold them despite its impractical size. "Stretch my legs, perhaps get some fresh air on the deck."

"Good idea, darling." Trevor offered his arm. "You've had quite the winning streak. Best to quit while you're ahead."

They made their way through the crowded casino floor, Heidi walking obediently at Shea's side despite the overwhelming sensory assault of lights, sounds, and the press of humanity. Shea noticed Marcus Wade's gaze following their progress across the room, his expression unreadable but his attention unwavering.

As they approached the door leading to the exterior promenade deck, a woman materialized from the shadows near a decorative pillar. It was the striking woman in the red dress from earlier. Up close, she was even more impressive, with sharp cheekbones, intelligent dark eyes that missed nothing, and an aura of controlled danger that Shea recognized from her own profession.

"Mrs. Harrison." The woman's voice carried a hint of an accent that Shea couldn't quite place. Spanish, possibly, or Portuguese. "Congratulations on your exceptional run at the tables. You play with remarkable skill."

"Thank you." Shea shifted into her wealthy persona. "I've always enjoyed games of strategy."

"I'm Elena Reyes." The woman extended a perfectly manicured hand. "I work as a consultant for the casino, helping to identify patterns and... irregularities in gameplay." Her smile was sharp and knowing. "Though I must say, there's nothing irregular about your technique. You're simply very good at reading people."

"Years of practice in business negotiations." The lie rolled smoothly off Shea's tongue. "You learn to spot tells when millions of dollars are at stake."

"Indeed." Elena's gaze shifted briefly to Trevor, then back to Shea with an intensity that felt like being examined under a microscope. "Real estate development, isn't it? Your husband mentioned you have properties across Arkansas and Tennessee."

Warning bells rang in Shea's mind. Elena knew their cover story. Had she been researching them, or was she making conversation based on what they'd told Amy during the tour?

"That's correct," Trevor interjected. "Commercial and residential. We've been fortunate with our investments."

"Fortune favors the bold." Elena's lips curved into a smile. "Though I've always believed that careful observation and strategic thinking trump luck every time. Wouldn't you agree, Mrs. Harrison?"

The emphasis on Shea's cover name felt deliberate, almost mocking. This woman knew something. The question was what, and whether she posed a threat to their investigation.

"I'd say both play a role," Shea replied carefully. "The key is knowing when to bet big and when to fold."

"Wise words." Elena glanced around the casino floor before lowering her voice slightly. "I wonder if I might speak with you privately. I have some information that might interest someone with your particular... talents."

Every instinct Shea had developed over years in law enforcement screamed that this was a pivotal moment. Elena was offering something—information, an alliance, or possibly a trap.

"What kind of information?" Shea asked.

"The kind best not discussed in public spaces

where everyone has ears." Elena's gaze flickered toward the security cameras positioned throughout the casino. "There's a private lounge on the observation deck. Very exclusive, very quiet. Perhaps we could meet there in thirty minutes? I promise it will be worth your time."

Before Shea could respond, Elena produced an elegant card from her small evening bag and pressed it into Shea's hand. The card was simple black with silver lettering: "Elena Reyes - Private Consultant" followed by a phone number.

"Thirty minutes," Elena repeated, then turned and walked away, her red dress drawing appreciative glances as she moved through the crowd with the grace of someone comfortable in her own skin.

Shea waited until Elena disappeared before examining the card more closely. "What do you think?" she asked Trevor quietly.

"I think she knows exactly who we are and why we're here." Trevor's hand rested protectively on the small of Shea's back. "The question is whether she's part of the syndicate or something else entirely."

"Only one way to find out." Shea tucked the card into her clutch. "But I want you to do something while I'm meeting with Elena."

"Investigate the lower decks," Trevor said, following her train of thought. "Amy mentioned during the tour that the crew quarters and storage areas are restricted to guests, but she was vague about what else might be down there."

"Exactly. Bill's photo was on that banned list, which means he was involved with this casino somehow. And if there's a secondary operation like Agent Martinez suggested, something beyond the regular gambling, it would be hidden somewhere guests don't normally go."

They found a relatively private corner of the promenade deck where they could talk without being overheard. The Mississippi River stretched dark and wide around them, its surface reflecting lights from the shore and the occasional passing barge.

"Be careful," Shea said, her hand finding Trevor's. "If this syndicate is as dangerous as the FBI believes, they won't hesitate to eliminate anyone who threatens their operation."

"Same goes for you," Trevor countered. "This Elena knows we're not who we claim to be. That makes her extremely dangerous, even if she's offering to help."

"I'll have Heidi with me. She'll alert if Elena tries anything hostile." Shea glanced down at the German Shepherd, who sat attentively at her side. "And I'll be in a semi-public space. You're the one going into restricted areas where no one will hear you if things go wrong."

"I'll be fine." Trevor squeezed her hand gently. "I've talked my way out of worse situations. Besides, I'm just a wealthy tourist who got lost looking for the bathroom."

Despite the tension, Shea smiled at the cover story. "Thirty minutes. If I'm not back in the suite within an hour, assume something went wrong."

"And if I'm not back in ninety minutes, same assumption." Trevor checked his watch. "We should split up now. The longer we stand here having intense conversations, the more suspicious we look."

~

Twenty-eight minutes later, Shea pushed open the door to the observation deck lounge that Elena had indicated. The space was exactly as promised— exclusive, quiet, and currently empty except for Elena herself, who stood near the floor-to-ceiling windows with a glass of red wine in hand.

"Punctual," Elena observed with approval. "I appreciate that quality in a person."

"You said you had information," Shea replied, not bothering with social niceties. Heidi moved to position herself between Shea and Elena, the dog's training asserting itself even in this supposedly friendly meeting.

"Direct. I appreciate that too." Elena took a sip of her wine before setting it carefully on a nearby table. "Let me be frank, Sheriff Callahan. Your cover is adequate for casual scrutiny but wouldn't survive a deeper investigation. The legend your contact created is good, but not perfect."

Shea's hand drifted toward her clutch, where she'd concealed a small firearm—illegal to bring aboard, but she'd never felt comfortable being completely unarmed in dangerous situations.

"Don't." Elena raised her hands slightly. "I'm not your enemy. In fact, I'm probably the only ally you have on this boat."

"Who are you really?" Shea demanded.

"Exactly who I claimed to be—Elena Reyes, consultant. Though my employer is the Drug Enforcement Administration rather than the casino." She pulled aside the neckline of her dress slightly to reveal a small tattoo on her collarbone—a stylized eagle that Shea recognized as a DEA identifier used by deep cover operatives.

"You're DEA?" Shea's mind raced through the implications. "How long have you been undercover here?"

"Two years." Her expression hardened. "My husband was murdered by this syndicate three years ago when he tried to infiltrate their operation. I've been working my way into their inner circle ever since, gathering evidence that might actually stick in court rather than getting thrown out on technicalities."

"I'm sorry about your husband," Shea said sincerely. "But why reveal yourself to me?"

"Because you're here looking for Bill Miller and his son, Ryan. And your presence has created ripples that might destroy years of careful work if we don't coordinate." Elena moved closer, her voice dropping. "The syndicate is run by a man known only as 'The

Banker.' He never appears in person and conducts all business through intermediaries. Bill Miller got involved with them about eight months ago— when he started gambling here on the regular casino floor, ran up debts he couldn't pay."

"Let me guess," Shea interjected. "The Banker offered him a loan at predatory interest rates."

"Worse. Bill is a software engineer specializing in security systems. The Banker discovered this and offered to forgive his entire debt if Bill would use his skills for one job." Elena's expression was grim. "I don't know what the job is yet, but it's big. Important enough that they took his son as collateral to ensure his cooperation."

Shea felt her stomach drop. "Ryan's alive?"

"As of three days ago, yes. They're keeping him with several other children whose parents are also being coerced into working for the syndicate. It's a pattern they've used before. They find desperate people with useful skills, get them into debt, then force them to commit crimes by threatening their families."

"Where are they holding the children?"

"I don't know yet. That information is kept extremely compartmentalized. Only The Banker and a few trusted operatives know the location. But I'm working on finding out." Elena pulled a slim phone from her bag and showed Shea a series of photographs. "These were taken from security footage. Bill being escorted onto the boat two weeks ago. Bill working on something in the lower deck areas where the private games are held. And this—"

The final photo showed Bill leaving the casino with Marcus Wade and another man Shea didn't recognize. Bill looked haggard, his face gaunt and his eyes haunted.

"Your friend's ex-husband made a terrible mistake getting involved with these people," Elena said softly. "And now his son might pay the price for that mistake. Unless we can find a way to take down the entire operation before The Banker decides Bill has outlived his usefulness."

~

In the lower deck, Trevor moved carefully through a dimly lit corridor that smelled of diesel fuel and river water. The opulent decoration of the upper levels had given way to purely functional spaces— metal walls painted industrial gray, exposed pipes, and the constant thrum of engines that kept the massive boat moving.

He'd slipped past the restricted area sign by following a crew member through a door, then simply acting like he belonged whenever someone looked his way. The wealthy tourist persona helped. Most crew members assumed anyone in expensive clothes had permission to be wherever they were.

The corridor opened into a larger space that made Trevor stop in his tracks. This wasn't storage or crew quarters. This was a casino, but unlike anything on the upper decks. Five poker tables were arranged in the center of the room, each one surrounded by players and onlookers. But these weren't casual gamblers or even typical high rollers.

Trevor recognized criminal types when he saw them. The hard faces, the bulges of concealed weapons, the wary postures of men accustomed to violence. And the amounts being bet made the upper casino look like a church bingo game. He watched as one player casually pushed forward stacks of chips that had to represent at least half a million dollars.

"Can I help you?" A cold voice spoke from behind him.

Trevor turned to find a muscular man in a dark suit blocking his exit. The man's jacket was tailored to hide a shoulder holster, but Trevor's trained eyes spotted it anyway.

"I'm afraid I got turned around." Trevor gave an embarrassed laugh. "Looking for the restroom and took a wrong turn. This boat is a maze!"

"Guests aren't allowed in this area." The man's hand moved meaningfully toward his jacket.

"Completely understand. My apologies." Trevor gestured back toward the corridor. "If you could just point me toward the nearest—"

"Marcus should know about this." The man pulled out a radio.

Trevor's mind raced. If they brought Marcus Wade into this, their cover would be thoroughly examined. He needed to de-escalate immediately.

"Look, no need to bother your boss," Trevor pulled out his wallet and extracted a five-hundred-dollar bill. "I made a mistake, wandered where I shouldn't have. Let's just forget this happened." He held out the cash.

The security guard looked at the money, then at Trevor's expensive watch and clothes. After a moment of calculation, he pocketed the bills. "The stairs at the end of the corridor. Up two levels, then follow the signs. And next time you get lost, maybe get lost somewhere less restricted."

"Absolutely. Won't happen again." Trevor walked past the guard with deliberate casualness, his heart pounding but his expression relaxed. Only when he reached the stairs did he allow himself to breathe normally.

He'd seen enough. The lower deck operated high-stakes private games catering to criminals and avoiding oversight. But more importantly, he'd seen several doors marked with electronic locks and keypad entries. The kind of security used for valuable storage or restricted areas.

If they were holding Bill Miller somewhere on this boat, those locked rooms would be the place to look.

~

Shea returned to their suite to find Trevor already there, his jacket off and his expression troubled. They stood on the balcony where conversations couldn't be overheard, the sound of the river masking their voices from any potential listening devices.

"Elena is DEA," Shea said without preamble. "Deep cover for two years. She knows who we are and why we're here."

"The lower deck has a second casino," Trevor reported. "High-stakes private games with no limits, catering to what looked like organized crime figures. Heavy security, electronic locks on multiple doors."

They shared their discoveries, piecing together a picture that was far more complex and dangerous than they'd anticipated. This wasn't just a gambling operation. It was a criminal empire using the casino as a cover for money laundering, loan sharking, and apparently coercing skilled individuals into committing crimes by holding their children hostage.

"Elena said Bill's being forced to use his skills for some kind of job," Shea said. "Something big enough that they took Ryan as insurance. She doesn't know what the job is yet, but she's working on finding out."

"We need to find those children," Trevor said firmly. "Even if it compromises our cover or the DEA's investigation. We can't leave Ryan and the others in danger."

"Agreed." Shea looked out over the dark river, thinking of Becky waiting desperately for news in Little Rock. "But we need to be smart about this. One wrong move and everyone, Bill, Ryan, the other children, and us, end up dead."

Her phone buzzed with a text message from Elena: "Meet me tomorrow, 6 AM, observation deck. I have more information. Come alone. Your friend's ex-husband made a mistake. His son is paying the price. We can still fix this, but time is running out."

Shea showed the message to Trevor, and they both understood the unspoken warning. Whatever Bill had gotten involved in, whatever job The Banker needed him to complete, a deadline was approaching. And when that deadline passed, there would be no more reason to keep Ryan alive.

Chapter Six

The invitation arrived at their suite just after dawn, delivered by a uniformed steward who knocked discreetly and then disappeared before Shea could answer the door. She found the heavy cream-colored envelope lying on the threshold, her cover name written in elegant calligraphy across the front.

Trevor watched as Shea opened the envelope with careful fingers, extracting a single card printed on expensive stock that felt substantial in her hand.

"Mrs. Catherine Harrison," Shea read aloud, "You are cordially invited to participate in an exclusive private gaming event this evening at 9 PM. Table stakes: $50,000 entry. Limited to eight players. Business formal attire required. RSVP by noon."

She handed the card to Trevor, who examined it with the same careful attention he'd give evidence at a crime scene. "This is it. This is your way into the inner circle."

"Fifty thousand dollars is the problem," Shea

pointed out, moving to the coffee maker and starting a pot despite her churning stomach. "Good thing I won that money yesterday." She really didn't want Becky footing the entire bill of the operation.

She poured herself a cup once the coffee finished brewing, wrapping her hands around the warm ceramic as she stared out at the river. The morning sun was beginning to burn off the mist that clung to the water's surface, creating an almost ethereal landscape that felt disconnected from the dangerous game they were playing.

"What about the money we seized from Gary Richardson?" Trevor suggested, referring to the arson case that had consumed their lives just months ago. "The court ordered it forfeited to the department for investigative use. There's at least seventy thousand in that account."

Shea turned to face him, considering the implications. "That money is supposed to be used for equipment, training, and operational expenses. Using it for a poker game, even an investigative one, would raise serious questions from the town council and probably the state oversight board. Especially since we're out of our jurisdiction."

"Only if they find out about it," Trevor countered. "And only if we don't get results. If we successfully dismantle a multi-state gambling syndicate and rescue kidnapped children, I doubt anyone's going to complain about how we funded the operation."

"That's a big 'if,'" Shea said, but she was already mentally running through the logistics. "We'd need to move the money into our operational account, then withdraw it as cash without raising red flags. And we'd need to have a very solid explanation if things go sideways and I lose it all."

"You won't lose it all." Trevor's confidence in her abilities was both touching and terrifying. "You're good enough to hold your own against professionals. And remember, the goal isn't to win. It's to gather intelligence, make connections, and get closer to whoever runs this operation."

Shea took a long drink of her coffee, feeling the caffeine begin to work its magic on her tired mind. "Losing deliberately is harder than winning honestly. I'll have to play well enough to be taken seriously but not so well that I dominate the table and attract the wrong kind of attention."

"Elena can help." Trevor pulled out his phone. "If she's been undercover here for two years, she probably knows who'll be at this game and what their tells are. Any advantage we can get increases our chances of walking out of there with useful information."

A soft knock at their door made both of them freeze. Shea glanced at the clock. Barely six-thirty in the morning, earlier than room service would typically deliver breakfast. She approached the door and checked the peephole before opening it.

Elena stood in the corridor, dressed casually in

jeans and a simple blouse. A stark contrast to the elegant red dress from the previous evening. She carried three coffee cups in a cardboard tray from what appeared to be a local Memphis shop rather than the boat's service.

"May I come in?" she asked quietly. "I saw the steward deliver your invitation. We need to talk."

Once Elena was inside with the door securely closed, she handed one of the coffees to Shea and another to Trevor. "I took the liberty of getting you something better than the swill they serve on this boat. Figured you could use it after the morning you're about to have."

"You know about the game. It wasn't a question.

"I know about all the games." Elena settled into one of the suite's expensive chairs. "This particular one is special. It's a testing ground. The Banker uses these exclusive events to evaluate potential assets—people with money, connections, or skills he might want to exploit. If you perform well and show the right combination of intelligence and moral flexibility, you'll get invited deeper into the organization."

"And if I perform too well?" Shea asked.

"Then you become a threat rather than an asset, and threats don't typically leave this boat alive." Elena's blunt assessment hung in the air like smoke. "You need to be impressive but not dominant. Win some hands, lose others, show you're smart enough to be useful but not so smart you're dangerous."

Trevor sat forward, his elbows on his knees. "Who else will be at this game?"

"Six regulars and two newcomers. You'll be one of them. The regulars include Victor Swanson, whom you've met. He's decent at poker but relies too heavily on aggression. There's Amanda Channing, a real estate developer from New Orleans who launders money through property deals. Gerald Hawthorne runs a logistics company that moves everything from luxury goods to human cargo. Patricia Wade, Marcus Wade's sister, who manages several 'consulting firms' that are actually fronts for the syndicate's operations."

Elena paused to sip her own coffee. "And then there's James Rothmore."

The way she said the name made Shea's instincts prickle. "Tell me about Rothmore."

"He's the one you need to watch most carefully. Rothmore is a hedge fund manager from Chicago, at least publicly. But I've been tracking him for eighteen months, and I'm ninety percent certain he's actually The Banker himself." Elena pulled up several photos on her phone, showing a distinguished man in his fifties with silver hair and cold gray eyes. "He rarely plays in these games. He usually observes and makes assessments. If he's actually sitting at the table tonight, it means he's specifically interested in you."

"Why would The Banker be interested in me?" Shea suspected she already knew the answer.

"Because you won over a hundred thousand dollars

at the public tables yesterday with the kind of skill that suggests professional training or natural talent. Because you're supposedly wealthy enough to afford the entry fee without blinking. And because—" Elena's expression grew serious, "—I think Marcus Wade did a deeper background check on the Harrisons and found some inconsistencies. Not enough to blow your cover completely, but enough to make them curious about who you really are and what you really want."

"How much danger is she in?" Trevor frowned.

"That depends entirely on how she handles herself tonight. If she plays the role perfectly and gives them no reason to dig deeper, she'll be fine. If she makes even one mistake that confirms their suspicions..." Elena didn't need to finish the sentence.

Shea felt the weight of responsibility settling on her shoulders. "What about surveillance? Can you monitor the game somehow?"

"There's a security office where Victor reviews all the camera feeds. I can get access through my consultant position, and I can bring one guest." Elena looked at Trevor. "You'll need to stay out of sight during the actual game. We can't have the devoted husband hovering when his wife is supposed to be an independent operator, but you can watch from the security office and alert me if you spot anything suspicious."

"What about communication?" Trevor asked. "If something goes wrong, how do we coordinate?"

Elena produced two small devices that looked like expensive earrings. "Micro-transmitters disguised as jewelry. They're directional and encrypted, so the casino's standard surveillance won't detect them. Shea wears one, I wear the other, and we can communicate through a receiver Trevor will have. We won't be able to talk during the actual gameplay. Too risky. But before and after, we'll have a direct line."

Shea scrutinized the earring. The technology was impressive, clearly government-issue rather than commercially available. "How much experience do you have coordinating undercover operations?"

"More than I'd like," Elena replied with a bitter smile. "My husband and I worked together for five years before he died. I learned from the best, and I've stayed alive for two years in one of the most dangerous infiltration assignments DEA has ever attempted. I know what I'm doing, Sheriff."

The use of Shea's real title was deliberate. A reminder that Elena knew exactly who they were and held their safety in her hands.

~

By noon, Shea had confirmed her attendance at the evening's game. Trevor had arranged for fifty thousand dollars to be transferred from the seized assets account into an operational fund, then withdrawn it in cash. The money sat in the suite's safe, neatly stacked in hundred-dollar bills, representing more money than most Misty Hollow residents had seen in years.

The afternoon passed in careful preparation. Elena provided detailed profiles of each of the expected players—their gambling styles, business interests, known associates, and, most importantly, their weaknesses. Shea memorized it all, knowing that every piece of information could mean the difference between success and disaster.

At eight-thirty PM, Shea stood in front of the full-length mirror in their suite, barely recognizing herself. She wore a midnight-blue evening gown that had cost more than her monthly salary, her hair professionally styled at the boat's salon, and enough jewelry to look wealthy without being ostentatious. The micro-transmitter earring nestled invisibly among the other pieces.

"You look incredible,." Trevor stood behind her. His hands rested gently on her shoulders, and for a moment, they just looked at each other in the mirror. Two people pretending to be married who were finding it increasingly difficult to remember where the pretense ended and reality began.

"I'm scared," Shea admitted quietly, allowing herself a moment of vulnerability. "Not of the poker game or even of getting caught. I'm scared of what happens if I fail and we can't find Ryan in time."

"You won't fail," Trevor said with absolute conviction. "You're the most capable person I've ever met, Shea Callahan. Trust your instincts, play smart, and remember...we're right there with you, even if you can't see us."

A knock at the door announced the steward who would escort her to the private gaming room. Shea took a deep breath, let her poker face settle into place, and transformed herself into Catherine Harrison—wealthy, confident, and ready to gamble with the devil himself.

~

The private gaming room was located on the boat's lowest passenger deck, accessed through a series of corridors that grew progressively more exclusive. The steward led her through a final door that required both a keycard and a security code, then stepped aside to allow her entry.

The room was smaller than she'd expected, designed for intimacy rather than grandeur. A single octagonal poker table dominated the space, surrounded by eight leather chairs that probably cost more than her truck. Subtle lighting created pools of illumination over the table while leaving the rest of the room in tasteful shadow. A small bar occupied one corner, staffed by a silent bartender who moved like a ghost.

Five players had already arrived. Shea recognized Victor Swanson from their tour, along with the others Elena had described. Amanda Canning with her predatory smile, Gerald Hawthorne checking his expensive watch, Patricia Wade examining her manicured nails with studied disinterest, and a younger man Elena hadn't mentioned, who looked nervous and out of place.

And then there was James Rothmore.

He sat at the position directly across from where Shea's place card indicated she should sit, and the arrangement felt deliberate. He was exactly as Elena's photos had shown—distinguished silver hair, impeccable suit that whispered of bespoke tailoring, and eyes the color of a frozen lake. But the photos hadn't captured the intensity of his presence, the way he seemed to evaluate and calculate everything around him with predatory focus.

"Mrs. Harrison," he said as she approached, his voice cultured and smooth. "I've heard impressive things about your performance at the public tables. Please, join us."

Shea took her seat, acutely aware that she was now directly in The Banker's sightline. She placed her fifty thousand dollars in chips in front of her, accepted a glass of wine from the silent bartender, and prepared for the most important poker game of her life.

The final two players arrived. An oil executive from Texas and a woman who owned a chain of luxury hotels. Then the game began.

For the first hour, Shea played cautiously, feeling out the table dynamics and confirming Elena's assessments of each player. Victor was indeed overly aggressive, raising on weak hands and trying to bully the pot. Amanda was patient and calculating, waiting for premium hands before committing her chips. Gerald played too conservatively, folding to any significant pressure.

But it was Rothmore who commanded her attention. He played with the precision of a surgeon, never wasting a chip, always extracting maximum value from his strong hands while minimizing losses on his weak ones. He spoke rarely, but when he did, his comments carried layers of meaning that Shea suspected only she fully understood.

"Gambling is fascinating, don't you think?" he said during a break between hands, his gaze fixed on Shea. "It reveals so much about a person's character. Some people play recklessly, chasing losses and ignoring probability. Others play too cautiously, so afraid of losing that they never take the risks necessary to win."

"And what does my play reveal?" Shea met his eyes steadily.

"That you're intelligent enough to understand mathematics but confident enough to trust your instincts. That you know when to be patient and when to strike. And that you're searching for something beyond simple monetary gain." His smile didn't reach his eyes. "The question is what exactly you're searching for."

"Perhaps I'm just here for the entertainment." Her heart hammered in her chest.

"Perhaps." Rothmore studied his cards with the same intensity he'd directed at Shea moments before. "Though I find that the most interesting players are those with hidden agendas. They bring a certain...

tension to the table that mere money cannot provide."

The hand continued, and Shea found herself holding a strong pair of kings. Rothmore raised significantly, and she had to make a decision—fold and preserve her chips, or call and risk exposing the strength of her hand.

She called, and the flop came down showing another king along with two low cards. She'd flopped three of a kind—a powerful hand that would win most pots. But as she prepared to bet, Rothmore spoke again.

"You know what I find most tragic about this business?" he said conversationally. "It's the lost children. Not physically lost, you understand, but lost in other ways. Children whose parents make poor decisions, gamble with things they shouldn't gamble with, and then leave their offspring to pay the consequences."

Shea's blood turned to ice. He was talking about Ryan, about Bill, about the children being held hostage. And he was doing it while staring directly at her, watching for any reaction that might confirm his suspicions about who she really was.

She forced herself to remain calm, to keep her expression neutral. "That is tragic," she agreed neutrally. "Though I suppose the children of gamblers have always suffered for their parents' vices."

"Indeed. Though some suffer more than others." Rothmore pushed a large stack of chips forward. "I raise."

The bet was enormous, designed to force her either

to commit a substantial portion of her remaining chips or fold a strong hand. Shea looked at her three kings, looked at Rothmore's unreadable expression, and made her decision.

She folded.

A murmur went around the table—folding such a strong hand to a single bet was unusual, suggesting either weakness or extreme caution. But Shea knew what she was doing. She was showing Rothmore that she could be intimidated, that she wasn't the threat he might have suspected.

As Rothmore collected the pot, he revealed his cards. A pair of fours. He'd been bluffing, and Shea had let him win.

His eyes met hers across the table, and something shifted in his expression. Respect, perhaps, or recognition that she was playing a deeper game than it appeared.

The evening continued, and Shea deliberately lost more hands than she won, slowly diminishing her chip stack while gaining valuable intelligence. She observed who deferred to Rothmore, who seemed afraid of him, and most importantly, she catalogued every word he spoke and every gesture he made.

When Rothmore mentioned "business associates who require creative solutions to logistical problems," she understood he was referring to the coercion operation. When he talked about "ensuring cooperation through proper incentives," he meant the kidnapped children. Every euphemism painted a clearer picture of the syndicate's operations.

By midnight, Shea had lost most of her fifty thousand dollars. She'd finished in sixth place out of eight players. Respectable but not threatening. As the game concluded and players began departing, Rothmore approached her.

"Mrs. Harrison, you play an interesting game. Conservative, but with flashes of boldness. I appreciate that." He handed her his card—heavy stock with simple engraving. "If you're interested in more... exclusive opportunities, please contact me directly. I'm always looking for intelligent people who understand the value of discretion."

"Thank you." She accepted the card. "I'll definitely consider it."

As Rothmore walked away, Shea realized with absolute certainty that she'd just been offered recruitment into the syndicate's inner circle. The question was whether she'd successfully convinced him she was a potential asset rather than a threat.

Only time would tell, and time was something Ryan Miller was rapidly running out of.

Chapter Seven

The ringing of her phone jolted Shea awake from the restless sleep she'd finally fallen into after the poker game with Rothmore. She fumbled for her phone, squinting at the bright screen that showed it was barely six in the morning. "Hello?"

"Shea!" The desperate cry from Becky pierced through Shea's eardrum.

"Settle down, Becky. I can't help you if I don't understand what you're saying." Shea swung her legs out of bed and sat up, her heart already racing with the adrenaline that came from hearing genuine terror in her best friend's voice. "What's wrong? What happened?"

"I got a package." Becky's voice broke on a sob that sounded like it had been torn from somewhere deep in her chest. "It was on my doorstep when I went out to get the newspaper. Ryan's baseball jersey—the one from his team, the one he wore to every single practice and game. Shea, it has blood on it. Fresh blood. Oh God, there's so much—"

Shea's own blood turned to ice in her veins, her stomach dropping as the implications crashed over her like a wave. "Is there anything else in the package? A note, a phone, anything?"

She heard Becky breathing hard, the sound of paper rustling. "A note. It says, 'Bill knows what we want. Clock is ticking.' That's it. Nothing else." The desperation in Becky's voice escalated to near hysteria. "Shea, please tell me you're getting close to finding my son. Please tell me he's okay. If that's his blood, what did they do to him?"

Trevor stepped out of the bathroom, his hair still wet from his shower, a towel wrapped around his waist. He took one look at Shea's face and immediately mouthed, "What's wrong?"

Shea held up a hand, focusing on keeping her voice steady despite her own rising panic. "We are getting close, Becky. I promise you." The lie tasted bitter on her tongue, guilt gnawing at her insides like acid. They were closer than they'd been days ago, but close wasn't good enough when a child's life hung in the balance. "Bill has been banned from the Lucky Dragon casino. We saw his photo posted with other restricted patrons. I'm not entirely sure that he and Ryan are still on the ship, but we're following every lead. We won't stop until we find them."

She almost told Becky about Elena, about the DEA investigation, and the revelation that Ryan was being held with other children as collateral. But the words died in her throat. The fewer people who knew about Elena's cover, the safer it was for the undercover agent who'd been working this case for two years. One careless word, one desperate phone call that might be monitored, and Elena's life would be worth nothing.

"Let us keep working on this, " Shea continued, her sheriff's training kicking in despite her emotional turmoil. "I'll keep you updated on everything significant. And listen to me carefully. I don't think they'll seriously harm Ryan. He's their bargaining chip to control Bill. As long as Bill is still useful to them, Ryan stays alive as leverage."

The logic was sound, but Shea knew firsthand that logic didn't always govern the actions of desperate criminals. Still, Becky needed something to hold onto, some thread of hope to keep her from completely falling apart.

"You need to take that jersey to the Little Rock police immediately," Shea instructed. "Tell them your son has been missing, and you received this in the mail. They'll process it as evidence and get the blood tested. Trevor has contacts with the Arkansas State Crime Lab. I'll have him pull some strings to expedite the analysis so we know exactly what we're dealing with."

Becky sniffed, trying to regain some composure. "Okay. Yes. I'll do that right now. Shea, I... I sure hope you're right about them keeping him alive. I can't lose my baby. I can't."

"You won't. I won't let that happen." Shea wished

she felt as confident as she tried to sound. "Call me after you file the police report."

The line went dead, and Shea sat staring at her phone, feeling the weight of responsibility crushing down on her shoulders. Across the room, Trevor had pulled on jeans and a T-shirt, his expression grave.

"Ryan's blood?" he asked quietly.

"On his baseball jersey. Sent to Becky with a threatening note." Shea stood and moved to the window, staring out at the Mississippi River without really seeing it. Dawn was breaking over the water, painting the sky in shades of orange and pink that should have been beautiful but felt like a mockery instead. "They're escalating, Trevor. Making it personal. Making sure Bill understands exactly what's at stake if he doesn't give them what they want."

Trevor crossed the room and wrapped his arms around her from behind, his chin resting on top of her head. "This isn't your fault," he said firmly, as if reading the guilt written across her face. "You didn't kidnap that child. You didn't force Bill into gambling debts or coerce him into working for criminals. You're trying to fix a situation you didn't create."

"But what if my investigation is making it worse?" Shea turned in his arms to face him, her eyes burning with unshed tears. "What if asking questions and playing poker with Rothmore has made them nervous? What if they decide Bill's not worth the trouble and they dispose of both of them as loose ends?"

"Then we find them before that happens." Trevor's hands framed her face gently. "You heard what Elena said. Bill is working on something big for The Banker. Something that requires his specific skills. They won't kill him until that job is complete, and they won't kill Ryan while they need leverage over Bill."

"But hurting him sends a message without eliminating their leverage." Shea pulled away and began pacing. "That blood could be from a minor injury or something much worse. We need to know."

"I'll call my contact at the state lab right now." Trevor checked his watch. "He owes me a favor from a case three years ago. I can get him to prioritize the analysis and have preliminary results by this afternoon."

While Trevor made the call, speaking in low, urgent tones to his contact, Shea pulled up the security footage Elena had provided the night before. The DEA agent had managed to copy several days' worth of recordings from the casino's surveillance system, looking for any trace of Bill Miller or leads to where he might be now.

Shea had been too exhausted after the poker game to review them properly, but now she forced herself to focus, scanning through hours of footage at accelerated speed. The casino floor, the restaurants, the corridors, the exterior loading docks where supplies came aboard—

There. She hit pause and backed up the footage frame by frame.

The timestamp showed three days ago, just before midnight. A service entrance on the lower deck that crew members used to load provisions. Two men in dark suits, not crew uniforms, were escorting a third man between them. The third man's head was down, his hands bound behind his back, and though the angle wasn't perfect, Shea recognized the thinning brown hair and defeated posture from Bill's photo on the banned patron's wall.

They were moving him off the boat.

"Trevor, come look at this." Shea replayed the segment, watching as the men bundled Bill into the back of a black van with no visible plates or identifying marks. The van pulled away from the dock and disappeared into the Memphis night.

Trevor leaned over her shoulder, his body tense. "That's definitely Bill. But where are they taking him?"

"Not sure, but look at this." Shea advanced the footage several frames. As the van pulled away, one of the men had turned slightly toward a security camera, giving them a clear view of his face. "Recognize him?"

Trevor studied the image, then pulled out his phone and began scrolling through photos. "That's one of the men I saw in the lower deck casino. The high-stakes private games area. He was standing guard near one of those locked doors with electronic keypads."

Shea felt a spark of hope cut through her anxiety.

"Which means he's part of the inner security team. The kind of people who handle sensitive operations for the syndicate."

"Elena might know who he is." Trevor glanced at the clock. "It's barely six. Think she's awake?"

As if summoned by the mention of her name, Shea's phone buzzed with a text from Elena: "Need to meet. Now. Observation deck. Important development."

They found Elena already waiting when they arrived at the observation deck five minutes later, bundled in a jacket against the morning chill. Her usually composed expression showed cracks of strain, and Shea knew immediately that something significant had happened.

"I accessed The Banker's private communications last night after your poker game," Elena said without preamble, keeping her voice low despite the deck being deserted at this hour. "He was impressed with you, which is good. But I also intercepted messages about Bill Miller."

"We have footage of him being taken off the boat three days ago," Shea interjected. "Two men escorting him to a van."

"That tracks with what I found. They moved him to a warehouse district in South Memphis. An area controlled by the syndicate, where police rarely patrol and witnesses keep their mouths shut. The warehouse is used for multiple operations: storage for smuggled goods, a temporary holding facility for people they're moving, and apparently as a workspace where they're forcing Bill to complete whatever technical job they need done."

Elena pulled up a map on her phone, showing an industrial area near the river. "This is the complex. Six warehouses in total, all owned by shell companies that trace back to The Banker's organization. Bill is in warehouse three, based on the communications I intercepted. They're keeping him isolated, working around the clock on what appears to be hacking into some security system."

"What about Ryan?" Trevor asked. "Is he there too?"

Elena shook her head, and Shea's heart sank. "The children are kept at a separate location for security reasons. The syndicate learned a long time ago not to keep all its leverage in one place. If law enforcement raids one location, they still have bargaining chips at the other."

"So even if we find Bill, we won't have Ryan." The defeat in Shea's voice was palpable.

"Not immediately, no. But Bill knows where Ryan is being held—he has to, because they use video calls to show him his son is alive and unharmed. If we can extract Bill from that warehouse, he can lead us to Ryan."

"Extract him how?" Trevor's asked. "You're DEA, we're local law enforcement from another state, and we have no jurisdiction or legal authority to conduct a raid on a warehouse in Memphis. Going in without backup or proper authorization could get us all killed."

"Or it could save Bill and Ryan's lives." Shea's voice had taken on the determined edge that Trevor recognized from the arson case. "Elena, what kind of security are we talking about at this warehouse?"

Elena hesitated, clearly torn between her duty to run this operation by the book and her understanding that Ryan was running out of time. "From what I can tell, minimal. They're relying on location and intimidation rather than a heavy guard presence. Maybe two or three men are actually inside the warehouse, probably armed. More problematic is the camera system and electronic locks."

"Which Bill could disable if we could communicate with him." Shea's mind was already formulating a plan. "Can you get us a building schematic? Entry and exit points?"

"Shea, we need to think about this carefully," Trevor cautioned. "If we go in half-cocked and it goes wrong, we lose our only chance to find Ryan. Maybe we should loop in the FBI, get Agent Martinez's team involved—"

"There's no time." Shea pulled up the photo Becky had texted her—Ryan's blood-stained jersey, the threatening note. "They're hurting him, Trevor. That blood proves they're willing to escalate. Every hour we spend going through proper channels is another hour Ryan spends terrified and in pain."

"The blood analysis came back while we were coming up here," Trevor said quietly. "My contact put a rush on the preliminary test. It's definitely Ryan's blood type, but the volume suggests a non-fatal injury. Probably a cut or controlled bleeding designed to frighten rather than seriously harm."

The information should have been reassuring, but Shea felt her resolve harden instead. "So, they're torturing a ten-year-old child to keep his father compliant. That's who we're dealing with. That's who we're supposed to trust will keep their word and release Ryan once Bill finishes their job?"

She turned to Elena. "What happens when Bill completes this hacking work, or security system bypass, or whatever they have him doing? What's their standard procedure?"

Elena's silence was answer enough. The syndicate didn't leave witnesses or loose ends. Once Bill finished his work, both he and Ryan would be liabilities rather than assets.

"We don't have a lot of time," Elena finally said. "Based on the communications I intercepted, the job Bill's working on has a deadline. After that, they won't need him anymore."

"Then we go tonight." Shea's tone left no room for argument. "We extract Bill from that warehouse, we make him tell us where Ryan is being held, and we get that child back to his mother before this deadline expires and they become disposable."

Trevor ran a hand through his still-damp hair, clearly torn between supporting Shea and recognizing the enormous risks they were taking. "This could end our careers. Going in without authorization, conducting an operation outside our jurisdiction, potentially engaging in armed confrontation—"

"I don't care about my career if a child dies because I was too worried about the procedure to act." Shea shook her head. "You can sit this one out if you want, Trevor. I won't blame you. But I'm going into that warehouse tonight, with or without backup."

"You know I'm not letting you go alone." Trevor's voice was resigned but resolute. "If we're doing this, we do it together. Partners."

"Partners." She felt a surge of gratitude for this man who stayed by her side when things got dangerous and complicated.

Elena looked between them, seeming to measure their commitment and capability. "Okay. If we're doing this, we do it smart. I'll get building schematics and security details. We go in after midnight when the skeleton crew is most likely to be tired and complacent. We get Bill, we get the information about Ryan's location, and we get out before anyone can respond."

"What about The Banker?" Shea asked. "If we raid that warehouse, he'll know someone is targeting his operation."

"Let him know." Elena's smile was cold and vengeful. "I've been playing the long game for two years, building evidence case by case. Maybe it's time to make some noise and see what crawls out of the woodwork when The Banker realizes his organization is under direct attack."

They spent the rest of the morning planning, reviewing schematics that Elena obtained through her DEA resources, and preparing for what would likely be the most dangerous operation any of them had ever attempted. Shea felt the familiar pre-operation adrenaline building, the same heightened awareness and focused intensity that had served her well during the arson investigation. But this time felt different. This time, a child's life hung in the balance, and the margin for error was virtually nonexistent.

As the sun climbed higher over Memphis, Shea checked her phone and saw another message from Becky: "Police took the jersey. They said they'd investigate. But I know you're my best hope. Please find my baby."

Shea typed back a simple response: "I will. I promise."

And, she meant to keep that promise, no matter what it cost her.

Chapter Eight

Shea's heart hammered so hard under the Kevlar vest she wore that she swore she could see it beating through the heavy fabric. The vest was borrowed from Elena's DEA equipment stash, along with the tactical flashlights and communication earpieces they were all wearing. Her service weapon felt heavier than usual in her hand as she crouched behind a rusted dumpster, surveying the warehouse complex sprawled before them.

The industrial district was exactly as Elena had described—abandoned, isolated, and emanating the kind of menace that came from places where bad things happened on a regular basis and no one asked questions. Sodium vapor lights cast sickly orange pools of illumination across cracked asphalt, leaving large swaths of shadow perfect for their approach. A chain-link fence with a broken gate supposedly secured the perimeter, but the multiple tire tracks and cigarette butts suggested plenty of people came and went without authorization.

She glanced at Elena and Trevor, both dressed in dark tactical clothing that helped them blend into the night. Elena gave a curt nod, her DEA training evident in her calm readiness. Trevor's jaw was set with determination, though Shea caught the concern in his eyes when he looked at her. They'd been over the plan three times, but everyone knew plans rarely survived contact with reality.

Shea motioned forward, and they moved as one through the shadows toward the warehouse. A squat concrete structure with boarded windows and a loading dock entrance that hung partially open. The building looked abandoned from the outside, but fresh tire marks in the dirt and the absence of accumulated debris near the door told a different story.

Once inside, they paused to let their eyes adjust to the deeper darkness. The room smelled of industrial solvents, old motor oil, and beneath it all, the distinctive copper tang of blood. Not fresh, but recent enough to set her nerves further on edge.

Trevor clicked on his flashlight, keeping the beam low, and the others followed suit. Shea swept her light around the cavernous space. The warehouse's main floor was enormous, easily fifty yards square with exposed ceiling joists two stories overhead. Boxes and wooden crates lined the opposite wall, some marked with shipping labels in languages she didn't recognize. Metal desks and chairs sat shoved haphazardly in the far corner as if someone had cleared space in a hurry. A metal staircase led to a second story that appeared to be office space or a storage loft.

The warehouse might have been legitimately in use once, maybe decades ago, when this industrial area was thriving, but those days were clearly long past. Now it served darker purposes for people who needed locations that official eyes never saw.

"Clear down here so far," Trevor whispered into his comm, his light sweeping across the space. "No movement, no guards."

Elena moved toward the crates. "These are recent. Shipping dates from last week. I'm seeing labels from Central America, Southeast Asia. This is definitely an active operation."

Shea motioned that she was heading upstairs while pointing at them to continue searching the ground floor. She needed to see what was up there, needed to confirm whether Bill had been held in this location or if Elena's intelligence had been wrong.

She climbed the metal staircase slowly, placing each foot carefully to minimize noise despite the sound-dampening effect of her tactical boots. The stairs creaked softly under her weight, each sound making her hyper-aware that if anyone was still in this building, they'd hear her coming.

At the top, she paused and peered over the edge into the second-floor space. Her flashlight beam cut through the darkness, revealing a room smaller than the warehouse floor below—maybe twenty by thirty feet with a low ceiling and concrete walls.

In the center sat a lone chair, wooden and scarred with age. A length of rope hung over the back, its ends frayed where it had been cut. The implications made Shea's stomach turn.

She swept her light across the rest of the room. A card table stood against one wall with the remains of fast food scattered across its surface. Empty burger wrappers, cold fries, paper cups half-filled with flat soda. Someone had been here recently, multiple someones based on the amount of trash.

But it was the other side of the room that made her freeze. A sleeping bag lay crumpled in the corner next to a bucket that had clearly been used as a makeshift toilet. A desk had been positioned near an electrical outlet, and even from here, Shea could see the setup. Laptop, external hard drives, cables snaking everywhere, and a printer that had run out of paper mid-job, leaving several sheets curled on the floor.

This was where they'd kept Bill. Where they'd forced him to work while holding him prisoner.

"Found something," Shea said quietly into her comm. "Second floor. Looks like a workstation. Someone was definitely held here."

She heard Trevor and Elena's footsteps on the stairs as she moved closer to investigate. The laptop was gone. They'd taken it when they moved Bill, but they'd left behind scattered evidence of what he'd been working on. Technical manuals for security systems, printed diagrams of buildings and street layouts, and handwritten notes in margins showing calculations and timelines. Shea doubted anyone had expected someone to find these things.

Trevor reached the top of the stairs first, his light joining hers as they examined the makeshift prison. "This is where they held him," he confirmed, pointing to the rope and chair. "Restrained him when he wasn't working, kept him isolated."

Elena crouched next to the desk, carefully gathering the papers that remained. Her expression grew increasingly grave as she read. "These are route maps. Armored car routes." She held up a diagram showing streets marked with timing notations and security camera locations. "And this," she grabbed another sheet, "This is a schedule for Federal Reserve transfers."

The words hung in the air like a bomb waiting to explode. Shea felt her pulse spike as the implications crystallized. "They're planning to rob a Federal Reserve armored car."

"Not just planning. They're well into preparation." Elena spread the papers on the desk, her flashlight illuminating details that painted a chilling picture. "These routes, these schedules...this is the kind of intelligence that takes months to gather. Guard shift changes, traffic patterns, blind spots in camera coverage, response times for backup units."

Trevor picked up one of the technical manuals, flipping through pages marked with sticky notes. "High-security electronic locks, GPS tracking systems, vehicle immobilization protocols. Bill's not just a software engineer. He specializes in security systems. They need him to hack the armored car's defenses."

"Which means they can't do this without him." Shea's mind raced through the tactical implications. "As long as Bill is alive and working on this, Ryan stays alive as leverage. But once the heist is complete..."

"They become liabilities," Elena finished grimly. "Standard operating procedure for The Banker. No witnesses, no loose ends."

Shea moved around the perimeter of the room, her light sweeping across walls that were covered in graffiti and water stains. Near the corner where the sleeping bag lay, something caught her eye. Fresh scratches in the concrete wall, deliberate marks that formed words rather than random damage.

"Over here." She crouched to examine the message more closely. The letters were crude, obviously carved with something improvised like a nail or piece of metal, but the message was clear:

"Ryan—Boathouse—Safe"

Trevor knelt beside her, reading the desperate message Bill had left. "He's telling us where Ryan is. Or at least where he thinks Ryan is safe."

"The boathouse." Elena pulled out her phone, accessing a map of the Memphis area. "There are dozens of boathouses along the river, private and commercial. We need more specifics."

Shea studied the wall, looking for additional clues. Below the main message, almost hidden by the angle of her light, were numbers: "35.1" and then a symbol that might have been a degree marker, followed by "90.0"

"Coordinates." Trevor peered over Shea's shoulder. "Latitude and longitude. Not complete, but enough to narrow the search considerably."

Elena was already inputting the partial coordinates into her phone's mapping application. "If I assume these are for the Memphis area and fill in the missing digits based on standard coordinate format, then that gives us a search radius along the river approximately fifteen miles south of here. Rural area, lots of private property and abandoned structures."

She zoomed in on the map, satellite imagery showing a winding section of the Mississippi with scattered buildings along the shoreline. "Three structures identified as boathouses in this radius. One is part of a private estate that's clearly occupied, and another is a commercial marina. Too public for what they'd need. But this one." She highlighted a structure that appeared isolated, accessed only by a single dirt road. "This one is listed as abandoned property, tax lien, no official owner of record."

"That's it," Shea said. "That's where they're keeping Ryan."

Trevor examined the other papers scattered around the desk. "According to these timelines, the Federal Reserve transfer they're targeting happens in five days. Friday afternoon is the peak traffic time when response will be slower."

He looked up at Shea. "If we stop the heist, we tip our hand. The Banker will know we're onto him, and he'll likely kill both Bill and Ryan as a precaution before we can locate them."

"But if we let the heist proceed, we're accomplices to a federal crime," Elena added, her voice tight with frustration. "Not to mention the danger to innocent people—armored car drivers, bystanders, responding officers. Federal Reserve robberies typically end in violence."

Shea stood, her mind working through scenarios and possibilities, weighing lives against laws and outcomes against consequences. This was the kind of impossible choice that kept law enforcement officers awake at night. The trolley problem made real, with no good answers.

"We find Ryan first," she decided. "Before we do anything about the heist, before we approach Bill or The Banker or anyone else, we locate Ryan and get him to safety. Once he's safe, Bill loses his primary motivation to cooperate with these people."

"And if they've moved him from the boathouse?" Trevor asked. "If this information is outdated?"

"Then we make them tell us where he is. One way

or another."

Elena gathered the papers, photographing each one with her phone before collecting them as evidence. "I'll run these through DEA's database, see if we can identify other players involved in this operation. The level of planning here suggests multiple people with specific expertise—the muscle to execute the robbery, the intelligence to plan it, the technical support to bypass security systems."

Trevor had moved to the area near the stairs, examining something that had caught his attention. "Shea, look at this."

She joined him where he'd discovered a bulletin board that must have been used to coordinate the operation. Photos were pinned to the board. Several surveillance shots of an armored car on its route, close-ups of the vehicle's locking mechanisms, pictures of the drivers and guards who would be on duty during the targeted transfer.

But it was the other photos that made Shea's blood run cold. Children. At least four different children, each photo labeled with a name and a notation. Ryan's photo was there, marked "Miller—Primary leverage—Boathouse 3." A girl, maybe eight years old, was labeled "Larson—Secondary leverage—Location 7." Two boys who looked like brothers were marked "Hawthorne twins—Primary leverage—Location 2."

"They're not just holding Ryan," Elena breathed. "This is their entire collateral system. Parents with useful skills, coerced into working through kidnapped children."

The scale of the operation was staggering. How many Federal Reserve transfers had The Banker's organization already successfully robbed? How many coerced experts had committed crimes to save their children, only to be eliminated afterward as loose ends?

Shea photographed the board with her phone, making sure to capture every detail that might help them identify and rescue the other children. This was bigger than just finding Ryan. This was a criminal enterprise that had likely been operating for years, perfecting its method of coercion.

"We need to get out of here." Trevor glanced at his watch. "We've been inside almost thirty minutes. That's pushing our margin for safety."

Elena was already moving toward the stairs, her practiced movements suggesting this wasn't her first time conducting an unauthorized search of a criminal facility. "I'll take these papers back to my contact at the DEA field office. We need to start building a case that will actually stick. Something that goes beyond just this robbery and takes down the entire network."

Shea took one last look around the room where Bill had been held prisoner, where he'd worked under duress while his son remained captive as insurance. She tried to imagine the desperation he must have felt, the impossible choices between cooperating with criminals or risking his child's life.

The message scratched into the wall seemed to glow in her flashlight beam: "Ryan—Boathouse—Safe"

A father's desperate attempt to leave a trail, to give someone a chance to find his son, even if he couldn't do it himself. Bill had probably known that leaving this message was dangerous, that if his captors discovered it, they might hurt Ryan as punishment. But he'd done it anyway, clinging to the hope that someone would come looking, that someone would care enough to search.

"I'm coming for him," Shea whispered to the empty room. "I'm coming for all of them."

They made their way back out of the warehouse, moving quickly but carefully through the shadows. The parking lot remained empty, the industrial district silent except for the distant sound of river traffic and the occasional bark of a dog from somewhere blocks away.

As they reached their vehicle, Elena's nondescript sedan parked three blocks away in the lot of an abandoned gas station, Shea felt her phone buzz with an incoming call. Becky's name appeared on the screen, and her stomach dropped.

"I have to take this." She stepped away for privacy.

"Shea?" Becky's voice sounded raw from crying, exhausted from days of constant fear. "The police called. They analyzed the blood on Ryan's jersey. It's definitely his, but they said the amount suggests a minor injury rather than a life-threatening one. They asked me if Ryan has any blood disorders or medical conditions that might cause excessive bleeding, but he doesn't. He's never even had a serious nosebleed."

The information aligned with what Trevor's contact at the state lab had reported, but hearing it from Becky made it feel more real somehow. "That's actually good news," Shea said gently. "It means they're trying to frighten Bill into compliance, not actually harm Ryan seriously. They need him healthy."

"Did you find anything? Any leads?" The desperate hope in Becky's voice was painful to hear.

Shea thought about the message on the warehouse wall, the coordinates pointing to a boathouse, the photos of children being held as collateral. How much should she tell her friend? How much hope could she offer without making promises she might not be able to keep?

"We found evidence that Bill was being held at a location in Memphis, but he's been moved," Shea said carefully. "We also found information that gives us a much better idea of where Ryan might be. We're going to check it out first thing tomorrow."

"Tomorrow?" Becky's voice cracked. "Why not now? If you know where he is—"

"Because going in blind in the middle of the night with no backup and no intel on what security they have is the surest way to get Ryan hurt," Shea said firmly. "I know waiting is agony, Becky. But I need you to trust me. We're going to bring him home, but we're going to do it smart. Okay?"

The silence on the other end stretched long enough that Shea wondered if the call had dropped. Finally, Becky spoke, her voice barely a whisper. "Okay. I trust you. Just... please hurry."

"I will. I promise."

After ending the call, Shea climbed into the back seat of Elena's sedan. Trevor took the front passenger seat, and Elena drove, pulling out of the gas station lot with her headlights off until they were several blocks away from the warehouse district.

"The boathouse tomorrow?" Trevor asked, though it wasn't really a question.

"The boathouse tomorrow," Shea confirmed. "We scout the location, assess security, and figure out how to extract Ryan without getting him or anyone else killed."

"And then we deal with The Banker," Elena added. "Once Ryan is safe, we take down the entire organization. No more children held hostage. No more desperate parents forced into committing federal crimes."

Shea looked out the window as they drove through Memphis's empty early-morning streets, heading back toward the casino boat where their cover identities waited. The sun would be rising soon, bringing another day closer to the Friday deadline when Bill would be forced to help rob a Federal Reserve armored car.

Five days to find Ryan. Five days to figure out how to stop a federal heist without getting anyone killed. Five days to take down a criminal syndicate that had operated with impunity for years.

It should have felt impossible.

But Shea Callahan had never been very good at accepting impossible odds.

Chapter Nine

The abandoned boathouse sat at the end of a rutted dirt road that hadn't seen maintenance in at least a decade. Shea navigated her truck carefully around potholes filled with murky water from recent rain, while Trevor studied the satellite images on his phone, comparing them to what they could see through the windshield.

"That's definitely the structure from Bill's coordinates." He zoomed in on the map. "Abandoned since 2018, according to property records. Previous owner died, property went into limbo with the county, nobody's paid taxes on it since."

"Perfect place to hide someone nobody's supposed to find." Shea parked the truck in a grove of trees about fifty yards from the boathouse, concealing it from the road and the river. She'd left Heidi with Elena back at the casino boat. The dog's presence would be too noticeable during reconnaissance.

The morning air was thick with humidity,

promising afternoon storms. Mosquitoes hummed in clouds near the water's edge, and the smell of river mud and rotting vegetation was almost overwhelming. This section of the Mississippi River felt isolated, cut off from civilization despite being less than an hour's drive from Memphis.

They'd left before dawn, telling Elena they needed to check out the boathouse location before it got too hot. The truth was that Shea had barely slept. Her mind had raced with plans and contingencies and worst-case scenarios. When she'd finally dozed off around three AM, she'd dreamed of Ryan calling for help from somewhere she couldn't reach.

"Ready?" Trevor asked, checking his service weapon and adjusting the radio on his belt.

"As I'll ever be." Shea took a deep breath, pushing down the anxiety that had been building since they'd found Bill's message. "If Ryan's not here, if they've moved him again..."

Trevor's hand found hers, warm and solid. "Then we follow the next clue. But Shea, we're close. I can feel it."

His touch steadied her more than she wanted to admit. Over the past few days, the lines between their professional partnership and something deeper had blurred almost completely. She found herself reaching for him in moments of stress, seeking the comfort of his presence in ways that had nothing to do with being fellow officers.

"When this is over," she said quietly, not quite meeting his eyes, "when Ryan is safe and we're back in Misty Hollow... we need to talk about what this is. What we are."

"I know exactly what we are." Trevor's voice was gentle but certain. "The question is whether you're ready to admit it."

Before she could respond, he released her hand and moved toward the boathouse, forcing her to follow. The moment passed, but the warmth of his touch and the promise in his words stayed with her.

The boathouse was a simple structure. Weathered wood that had once been painted red but now mainly showed gray, a tin roof with rust blooming in patches, and a covered dock that extended over the water. The main building was maybe twenty feet square, probably used originally for storing equipment and providing shelter during storms.

The door hung crooked on broken hinges. Shea drew her weapon and pushed it open. The hinges protested with a screech that sent birds exploding from nearby trees. Trevor moved in behind her, covering her blind spots.

The interior was dim despite morning sunlight filtering through gaps in the walls. The smell hit her immediately—not pleasant, but not the worst she'd encountered. Stale food, body odor, fear-sweat, and beneath it all, the scent of a child who hadn't been able to bathe properly.

"Someone was definitely here." Trevor swept his light across the space.

Evidence of recent occupation was scattered on the wooden floor. A child-sized sleeping bag lay crumpled in one corner. Empty food wrappers—granola bars, juice boxes, crackers—the kind of things you'd feed a kid who needed to be kept quiet and compliant. A bucket in the corner confirmed that whoever had been held here hadn't been allowed outside for basic necessities.

But it was the drawings that made Shea's throat tighten with emotion.

Taped to the walls were at least a dozen sheets of paper covered in crayon drawings. A child's artwork, rendered with the kind of careful detail that suggested hours of bored concentration. Some were clearly attempts to document his surroundings—the boathouse interior, the view of the river through the window, the trees outside.

Others were more personal. A house with flowers in front, probably Ryan's home. A woman who had to be Becky, her smile exaggerated and bright. A smaller figure that might be Jaime. And a man standing apart from the family, his face sad, his posture defeated. Bill, already separated by divorce but clearly still loved by his son.

"He was trying to leave a trail." Trevor examined one of the drawings more closely. "Look at this one. That's not random. That's a map."

The drawing showed the boathouse from an aerial perspective, with lines representing the road leading to it and the river beside it. Stick figures stood near a vehicle, presumably his captors. But what caught Shea's attention was the notation written in careful printing across the top: "They talk about the compound. Friday is important."

"He was listening." Shea grinned. "Smart kid, paying attention to everything they said around him."

She moved to another drawing. This one showed a view through what appeared to be a window. Trees, water, and in the distance, a structure that stood above everything else. A water tower painted in a distinctive blue and white checkerboard pattern.

"Trevor, look at this." She pointed to the tower. "This is what Ryan could see from wherever they kept him. If we can identify that tower—"

"I can do better than identify it." Trevor was already pulling up his phone, accessing a database of water towers in the region. "That checkerboard pattern is unusual. Most water towers are solid colors or have town names. This design is specific."

His fingers flew across the screen, searching and filtering. "Got it. There's only one water tower with that exact pattern within a hundred miles. Chesterfield Heights, about fifty miles northeast of Memphis. Small unincorporated area, mostly rural, no real law enforcement presence except the county sheriff, who's stretched thin."

He pulled up satellite imagery and zoomed in on the area around the water tower. "And look what's about a quarter mile from that tower. A compound. Fenced perimeter, multiple buildings, accessed by a single private road. Property records show it belongs to a holding company that traces back to... It's buried under six layers of corporate shells, but I'd bet my badge it ultimately connects to The Banker's organization."

Shea felt a surge of hope so intense it was almost painful. "That's where they're keeping the children. All of them, not just Ryan."

"Probably," Trevor agreed. "Makes sense to centralize their leverage in one secure location. Easier to guard, easier to control."

Shea photographed every drawing, making sure they had documentation of everything Ryan had created. Each piece of art was evidence not just of the crime but of a child's resilience, his refusal to give up even when he must have been terrified.

Trevor moved to a corner where the previous occupants had abandoned their fishing equipment. Old, rusted tackle boxes sat stacked against the wall, decaying. He opened them, finding nothing but ancient lures and tangled line until he reached the fourth box.

"Shea."

Something in his voice made her turn immediately. He held up a small USB drive, the kind that held maybe sixteen gigabytes, carefully sealed in a plastic baggie to protect it from moisture.

"Bill was here," Trevor said. "He left another breadcrumb."

Shea took the drive, turning it over in her hands. "If he managed to leave this here, maybe he left other clues at the compound. Evidence we can use to build a case."

"First, we need to see what's on this drive." Trevor pulled out his laptop from the bag he'd brought. "Let's hope it's not encrypted, or at least not with something I can't crack."

He plugged in the drive, and they waited as the computer recognized it. A folder appeared, labeled simply "Insurance." Inside were multiple files—documents, spreadsheets, and video files.

Trevor opened one of the documents, and they both leaned close to read. It was a detailed accounting of transactions, names, dates, and amounts that clearly represented money laundering operations. Millions of dollars moving through shell companies, legitimate businesses used as fronts, the whole complex web of The Banker's financial empire laid bare.

"Bill's been documenting everything," Shea said softly. "Every transaction, every meeting, every person involved. This isn't just evidence of the robbery they're planning. This is evidence of the entire operation."

Trevor opened another file, this one showing route maps and security protocols for not just the upcoming Federal Reserve transfer but for at least a dozen previous robberies. Dates going back three years, each meticulously documented with before-and-after analysis.

"The Banker's been doing this for years," Trevor said grimly. "Forcing experts to commit federal crimes using their kidnapped children as leverage. Bill's not the first software engineer they've coerced. Look at these names—network security specialists, explosives experts, logistics coordinators. They've built an entire criminal enterprise on the backs of desperate parents."

But when Trevor tried to open the video files, an encryption prompt appeared. "These are locked." He tried several standard passwords without success. "I can probably crack it given enough time, but it's going to take specialized software and expertise I don't have."

"We need a hacker," Shea concluded. "Someone who can decrypt these files without damaging them."

"I might know someone," Trevor said slowly. "Jack Morrison—the Memphis PD contact I mentioned before. He has a friend in their cybercrimes unit who owes him a favor. But Shea, bringing in another person means expanding the circle of people who know what we're doing."

"Do we have a choice?" She looked at the encrypted files, knowing they probably contained the most damaging evidence against The Banker's organization. "Whatever's in those videos, Bill thought it was important enough to encrypt and hide. We need to see what he risked his life to document."

The sound of a vehicle approaching made them both freeze. Through gaps in the boathouse walls, Shea spotted a dark SUV navigating the rutted road toward them.

"Out the back," Trevor whispered, already moving toward the door that opened onto the dock. "Now."

Shea grabbed the USB drive, shoving it deep in her pocket as they slipped out onto the weathered dock. The Mississippi River flowed dark and fast beside them, and for a moment, Shea thought they might have to go into the water to avoid detection.

But Trevor pointed to a narrow gap between the boathouse and the overgrown vegetation on the shore. They squeezed through, thorns catching on their clothes, and crouched in the undergrowth just as they heard voices approaching the boathouse.

"—told you we should have burned this place down," a man's voice said. "Too many tracks, too much evidence left behind."

"Boss said to check for anything the kid might have left," another voice replied. "Make sure there's nothing that could lead them to the compound."

Shea's heart hammered as the men entered the boathouse. Through the vegetation, she could see their silhouettes moving around inside, examining the space with flashlights despite the daylight.

Trevor's hand found hers in the underbrush, squeezing gently. They were close enough that she could feel his breath on her cheek, could smell his familiar scent beneath the sweat and adrenaline. In that moment, crouched in the mud and mosquitoes with danger twenty feet away, she realized how much she'd come to depend on him—not just as a partner, but as something more fundamental to her life.

"Here," one of the men said, and Shea heard the sound of paper being torn from the walls. "Kid's drawings. Cute. Boss is gonna want to see these, make sure the kid didn't give away too much."

"What about that tackle box? The one that's been moved?"

Shea's blood ran cold. They'd noticed the disturbance in the fishing equipment.

"Probably just animals. Raccoons get into everything out here." A pause. "But we should tell Marcus, let him decide if it's worth investigating."

Marcus Wade. The head of security from the Lucky Dragon. Further confirmation that the casino operation and the kidnapping ring were connected at the highest levels.

The men spent another ten minutes searching the boathouse, but eventually they left, taking Ryan's drawings with them. Shea and Trevor waited another twenty minutes, making sure the SUV was gone, before emerging from their hiding spot.

"That was too close." Trevor helped her brush mud and leaves from her clothes. His hands lingered on her shoulders, and for a moment, they just looked at each other, the shared danger heightening the awareness that had been building between them for months.

"Thank you," Shea said softly. "For being here. For having my back. For..." She trailed off, not quite ready to put all her feelings into words.

"Always," Trevor replied, and the promise in that single word carried weight beyond their professional partnership. "When this is over, when Ryan is safe and we're back home, I'm taking you on a proper date. Not undercover work pretending to be married. A real date where we can just be Trevor and Shea."

"I'd like that." Warmth spread through her chest despite their muddy, uncomfortable situation. "A lot."

They made their way back to the truck, moving carefully to avoid leaving obvious tracks. As Shea drove back toward Memphis, her mind already worked through their next steps.

"We need to get this USB drive to your cybercrimes contact," she said. "The videos are too important to ignore. But Trevor, we can't wait for a full investigation to play out. Those children are in that compound, and we're running out of time."

"I know." Trevor studied the satellite images of the compound again. "We have four days until the heist on Friday. If we're going to extract those kids, we need to do it before then. Before Bill completes his work and becomes expendable."

"Elena's going to want to coordinate with DEA, bring in a tactical team with proper authority and backup." Shea navigated around a particularly deep pothole, her knuckles white on the steering wheel. "But that takes time we don't have."

"What are you thinking?"

Shea glanced at him, seeing her own determination reflected in his expression. "I'm thinking we scout that compound tomorrow. Get eyes on the location, figure out their security, and identify where the children are being held. And then we go in and get them ourselves if we have to."

"That's a lot of 'ifs' and 'maybes,'" Trevor pointed out. "But I'm with you. Whatever it takes."

His hand found hers on the center console, and this time, neither of them pulled away. They drove back to Memphis in comfortable silence, fingers intertwined, both knowing they were committed to a course of action that could cost them their careers or their lives.

But some things were worth any cost. And bringing Ryan Miller and the other kidnapped children home safely was one of those things.

As they crossed back into the city limits, Shea's phone rang. Elena's name appeared on the screen.

"We have a problem," Elena said without preamble when Shea answered on speaker. "The Banker wants to meet with you. Tomorrow night. Private dinner, just you and him. He said to tell Mrs. Harrison that he has a business proposition that could be very lucrative for someone with her particular talents."

Shea and Trevor exchanged glances. The Banker was making his move, trying to recruit her deeper into his organization. It was an opportunity they couldn't pass up, but also a danger that could expose their entire investigation.

"Tell him I accept." Her voice was steady despite her racing heart. "Time to see exactly what kind of proposition The Banker has in mind."

Chapter Ten

Elena's contact lived in a converted warehouse loft in a part of Memphis that real estate agents optimistically called "up and coming." Shea navigated through narrow streets lined with artist studios, craft breweries, and the occasional abandoned storefront that hadn't yet been claimed by the wave of renovation.

"Are you sure about this?" Trevor asked from the passenger seat, eyeing the graffiti-covered buildings with the wariness of someone who'd worked enough crime scenes to recognize trouble. "Trusting a hacker we've never met with evidence that could make or break this entire investigation?"

"Elena vouches for him," Shea replied, though she shared Trevor's concerns. "And she's been undercover with these people for two years. If she says he's trustworthy, I believe her."

They'd left the casino boat two hours ago under the pretense of shopping for evening wear—Shea needed something appropriate for her private dinner with The Banker tomorrow night. Instead, they'd driven to this decidedly non-shopping district to meet someone Elena called "the best hacker she'd ever worked with who wasn't currently in federal prison."

The address Elena had provided led them to a loading dock behind a building that had once been a textile factory. Elena was already waiting, leaning against her car with the studied casualness of someone who'd learned to look comfortable in uncomfortable situations.

"He's expecting us." She gestured toward a metal staircase that led to the upper floors. "But fair warning…Pixel is brilliant but socially awkward. Don't take anything he says personally."

"Pixel?" Trevor raised an eyebrow.

"It's what he calls himself. His real name is Landon Lewis." Elena started up the stairs, her footsteps echoing on the metal treads. "And before you ask—yes, he's related to Victor Swanson. "

Shea felt her stomach tighten. "We're trusting evidence to someone whose brother works directly for The Banker?"

"Which is exactly why Pixel wants to help," Elena replied. "Family drama goes deep with the Swansons. Trust me on this."

The loft was exactly what Shea expected from a hacker's lair. Exposed brick walls covered with multiple monitors, servers humming in the corner generating enough heat to make the space uncomfortably warm, empty energy drink cans forming pyramid structures on every available surface, and the bluish glow of screens providing most of the illumination.

A young man who couldn't be more than twenty-five looked up from a workstation that would have made NASA envious. He was slight, with black hair that stuck up in multiple directions, thick-framed glasses, and a Pokémon t-shirt that had clearly seen better days.

"Elena. You brought company." His voice carried no inflection, stating facts without judgment. "Sheriff Shea Callahan and Deputy Trevor Bolton, assuming the facial recognition software I just ran is accurate, which it is ninety-nine-point seven percent of the time."

"You ran facial recognition on us?" Trevor's hand drifted toward his weapon.

"Of course. I run it on everyone who enters this space. Can't be too careful when you're a reformed black-hat hacker working off a plea deal by consulting for law enforcement." Pixel pushed his glasses up his nose. "Elena said you have encrypted files you need cracked. Let me see the drive."

Shea exchanged glances with Trevor, then pulled the USB drive from her pocket. "Before we hand this over, we need to understand something. Elena said you're Victor Swanson's brother. How do we know you won't take this evidence straight to him?"

For the first time, emotion flickered across Pixel's

face. A mix of anger and pain that suggested old wounds not yet healed. "Because Victor destroyed our family. Our parents owned a small restaurant in Chinatown. Good people, worked every day of their lives, put both their sons through college. Victor was supposed to be the success story—business degree, good job, made them proud."

He stood and walked to the window, staring out at the Memphis skyline. "Then he got involved with The Banker's organization. Started using the restaurant to launder money. When our parents found out, they confronted him, threatened to go to the police. Two weeks later, the restaurant burned down. Electrical fire, the investigation said. But I know better. I know my brother ordered it."

"Did your parents survive?" Shea asked gently.

"Physically, yes. But the restaurant was everything to them. They lost their business, their savings, their purpose. My mother had a stroke six months later. She's in a care facility now, barely recognizes me. My father... he drinks. Can't hold a job. Won't speak Victor's name."

Pixel turned back to face them, and Shea saw the determination burning behind his awkward exterior. "Victor chose his criminal empire over his family. I've spent three years gathering evidence on The Banker's operation, feeding information to Elena's investigation. If this USB drive contains what I think it contains, it might finally be enough to bring the whole organization down. Including my brother."

"Even if it means Victor goes to prison?" Trevor pressed.

"Especially if it means that. Maybe prison will give him time to remember who he used to be before greed and power corrupted him." Pixel held out his hand. "The drive, please. And Elena said something about wanting immunity for Victor in exchange for my help?"

Elena stepped forward, her expression apologetic. "I thought it might be a negotiating point. Your expertise in exchange for leniency for your brother."

"No deal," Pixel said flatly. "I'll decrypt your files because it's the right thing to do. Because those encrypted videos probably show crimes that deserve justice. Because children are being held hostage, and federal robberies are being planned. Victor made his choices. He doesn't get immunity from consequences."

The statement hung in the air, revealing a core of integrity beneath Pixel's awkward exterior. This wasn't someone looking to profit or protect family. This was someone committed to stopping a criminal organization regardless of personal cost.

"All right." Shea handed over the drive. "But we need this done fast. We have four days before everything comes to a head."

Pixel plugged the drive into his system, and screens lit up with cascading code as his software went to work. "The encryption is military-grade, probably something Bill learned from his security systems work. Ironically, that makes it easier for me to crack because I know the likely algorithms. Give me thirty minutes."

While Pixel worked, Shea, Trevor, and Elena gathered around a different monitor where Pixel had pulled up files they'd already decrypted. The financial records and robbery documentation.

"This is incredible." Trevor scrolled through transaction records. "Bill documented every single operation. Dates, amounts, people involved. This is enough to bring down fifty people minimum, maybe more."

"Look at this," Elena pointed to a spreadsheet showing coerced experts. "Twelve different specialists forced to work for the syndicate over the past three years. Network security, explosives, logistics, financial fraud. And here—" she clicked to another tab, "—what happened to them after they completed their assigned crimes."

The column labeled "Status" told a grim story. Every single person listed was marked "Deceased" with dates shortly after their job completion. The syndicate's pattern was clear: use desperate parents through kidnapped children, force them to commit crimes, then eliminate them as loose ends.

"Bill knew this," Shea said, her voice tight. "He knew that cooperating wouldn't save him or Ryan. That's why he's been documenting everything, leaving clues. He's been trying to build a case even while being forced to work for them."

"Got it," Pixel announced, and his screens filled with thumbnail images of video files. "Forty-seven video recordings, ranging from two minutes to twenty minutes each. Looks like Bill recorded every meeting, every conversation he could capture without being detected."

He opened the first file, and Bill Miller's haggard face filled the screen. The footage was clearly shot on a hidden camera. Possibly his phone concealed in his shirt pocket based on the angle. He was in what looked like the warehouse office, speaking in a low, urgent whisper.

"My name is Bill Miller. If you're watching this, I'm probably dead. But I'm leaving this evidence for my son, Ryan, so he knows I tried. I won't let these people use my skills to hurt innocent people. I won't let them turn me into a criminal without fighting back."

Bill's voice cracked with emotion. "Ryan, buddy, I'm so sorry. I made terrible mistakes with gambling and got us both into this mess. But I want you to know that every day they held you, every day they threatened you, I was working on a way to bring them down. I've been sabotaging the heist preparation—planting errors in the security bypass code, feeding them faulty timing data, making sure that when they try to execute this robbery, things will go wrong."

The video showed Bill wiping tears from his eyes. "I know they'll probably kill me once they realize what I've done. But if I die making sure this robbery fails, if I die protecting you from these people, then it's worth it. You're worth everything, son. Never forget that."

The screen went dark, and Shea realized she had tears on her own cheeks. Trevor's hand found hers, squeezing gently.

"Play the next ones," Elena said, her voice rough with suppressed emotion.

The subsequent videos showed meetings between Bill and various members of The Banker's organization. Victor Swanson appeared frequently to discuss logistics and timelines. Marcus Wade featured prominently, delivering threats and intimidation. But it was the conversations Bill captured about the heist itself that proved most revealing.

"This Federal Reserve transfer is just the cover story," Bill's voice-over explained in one video. "The real target is a different vehicle in the convoy. One carrying something much more valuable than cash."

Pixel paused the video. "Wait. Did he just say the Federal Reserve robbery is a diversion?"

Elena leaned forward, her training kicking in. "Play that part again."

They watched as Bill's hidden camera captured a conversation between Victor and an unidentified man reviewing route maps. "The armored car carrying bearer bonds will be in the third position," Victor said. "Worth over fifty million in untraceable securities. The Federal Reserve vehicle is just bait to draw law enforcement response away from the real target."

"Bearer bonds," Trevor breathed. "Those are as good as cash, completely untraceable if you know how to move them."

"And worth killing for," Shea added. "This isn't about robbing a government transfer. It's about stealing securities that can be liquidated anywhere in the world."

Pixel typed furiously. "If they're targeting bearer bonds, that means the company transporting them would have filed security paperwork with federal regulators. Let me cross-reference Friday's scheduled transfers with known bond movements..."

His screens filled with data as he worked. Minutes passed in tense silence until Pixel let out a low whistle. "Found it. Wexler Financial is moving fifty-three million in bearer bonds from its Memphis vault to its New York office on Friday. The transfer is buried in routine armored car schedules, deliberately obscured to avoid attracting attention."

"How did The Banker's organization find out about it?" Trevor asked.

"Inside information," Elena said grimly. "Someone with access to Wexler Financial's security protocols fed them the intelligence."

Pixel opened another of Bill's video files, this one showing a different kind of meeting. Bill's camera had captured an elegantly dressed older woman sitting across from Victor Swanson, discussing security details with the casual familiarity of longtime associates.

"Facial recognition says that's Margaret Thornton," Pixel reported. "Senior VP of security for Wexler Financial. She's been with the company for twenty years."

"So, we have a corrupt executive providing inside intelligence," Shea said, the pieces falling into place. "The Banker pays her for information, uses that information to plan robberies, then splits the take with her and whoever else is on the inside."

Elena's phone buzzed, and she stepped away to answer it. When she returned, her face was pale. "That was my DEA handler. We have a problem. A big one. The FBI task force investigating money laundering in Memphis just raided three shell companies connected to The Banker's organization. Simultaneous raids, perfect timing, should have caught multiple targets."

"But?" Trevor prompted.

"Everyone was gone. Offices cleaned out, files destroyed, like they knew exactly when and where the raids would happen." Elena's voice was tight with anger. "There's a mole in the FBI feeding information to The Banker. Someone high enough to have access to operational planning."

The implications hit Shea like a punch. "Which means we can't trust federal law enforcement with any of this evidence. If we turn over Bill's videos to the FBI, the mole will warn The Banker, and everyone involved will disappear. Including the children."

"Worse than that," Pixel interjected, still analyzing

the video files. "Look at this timestamp. Bill recorded this conversation three days ago. After you started investigating, after you boarded the Lucky Dragon. Victor and Marcus are discussing a female sheriff from Arkansas asking questions, playing poker too well, winning too much money."

He played the video. Shea's blood chilled as she listened to Victor Swanson describing her undercover persona with unsettling accuracy. "This Mrs. Harrison is trouble. The background check shows some inconsistencies. The Banker thinks she might be law enforcement, but he wants to test her first. The dinner invitation is a trap."

The video continued with Marcus Wade adding his assessment. "If she's really an investigator, she'll have backup, maybe surveillance. We take her to dinner, interrogate her, find out who else knows about our operation, then dispose of her and anyone working with her."

Trevor was on his feet immediately. "You can't go to that dinner. It's an ambush."

"Actually," Elena said slowly, her tactical mind working through possibilities, "this might be exactly the opportunity we need. If The Banker is expecting Shea, if he's planned this elaborate trap, he'll be distracted. Focused on her while we're somewhere else."

"Somewhere else, like the compound where the children are being held." Shea understood Elena's logic even as her pulse raced at the prospect of walking into a trap.

"That's insane," Trevor protested. "You'll be walking into a situation where they plan to torture and kill you. We can't risk that."

"What we can't risk is letting those children remain hostages while we wait for perfect circumstances," Shea countered. "If The Banker and his top people are focused on me, that's when we hit the compound. Simultaneous operations. I keep them busy at the dinner while you and Elena extract the kids."

Pixel had been working while they argued, his fingers flying over keyboards. "I can help with that. I've been mapping The Banker's communication network for months. I can feed them false information, make them think Shea is bringing backup to the dinner, and force them to concentrate even more resources on the ambush. That leaves the compound more vulnerable."

"It's still too dangerous." Trevor moved to stand directly in front of Shea. "I won't let you walk into a death trap alone."

"You don't get to 'let' me do anything," Shea replied gently but firmly. "This is what we came here to do. Save Ryan and the other children. If using myself as bait accomplishes that mission, then that's what I'll do."

Their eyes locked. Trevor's hands came up to frame her face, and he spoke with quiet intensity. "When this is over, we're having that talk. The one about what we are and where we're going. Because I'm not going to lose you before we figure that out."

"Deal." Shea rested her forehead against his for a moment.

Elena cleared her throat. "We only have a few days to plan two simultaneous operations. Pixel, I need you to decrypt every remaining video file, map The Banker's entire organization, and find any other intelligence Bill left behind. Shea, you need to play along with this dinner invitation, seem eager and unsuspecting. Trevor and I will coordinate with my DEA tactical team—off the books, no FBI involvement until we know who the mole is."

"What about Bill?" Shea asked. "If he's been sabotaging the heist, they might have figured it out by now."

"Or they might kill him the moment they realize we're onto them," Elena added grimly. "We need to find where he's being held and extract him during the compound raid. He's the only one who can testify to everything that's happened, the only living witness to the entire operation."

Pixel pulled up one final video file, this one much shorter than the others. Bill's face filled the screen, and this time he looked directly into the camera with the resigned expression of a man who knew he was recording his final message.

"Ryan, if you're watching this and I'm gone, I need you to be strong. Take care of your mother and brother. Don't hate me for the mistakes I made. And remember, even when everything seemed hopeless, even when they threatened you every day, I was fighting back the only way I could. I love you, son. Forever and always."

The screen went dark, and for a long moment, no one spoke.

Then Shea squared her shoulders with renewed determination. "We're bringing him home. Bill and Ryan both. Whatever it takes."

Chapter Eleven

Shea stared at the stranger in the mirror. A woman in an ice blue dress that matched her eyes and hugged her curves in ways that made her feel both powerful and exposed. She'd swept her hair up into an elegant chignon and secured it with an imitation diamond-studded hair comb that Elena had provided from her DEA costume collection. Matching earrings caught the light, sending tiny sparks of reflection across her bare shoulders. The whole ensemble was a far cry from her sheriff's uniform.

"You're stunning." Trevor's voice came from behind her, rough with emotion he wasn't quite hiding. He stepped up and wrapped his arms around her from behind, resting his chin on the top of her head. Their eyes met in the mirror, and Shea saw fear mingled with the admiration in his gaze. "You're always beautiful to me, but wow, Shea. You take my breath away."

She smiled despite her nerves as heat infused her face at genuine appreciation in his voice. "Stunning enough to leave The Banker speechless?"

"He's a complete fool if he isn't." Trevor's expression sobered immediately, the fear overtaking the admiration. "This is dangerous. More dangerous than anything we've done so far. Walking into a known trap, surrounded by people who want to torture and kill you—"

"Yes," Shea interrupted gently, stepping from his embrace to collect the small designer clutch that matched her gown. The bag was absurdly tiny, barely large enough to hold a compact and lipstick, let alone anything useful. "It's dangerous. But it has to be done if we're going to save those children. While The Banker and his people are focused on me, you and Elena will have your best chance at the compound." She'd been in dangerous circumstances before.

Despite her brave words, her heart threatened to beat free from her chest. Her mouth had gone dry, and adrenaline made her hands shake. She forced herself to take a deep breath, center herself the way she did before any dangerous operation, and then planted a quick kiss on Trevor's lips—a promise and a goodbye in equal measure.

"Don't worry about me," she said, trying to inject confidence she didn't entirely feel. "I have a small derringer strapped to my inner thigh. Two shots, point-blank range. It won't stop an army, but it might buy me the seconds I need to escape."

"Yeah, that'll definitely stop the bad guys,"

Trevor said, his smile strained and not reaching his eyes. He pulled her close again, this time more desperately. "Shea, if something goes wrong—"

"It won't." She cut him off, not wanting to hear the end of that sentence. Not wanting to acknowledge that this might be the last time they stood together like this. "The wire I'm wearing will transmit everything to Elena's receiver. The moment things go sideways, she'll call in backup—Memphis SWAT, DEA tactical team, whoever can get there fastest."

"And if they kill you before backup arrives?"

"Then you make sure my death means something." Shea pulled back enough to look him directly in the eyes. "You get those children out. You bring Ryan home to Becky. You take down The Banker's entire organization. Promise me, Trevor. No matter what happens to me tonight, you finish this."

He was quiet for a long moment, his jaw working as he struggled with his emotions. Finally, he nodded. "I promise. But Shea, you need to promise me something too. Promise me you'll do whatever it takes to survive. Lie, cooperate, tell them whatever they want to hear. Your life is worth more than any case, any investigation, any arrest."

"I promise," she whispered, though she knew that promises made in desperate moments weren't always kept when circumstances demanded impossible choices.

~

Before leaving for dinner, Shea made a call that

had been weighing on her conscience since Pixel discovered the FBI mole. Agent Sarah Martinez answered on the second ring, her voice carrying the distracted tone of someone juggling multiple cases simultaneously.

"Shea? This is unexpected. I thought you were back in Misty Hollow dealing with small-town crime."

"I need to tell you something, and you're not going to like it." Shea took a breath, knowing this conversation could either help or destroy everything they'd worked toward. "There's a mole in the FBI. Someone high enough to have access to operational planning for money laundering task forces."

The silence on the other end stretched long enough that Shea wondered if the call had dropped. Then Sarah's voice came back, cold and professional. "That's a serious accusation. What evidence do you have?"

Shea explained the Lucky Dragon investigation, carefully omitting details that might compromise Elena's cover or reveal how much they knew. She described the recent failed raids and how The Banker's organization had known exactly when and where to evacuate its operations.

"The timing was too perfect," Shea concluded. "Someone with inside knowledge fed them intelligence about those raids. Sarah, we have video evidence of The Banker's people discussing their FBI source, bragging about having protection at the federal level."

"Send me those videos. Encrypted channel, highest security protocols." Sarah's voice had taken on the lethal calm of someone whose professional world had just been shaken. "If there really is a mole in my agency, I'll find them. And Shea? Watch your back. If they know you're investigating, if they've identified you as a threat..."

"They have. Which is why I'm about to walk into a meeting with The Banker himself." Shea checked her watch. Thirty minutes until the car service would arrive to take her to the restaurant. "Sarah, if something happens to me tonight, there's evidence hidden in three separate locations. Elena Reyes with the DEA has copies of everything. Whatever you do, don't shut down this investigation."

"What are you planning?"

"Saving some kids and taking down a criminal empire. Just another day." Shea tried for levity but heard how hollow it sounded. "I have to go. Start your mole hunt, Sarah. We're running out of time."

After ending the call, Shea found Trevor and Elena waiting in the suite's living area. Elena had a laptop open, showing real-time satellite imagery of the compound where the children were being held. The afternoon surveillance had confirmed what Bill's drawings suggested. Ryan and at least three other children were prisoners in the main building, under constant guard.

"The security is more extensive than we thought."

Elena zoomed in on various sections of the compound. "Six armed guards visible on rotation, plus whoever's inside with the children. Camera coverage on all approaches, motion sensors along the perimeter fence, and what looks like guard dogs in kennels near the main gate."

"Dogs complicate things," Trevor said. "Even if we avoid cameras and sensors, the dogs will smell us coming."

"Which is why we need the distraction of your dinner to pull resources away from the compound," Elena said to Shea. "Pixel is already feeding The Banker's organization false intelligence that you're bringing federal backup to the restaurant. He's made it seem like there will be a significant law enforcement presence, maybe even an arrest attempt. They'll concentrate their security there, leaving the compound more vulnerable."

Shea nodded, her mind already rehearsing the role she'd have to play. "How long do you need? How much time can I buy you at that dinner before they realize something's wrong?"

"Three hours minimum, four would be better." Elena's expression was apologetic. "I know that's a long time to maintain cover while surrounded by people planning to kill you."

"I've sat through worse," Shea lied. "Town council budget meetings go on for hours and feel just as life-threatening." She forced a laugh

Trevor didn't laugh at her attempt at humor. Instead, he moved to a duffel bag and extracted a small device no bigger than a button. "This is a panic trigger. Disguised as part of your jewelry but actually a GPS beacon with an emergency signal. You press it, and every law enforcement agency within fifty miles gets an alert with your exact location."

He fastened it carefully to her necklace, his fingers lingering at the base of her throat. "One press, Shea. Don't try to be a hero. The moment you feel genuinely threatened, you trigger this, and we come running."

"What about the children?" Shea asked. "If I trigger this while you're mid-extraction—"

"Then we adapt," Elena said firmly. "But Trevor's right. Your life isn't worth sacrificing for perfect timing. We'll get the kids out regardless of whether the diversion is still in play."

The car service arrived precisely on time. A black luxury sedan with a driver who looked more like private security than a chauffeur. He opened the door for Shea without speaking, his eyes hidden behind dark sunglasses despite the evening hour.

Before getting in, Shea turned back to Trevor. He stood on the sidewalk, hands shoved in his pockets, looking like he wanted to say a thousand things but couldn't find the words for any of them. She mouthed "I love you" before she could stop herself, then slid into the car before she could see his reaction. Those three words had never been spoken to a man before.

As the sedan pulled away from the curb, Shea caught his reflection in the side mirror. He stood where she'd left him, watching her disappear into the Memphis evening traffic.

~

The restaurant was the kind of place that didn't bother advertising because its clientele found it through personal connections and generational wealth. No sign marked the entrance, just a discreet brass plate with a street number. A valet whisked the sedan away the moment Shea stepped out, and a hostess in an elegant black dress materialized to escort her inside.

The interior was all dark wood and soft lighting, with tables spaced far enough apart that private conversations stayed private. Classical music played at a volume that suggested sophistication without demanding attention. Shea counted maybe a dozen other diners, all dressed in the kind of expensive, understated elegance that screamed old money.

James Rothmore, aka The Banker, waited at a corner table with perfect sight lines to every entrance, positioned against a wall that prevented anyone from approaching from behind. He stood as she approached, his silver hair immaculate, his charcoal suit perfectly tailored, and his smile warm, but his eyes calculating.

"Mrs. Harrison. You look absolutely stunning." He took her hand and brought it to his lips in a gesture that was somehow both courtly and vaguely threatening. "I'm delighted you accepted my invitation."

"How could I refuse such a personal request?" Shea allowed him to seat her, hyperaware of how her dress rode up slightly, how close his hands came to discovering the derringer strapped to her thigh. "Though I admit I'm curious what business proposition requires such formal circumstances."

"All in good time. First, let's enjoy some excellent food and wine." Rothmore signaled a sommelier who appeared with a bottle that probably cost more than Shea's monthly salary. "I took the liberty of ordering for us. I hope you don't mind. The chef here is a personal friend, and I asked him to prepare something special."

As the sommelier poured wine into crystal glasses, Shea noticed the other diners. Or rather, she saw that most of them were watching their table with varying degrees of interest. Some faces she recognized from the Lucky Dragon. High-level operatives in The Banker's organization. Others were strangers, but all had that distinctive awareness that came from people accustomed to violence.

She was surrounded. The restaurant wasn't neutral ground. It was another part of The Banker's empire, every staff member and patron carefully selected to serve his purposes.

"You seem nervous, Mrs. Harrison." Rothmore sipped his wine, those cold gray eyes never leaving her face. "Are you uncomfortable?"

"Just admiring the ambiance." Shea forced herself to relax her shoulders. "This is quite different from the restaurants I usually frequent in Little Rock."

"I imagine so. Tell me, how are you enjoying your stay aboard the Lucky Dragon? I understand you've been quite successful at the poker tables."

"Luck has been with me. Though I like to think skill plays a role as well."

"Indeed, it does. Skill, intelligence, the ability to read people and situations." Rothmore leaned back in his chair, steepling his fingers. "Which is why I wanted to speak with you privately. You see, Mrs. Harrison, or may I call you Catherine? I believe we could help each other immensely."

"I'm always interested in mutually beneficial arrangements." Shea took a small sip of wine, knowing she needed to stay sharp. "What did you have in mind?"

Before Rothmore could answer, the restaurant's front door opened, and Marcus Wade entered. He made brief eye contact with Rothmore, and some unspoken communication passed between them. Then Wade positioned himself near the entrance, effectively blocking the primary exit.

The trap was closing.

Rothmore's smile didn't waver, but something shifted in his eyes. A predatory gleam that made Shea's instincts scream warnings. "Actually, Catherine, before we discuss business, I have a confession to make. I know exactly who you are. Sheriff Shea Callahan of Misty Hollow, Arkansas. You've been investigating my organization under pretenses, working with a DEA agent who thinks she's been undercover all this time."

Shea felt ice flood her veins, but she kept her expression neutral. "I don't know what you're talking about."

"Please, don't insult my intelligence." Rothmore's voice hardened. "Did you really think I wouldn't discover your real identity? That I wouldn't investigate someone who appeared on my casino boat, asking too many questions and winning too much money?"

He pulled out his phone and showed her a screen displaying Shea's real sheriff's identification, along with photos of her in uniform, news articles about the Christmas arson case, everything that proved Catherine Harrison was a fiction.

"Now," Rothmore continued, his tone conversational despite the threat underlying every word. "I'm going to give you one chance to cooperate voluntarily. Tell me everything about your investigation. Who sent you, what you know, who else is involved. Do that, and you'll leave here tonight alive and unharmed."

Shea's hand drifted toward the panic trigger hidden in her necklace, but froze when Rothmore casually revealed a small device in his palm. "Before you trigger whatever emergency beacon your colleagues gave you, you should know that I have a man watching a live video feed of a room where four children are currently being held. The moment my device detects any emergency signal from this location, that man receives orders to eliminate all four children. Then he'll kill their parents. Then he'll disappear into a network of safe houses across three states."

He leaned forward, his voice dropping to barely above a whisper. "So, here's your choice, Sheriff. Cooperate with me now, answer my questions, and perhaps we can reach an accommodation that keeps everyone alive. Or trigger that beacon. Within minutes, four innocent children will be executed specifically because of your actions."

The world seemed to narrow to just that moment. Rothmore's cold eyes, the weight of impossible choices, the knowledge that Trevor and Elena were depending on her to buy them time, but also that children would die if she signaled for help.

Through the restaurant's window, the Memphis skyline darkened as night fell. Somewhere out there, Trevor and Elena were moving into position at the compound. Somewhere out there, Ryan Miller and other kidnapped children were waiting for rescue.

And here she sat, trapped between saving herself and saving them, knowing that whatever choice she made in the next few seconds would determine whether children lived or died.

"Well, Sheriff?" Rothmore pressed. "What's it going to be?"

Chapter Twelve

Trevor crouched in the tree line fifty yards from the compound's perimeter fence, his night-vision goggles turning the darkening landscape into shades of green. Beside him, Elena checked her tactical gear one final time, her movements precise.

"Radio check," Elena whispered into her comm. "Alpha team, report."

"Alpha in position," came the response from one of Elena's trusted DEA contacts.a tactical operator named Perez who'd agreed to help off the books. "South approach clear. Two guards visible on the compound's eastern perimeter."

"Bravo team?"

"Bravo ready," confirmed Jones, another of Elena's team. "Guard rotation just completed. We've got approximately twelve minutes until the next patrol circuit."

Trevor adjusted his earpiece, listening to the open channel that broadcasted Shea's wire from the restaurant. So far, it was just ambient noise—classical music, low conversation, the clink of silverware on china. His stomach churned with anxiety, knowing she was walking into a trap, but they'd all agreed this was their best chance.

"How's our sheriff holding up?" Elena asked quietly, noticing Trevor's tension.

"She hasn't said anything yet. Just got to the restaurant." Trevor forced himself to focus on the mission rather than his worry. "Once Rothmore starts making his pitch, we'll know if he suspects anything."

Elena pulled up a schematic of the compound on her tablet. "According to Pixel's intelligence, the children are being held in the main building, second floor, northwest corner. Two guards inside, maybe three. The rest of the security is focused on perimeter defense."

"Makes sense. They're not worried about the kids escaping. They're worried about someone getting in." Trevor studied the layout as his mind calculated approach angles and extraction routes. "Once we breach, we'll have maybe three minutes before reinforcements arrive. That's not enough time to get four children and any adults out safely."

"Which is why we wait for Shea's distraction to pull those reinforcements away." Elena checked her watch. "She needs to keep Rothmore engaged for at least two hours. Can she do it?"

"She can do anything she sets her mind to," Trevor

replied with absolute conviction. "The question is what it'll cost her."

They settled in to wait, monitoring the compound's security patterns while listening to Shea's wire. Trevor tried to calm his racing heart by reviewing their extraction plan for the hundredth time. Three vehicles positioned at different points around the compound perimeter. Six operators total. Enough to handle the guards and extract the targets, but not enough to wage a prolonged firefight if things went wrong.

Everything depended on timing, surprise, and Shea keeping The Banker's attention focused elsewhere.

Through his earpiece, Trevor heard the change in ambient sound as Shea was seated at her table. Then Rothmore's voice, smooth and cultured: "Mrs. Harrison. You look absolutely stunning."

Trevor's jaw clenched hearing another man compliment Shea, even knowing it was part of the operation. He forced himself to focus on the compound, scanning for any changes in guard positions or patrol patterns.

"Movement on the northwest corner," Rodriguez reported. "Single guard, making rounds with a dog."

"Copy that," Elena acknowledged. "Everyone, stay concealed. We're still thirty minutes from go-time."

The conversation from the restaurant continued. Pleasantries about wine, comments about food, Rothmore making small talk while presumably evaluating Shea. Trevor could hear the tension in her voice despite her attempts to sound relaxed, could imagine her sitting there in that stunning blue dress, surrounded by enemies, playing the role of her life.

Then Rothmore said something that made Trevor's blood freeze: "Tell me, how are you enjoying your stay aboard the Lucky Dragon?"

The question itself was innocent enough, but Rothmore's tone carried undertones that suggested he knew more than he was letting on. Trevor held his breath, waiting for Shea's response, praying she could navigate whatever trap Rothmore was setting.

"Guard change happening early," Jones's voice cut through Trevor's concentration. "Two new guards just arrived at the main gate. That's irregular."

Elena frowned, checking her notes. "The rotation isn't supposed to happen for another twenty minutes. Why would they—"

Rothmore's voice came through Trevor's earpiece again, and this time there was no mistaking the threat beneath the cultured words: "Actually, Catherine, before we discuss business, I have a confession to make. I know exactly who you are. Sheriff Shea Callahan of Misty Hollow, Arkansas."

Trevor was on his feet instantly, adrenaline flooding his system. "She's blown. Her cover's been compromised."

Elena grabbed his arm, pulling him back down into concealment. "Wait. Listen."

They listened as Rothmore laid out everything he

knew…Shea's real identity, the DEA investigation, even Elena's undercover presence. The man had clearly known all along, had been playing them while they thought they were playing him.

"He's known since we arrived." Elena's face paled even in the green glow of night vision. "The dinner invitation wasn't to recruit her. It was to capture her."

Through the wire, they heard Rothmore's ultimatum: cooperate voluntarily or face consequences. Then came the words that made Trevor's world tilt on its axis.

"I have a man watching a live video feed of a room where four children are currently being held. The moment my device detects any emergency signal from this location, that man receives orders to eliminate all four children."

"No," Trevor whispered. "No, no, no."

The implications crashed over him like a wave. If they attempted the extraction now, if anything went wrong and Shea triggered her panic beacon, those children would be executed. But if they didn't attempt the extraction, Shea was trapped in a restaurant with people who planned to torture and kill her.

Elena was already on her comm, her voice tight with controlled urgency. "All teams, stand down. Repeat, stand down. Do not approach the compound. We have a hostage situation."

"What?" Perez's confusion was evident. "We're in position, ready to breach."

"Stand down!" Elena hissed. "That's an order."

Trevor's mind raced through scenarios and possibilities, each one worse than the last. "We can't extract without them knowing. Even if we disable communications, if the man watching that video feed loses contact, he'll assume something's wrong and kill the children anyway."

"There has to be a way," Elena insisted, but her voice carried the same desperation Trevor felt. "Some way to get both Shea and the children out."

Through the earpiece, Shea's voice came—steady, calm, buying time even as she faced down The Banker's threat. "Before I answer your questions, Mr. Rothmore, I need proof the children are actually alive. For all I know, you're bluffing about having someone watching them."

"Smart woman," Rothmore replied with what sounded like genuine appreciation. "Marcus, show her the feed."

There was a pause, then Trevor heard Shea's sharp intake of breath. Whatever she was seeing on that video feed was real enough to convince her.

"Now," Rothmore continued, "let's start with something simple. Who else knows about your investigation besides your deputy and Agent Reyes?"

Trevor's hands clenched into fists. Every second Shea spent answering questions was one more second she was in danger, but every second she kept talking was a second they had to figure out a solution.

"We need Pixel," Trevor said suddenly. "If there's a video feed, he can trace it. Find where it's being transmitted from, identify the man watching it."

Elena was already dialing her phone. "Pixel? We have an emergency. I need you to trace a video signal, and I need it done in the next ten minutes."

While Elena coordinated with Pixel, Trevor kept his eyes on the compound. The additional guards who'd arrived early were now taking up positions around the perimeter. Not replacing the existing security, but augmenting it. Something had changed; some signal had been sent that they needed to increase protection.

"They know we're here," Trevor realized aloud. "Or at least they suspect we might attempt something. That's why the extra guards."

"Which means Rothmore's threat about killing the children isn't just to control Shea. It's also insurance against us trying to mount a rescue." Elena's voice was grim. "He's covering all his bases."

Perez's voice crackled over the comm. "We've got movement inside the main building. Lights are coming on in multiple rooms, including the second floor where the kids are supposedly held. They're increasing the alert status."

Through his earpiece, Trevor heard Shea's voice, still steady but with an undercurrent of fear he recognized because he knew her so well. She was stalling, asking clarifying questions, making Rothmore explain details while she tried to buy time for Trevor and Elena to come up with a plan.

"I understand your concerns, Mr. Rothmore," Shea was saying. "But you'll appreciate that I need to consult with my superiors before providing information about ongoing investigations. Surely you can give me a few hours to make some calls?"

"I'm afraid not, Sheriff." Rothmore's patience was wearing thin. "You have two options: cooperate now, or I make an example of you that will discourage any other law enforcement officials from investigating my operations. There is no third option. There is no rescue coming. Your deputy and Agent Reyes are currently watching my compound, debating whether to attempt an extraction. But they won't, because they know what will happen to those children if they try."

Trevor's breath caught. Rothmore knew they were here. He'd known all along, had anticipated their every move.

Elena's phone buzzed, and she answered on speaker. Pixel's excited voice came through: "I found the video feed. It's being transmitted from a location in downtown Memphis, not the compound. An apartment building on Riverside Avenue, unit 342. Whoever's watching that feed is not with the children. He's miles away."

Hope flared in Trevor's chest. "If we can take out the man monitoring the video without alerting anyone—"

"Then we can attempt the extraction without

triggering the kill order," Elena finished. "But we'd need split operations. Some of us handle the apartment while others stay ready to breach the compound the moment we secure the video monitor."

"And we'd need to do it without Shea knowing," Trevor added reluctantly. "If she thinks we're attempting something, her body language might give it away to Rothmore. She needs to keep believing we're standing down."

The decision was agonizing, but necessary. They couldn't save Shea by rushing into the restaurant. That would just get her killed faster and likely result in the children's deaths as well. But they could neutralize the immediate threat to the children, then coordinate with Memphis SWAT to extract Shea.

"Perez, Jones, hold position at the compound," Elena ordered. "Be ready to breach on my signal. Trevor and I are heading to Riverside Avenue. Pixel, I need you to shut down any remote communication from that apartment the moment we're in position. Nothing gets out. No calls, no internet, no signals of any kind."

"On it," Pixel confirmed. "I'll create a localized blackout. The guy won't even know he's been cut off until you're breaking down his door."

As Trevor and Elena sprinted back to their vehicle, Trevor forced himself not to listen to Shea's wire. He couldn't help her right now by monitoring every word. What he could do was move fast, hit their target hard, and eliminate the threat to those children so they could shift to extracting her.

The drive to Riverside Avenue took twelve minutes that felt like twelve hours. Elena navigated Memphis traffic while Trevor coordinated with the tactical team still at the compound.

The apartment building was a mid-rise structure typical of downtown Memphis. Probably built in the 1980s, showing its age but still respectable. Unit 342 was on the third floor, accessible by stairs or elevator. Elena and Trevor took the stairs, weapons drawn.

At the door to 342, they paused. Through the thin walls, they could hear a television playing and a man's voice speaking on a phone.

"Pixel, status?" Elena whispered into her comm.

"Signal blackout active in thirty seconds. All communications from that apartment are about to go dark."

Elena counted down silently on her fingers: three, two, one.

Trevor kicked the door just beside the lock, his boot connecting with enough force to splinter the frame. The door flew inward, and they were inside within seconds, weapons raised.

A man sat on a couch, laptop open in front of him that showed multiple video feeds. He reached for a phone, but Trevor was faster, knocking it from his hand.

"Federal agents!" Elena shouted, though she had no legal authority here. "Hands where I can see them."

The man complied, eyes wide with fear. On his laptop screen, Trevor spotted four children in a sparse room. Ryan Miller and three others, all looking scared but alive.

"Who gave you orders?" Elena demanded, her weapon steady on the man's forehead.

"I just watch the feeds," the man stammered. "I get paid to watch and report. That's all. I don't know anything else."

Trevor grabbed the laptop, quickly examining the video feeds and the associated software. "These feeds are from the compound. Real-time. But look…there's a delay built in, maybe fifteen seconds."

"Which means even if we breach now, he can't warn anyone fast enough," Elena realized. She grabbed her comm. "Perez, Jones—execute extraction. Go now!"

Through his earpiece, Trevor heard the tactical team spring into action. Breaching charges, shouted commands, the controlled chaos of a dynamic entry. Seconds ticked by, each one feeling like an eternity.

Then Rodriguez's voice, triumphant: "We have the children! Four kids, all alive, minimal security resistance. We're moving to extraction vehicles now."

Relief flooded through Trevor, so intense it was almost painful. The children were safe. Ryan was safe. At least that part of the mission had succeeded.

But Shea was still trapped in that restaurant, still at the mercy of The Banker and his threats.

"Pixel," Trevor said urgently, "we need every law enforcement unit in Memphis converging on that restaurant. Memphis PD, SWAT, FBI—everyone. Sheriff Shea Callahan is being held hostage by James Rothmore. Send them everything. Her location, the identities of everyone in that restaurant, the full evidence files Bill documented. Bring down the entire organization right now."

"On it," Pixel confirmed. "But Trevor, the FBI mole—"

"I don't care about the mole anymore," Trevor interrupted. "Shea's life is worth more than keeping one investigation compartmentalized. Send it to everyone. Make so much noise that the mole can't suppress it."

Elena was already coordinating with Perez. "Get those children to St. Francis Hospital. Full medical evaluation, then protective custody. And Perez? Find Bill Miller. He's being held somewhere near that compound. We need him for testimony."

As sirens began to wail across Memphis, dozens of emergency vehicles converging on the restaurant district, Trevor listened one more time to Shea's wire. She was still talking, still buying time even though she didn't know help was coming.

"Hold on," he whispered. "Just hold on a little longer. We're coming for you."

Chapter Thirteen

Shea leaned against the outside of her cabin door on the ship and fought to slow her racing heart and steady her breathing. Her hands shook as she fumbled with the key card, dropping it twice before successfully unlocking the door. Their carefully constructed plans to bring down Rothmore had taken a dangerous turn, veering into territory where control was slipping through their fingers like water.

For the first time in her law enforcement career, she genuinely believed she might fail to bring the bad guy to justice. Worse, people she cared about might die because of her failures.

The dinner with Rothmore replayed in her mind on a vicious loop. His cold gray eyes dissected every word she spoke, searching for lies. Marcus Wade had positioned himself at the exit like a human barrier. The video feed showed terrified children who'd been mere minutes from death. And then the final ultimatum that had sent her stumbling back to this cabin with her world tilting on its axis.

"Shea?" A familiar voice cut through her anxiety. "What happened? Is it Ryan?"

Shea's head snapped up to see Becky racing toward her down the corridor, her face pale with worry and exhaustion. The last thing she needed right now was her best friend appearing on a boat full of criminals who wouldn't hesitate to use her as additional leverage.

"What are you doing here?" Shea whirled to face Becky, her voice sharper than intended. "You shouldn't be here. This place isn't safe."

"I couldn't stay away any longer." Becky gripped Shea by the shoulders, her fingers digging in. "I've been going crazy in Little Rock, waiting for updates while my son is in danger. Now tell me what's wrong. You look like you've seen a ghost."

Shea glanced around the corridor, aware that the Lucky Dragon had cameras everywhere and people loyal to The Banker monitoring everything that happened on this boat. "I can't talk out here. Come inside. Quickly."

She opened the cabin door, her mouth dropping open at the scene that greeted her. Not only were Trevor and Elena present, but Ryan Miller sat on the couch, alive, safe, wrapped in a blanket that was far too large for his thin frame. His face was gaunt, his eyes haunted in ways no ten-year-old's should be, but he was here and breathing.

"Ryan!" Becky's scream of joy and relief could probably be heard throughout the entire deck. She launched herself across the room, dropping to her knees in front of her son and pulling him into her arms with the desperation of a mother who'd feared she'd never hold her child again.

Ryan buried his face in his mother's shoulder and started crying, not the quiet tears of a child trying to be brave, but the deep, body-wracking sobs of someone who'd been holding terror inside for too long. "Mom. Mom, they said they were going to hurt you. They said Dad was gone and I'd never see you again."

"I've got you, baby. I've got you." Becky rocked him back and forth, her tears flowing freely as she ran her hands over his hair, his face, his arms—checking that he was real and whole and actually here. "You're safe now. I'm here, and you're safe."

Shea closed the cabin door and leaned against it, watching the reunion with her own eyes burning. This was why they did the impossible. This moment right here, a mother and son reunited despite the odds, justified every risk, every dangerous choice, every line they'd crossed.

Trevor moved to stand beside her, his hand finding hers and squeezing gently. "We got all four kids out," he said quietly. "Ryan, two boys named Larson, and a girl named Katie whose father is a bank executive. They're all shaken up but physically okay. The medical team checked them out at the hospital before we brought Ryan here."

"Bill?" Shea asked, though she almost didn't want to know the answer.

"Still looking. He wasn't at the compound with the children. Elena's team is searching for other properties associated with The Banker's organization." Trevor's jaw tightened. "But Shea, we need to talk about what happened at that restaurant. What did Rothmore say to you after we lost the wire signal?"

Shea had switched off her wire before leaving the restaurant, unable to bear the thought of Trevor hearing what came next. "He knows everything. My real identity, the investigation, Elena's cover, all of it. He's known since we arrived on this boat. Maybe even before. We've been playing right into his hands the entire time."

Elena glanced up from where she'd been giving Becky and Ryan some space, her face neutral despite the devastating implications. "He said my cover is blown?"

"Not just blown. Someone recognized you. One of his contacts in Miami saw surveillance footage from the casino and identified you as DEA." Shea moved to pour herself a glass of water. Her hands shook so bad that water splashed over the rim. "Rothmore gave me forty-eight hours to prove my loyalty to his organization."

"Prove it how?" Trevor's voice carried the dangerous edge that appeared when he was barely containing his anger.

Shea met his eyes, seeing her own dread reflected back. "By giving him Elena. He wants me to identify her officially, expose her cover, and deliver her to him as proof that I've chosen his side over law enforcement. I played the role of a dirty cop. Or tried to, anyway."

The room went silent except for Ryan's quiet sobs and Becky's whispered reassurances. Elena stood.

"If you do that, I'm dead within hours," Elena stated matter-of-factly. "They'll torture me for information about other DEA operations, then kill me just like they killed my husband."

"I know." Shea's voice broke slightly. "That's why we need to accelerate every timeline. We can't give Rothmore forty-eight hours to consolidate his position or eliminate evidence. We need to bring down the entire organization now, tonight, before he can react."

"With what authority?" Elena challenged. "The FBI has a mole. Local law enforcement is either compromised or will take too long to mobilize. My DEA superiors won't authorize an operation this size on such short notice without going through channels that Rothmore probably has monitored."

"What if we give Rothmore exactly what he wants, but on our terms?" Trevor asked.

Everyone turned to face him. Ryan had quieted enough to pay attention, though Becky kept him pressed against her side protectively.

"Explain," Elena said carefully.

"Rothmore wants proof that Shea has turned, that

she's willing to betray law enforcement to join his organization. He specifically wants you delivered to him." Trevor's eyes were distant, calculating. "What if Shea does expose you, but you fake your death? Go completely dark in a way that makes Rothmore think you've been eliminated, but actually positions you to come back with overwhelming force."

Shea caught onto his thinking. "Stage your death, let Rothmore believe he's won, then use that false sense of security to bring in coordinated federal raids before he can react."

"But we'd need to make it convincing," Elena mused, her expression shifting from defensive to strategic. "Can't be an obvious fake or Rothmore will see through it. It needs to look like a genuine DEA agent being captured and killed by people protecting the syndicate."

"I can help with that," Becky interjected unexpectedly. Everyone looked at her, surprised. She was still holding Ryan, but her face had taken on the determined expression Shea remembered from their college days when Becky decided something needed to be done. "I'm nobody important to Rothmore's organization. Just a desperate mother who came looking for her son. What if I'm the one who identifies Elena?"

"Absolutely not," Shea said immediately. "You're not getting involved in the operational side of this."

"I'm already involved." Becky's voice was firm. "They kidnapped my child. They threatened to kill him.

I have every reason to want revenge on everyone associated with this organization. If I'm the one who accidentally reveals Elena's identity to the wrong people, it plays out perfectly. A grieving mother lashing out without understanding the consequences."

Elena nodded. "She's right. It creates distance between you and my exposure, Shea. Rothmore will still think you're trying to protect your cover, but circumstances outside your control led to my identity being revealed."

"And then what?" Trevor pressed. "Elena's identity is exposed, and then what happens to make it look like she's been killed?"

"A staged accident," Elena said. "Something public enough that Rothmore hears about it, but not so controlled that he can examine the body. A car crash, maybe, or a fire. Something that would destroy enough evidence to make the death believable, but that we can actually survive with DEA resources."

Ryan spoke up for the first time, his voice small but steady. "The man who watched us, the one with the video feeds, he talked about my dad a lot. He said they would move him tomorrow morning. Early, before sunrise. To someplace called the industrial yard."

Everyone froze. Becky looked at her son with surprise. "Ryan, baby, what did you hear?"

"A lot of things." Ryan's voice was stronger now. "They thought I wasn't listening, or that I was too scared to pay attention. But I heard them talking about locations, about people they were going to hurt, about when things were going to happen."

Trevor knelt in front of the boy, his voice gentle but urgent. "Ryan, this is really important. Do you remember anything else they said about your dad or where he might be?"

"They said he was causing problems. That the code he wrote had errors and was making them nervous. They wanted to move him someplace where they could watch him better." Ryan's eyes were wide but focused, like he understood the importance of what he was sharing. "And they mentioned a name a lot. The Banker. They said The Banker wanted to meet with Dad personally before the job on Friday."

"Which means Bill is still alive and The Banker still needs him," Elena concluded. "If we can find where they're moving him to, we can extract him before Friday's heist."

Shea's mind raced through the complexity of coordinating multiple operations with a ticking clock. "We have roughly thirty-six hours before Rothmore expects me to deliver Elena. In that time, we need to: find and extract Bill, stage Elena's death convincingly enough to fool The Banker's network, and position federal assets to take down the entire organization before they realize they've been played."

"That's a lot of moving parts," Trevor said. "A lot of things that could go wrong."

"Then we make sure nothing goes wrong." Shea

glanced at Elena. "Elena, contact your most trusted DEA supervisors. The ones you're certain aren't compromised. We need teams staged and ready to move the moment we give the signal."

She turned to Becky. "You and Ryan need to get off this boat and back to safety. The Lucky Dragon isn't secure anymore, and I won't risk either of you being caught in the crossfire."

"What about you?" Becky asked, fear evident in her eyes. "If Rothmore suspects you're playing him—"

"Then I'll deal with that when it happens." Shea cut her off, not wanting to think about the consequences of failure. "Right now, we have a narrow window to turn this entire situation around. We've been on the defense since we started this investigation, always responding to The Banker's moves. It's time we went on the offense."

Trevor moved to the cabin's small desk and pulled out a map of Memphis and the surrounding areas. "The industrial yard Ryan mentioned—there are three facilities in the Memphis area that match that description. If they're moving Bill early tomorrow, we need to figure out which one and have people in position."

"Pixel might be able to narrow it down." Elena pulled out her encrypted phone. "He's been monitoring The Banker's communications network. If there's chatter about the transfer, he'll catch it."

While Elena made her call, Shea sat down next to

Becky and Ryan. The boy had stopped crying but still clung to his mother .

"Ryan, you were so brave," Shea said softly. "What you did, listening, remembering, staying strong, that's going to help us save your dad and stop the people who hurt you."

"Are you really going to stop them?" Ryan asked, his voice small but hopeful. "The man who guarded us said nobody could stop The Banker. That he owned everyone, even the police."

"He doesn't own us." She squeezed Ryan's hand. "And we're going to prove that some things can't be bought or intimidated. Your dad's been fighting back this whole time, leaving clues and evidence. We're going to finish what he started."

Elena ended her call, her expression grim but determined. "Pixel intercepted communications about a transfer scheduled for oh-five-hundred hours tomorrow. They're moving a high-value asset to the Riverside Industrial Complex. That's the facility near the river where they store shipping containers."

"Perfect location for keeping someone hidden," Trevor observed. "Hundreds of containers, most of them empty, easy to move someone around if they suspect surveillance."

"Then that's where we'll be waiting." Adrenaline flooded through Shea. "Trevor, coordinate with Elena's tactical team. I want overwatch on that facility by midnight and assets ready to move the moment Bill appears."

She turned to Becky. "Take Ryan somewhere safe with protective custody. I need to know you're both far away from this boat and The Banker's reach."

Becky stood, still holding Ryan against her side. "Promise me you'll get Bill back. Promise me we'll have our family back, even if it's broken and needs fixing."

"I promise." Shea pulled her best friend into a fierce hug. "You've trusted me this far. Trust me a little further."

After Becky and Ryan left, escorted by one of Elena's trusted contacts, the three investigators stood in the cabin that had become their war room.

"This is it," Elena said quietly. "Tomorrow, we extract Bill, expose my identity, stage my death, and trigger the takedown of The Banker's entire organization. If anything goes wrong—"

"Nothing will go wrong," Trevor interrupted. "Because we don't have the luxury of failure. Too many people depend on us."

Shea looked at the two people who'd become not just colleagues but genuine partners in this impossible mission. "Tomorrow, we end this. One way or another."

Outside the cabin windows, Memphis glittered with lights, unaware that beneath its surface, a war was being waged between justice and corruption. Somewhere out there, Bill Miller was being moved like a chess piece in a game he'd never wanted to play.

Somewhere, The Banker sat in his empire, confident that his web of influence and intimidation would protect him from consequences.

Tomorrow, they would prove him wrong.

Tomorrow, they would bring him down.

Tomorrow, everything would change.

Chapter Fourteen

The abandoned warehouse on the outskirts of Memphis looked like a thousand other derelict industrial buildings with broken windows, graffiti-covered walls, and isolation. Perfect for what they needed.

Shea stood in the shadows across the street, watching as Elena's car—a nondescript silver sedan registered to one of her cover identities—pulled into the warehouse parking lot at exactly 2:47 AM. According to the script they'd carefully crafted, Elena was meeting a confidential informant who'd promised information about The Banker's operation.

According to the script, Rothmore would soon believe she was walking into an ambush.

"You sure about this?" Trevor's voice came through her earpiece. He was positioned three blocks away with a clear exit route, ready to extract Elena the moment the staged "death" was complete.

"As sure as I can be about faking someone's

murder." Shea adjusted the high-end camera Elena's DEA tech specialist had provided. The kind that news photographers used, capable of capturing images in low light that would look authentic on tomorrow's police reports.

Elena emerged from her car, moving with caution. She was dressed in dark clothes, her weapon visible in a shoulder holster. Everything about her body language screamed "federal agent conducting a dangerous meet."

Right on schedule, two vehicles pulled into the lot from opposite directions, boxing Elena's car in. Four men emerged—not actual members of The Banker's organization, but DEA agents playing the role with a commitment born of understanding how vital this deception was.

Shea began taking photos as the confrontation unfolded. Elena reaching for her weapon. The men surrounding her. A flash of muzzle fire from blanks that would photograph as real bullets. Elena falling, her body positioned to hide the blood pack she'd rigged under her shirt.

More photos as the men dragged her "body" into the warehouse. The silver sedan's windows being shot out with real bullets. Gasoline being poured. Then the explosion—carefully controlled by DEA demolitions experts, but photographed from an angle that made it look catastrophically violent.

Shea kept shooting, documenting every moment, knowing that Rothmore would have these images analyzed by experts. They needed to be perfect, needed to show exactly what The Banker expected to see: a federal agent exposed, ambushed, and eliminated.

As the warehouse burned, Shea triggered the next phase. Her phone call to 911, her voice shaking with perfect simulated panic: "There's been an explosion! I saw people shooting, then fire—oh God, I think someone's dead."

She stayed on the line long enough to give the address, then disconnected and melted back into the shadows. Fire trucks and police would arrive within minutes. They'd find exactly what Elena's people had staged. Evidence of a violent confrontation, a burned vehicle, enough DNA evidence in the wreckage to suggest a body had been present, and multiple witnesses (all DEA plants) who would corroborate seeing the shooting.

By dawn, Memphis news would be reporting the death of a federal agent in what appeared to be a targeted assassination. By mid-morning, that story would reach Rothmore's intelligence network.

And by afternoon, Shea would be summoned to explain exactly what she knew about the woman whose death she'd witnessed.

~

The call came at 2:00 PM, exactly as Elena had predicted. Victor Swanson's voice, professionally neutral: "Mrs. Harrison, Mr. Rothmore would like to meet with you. Today, 4:00 PM, his private office aboard the Lucky Dragon."

"Of course." Shea injected just the right amount of nervous eagerness into her voice. "I'll be there."

She spent the next two hours preparing. The right clothes, expensive but subdued, suggested someone who'd crossed a moral line and was trying to project confidence despite inner turmoil. Minimal makeup that made her look slightly tired, like someone who'd witnessed violence and hadn't slept well. Every detail mattered.

Trevor helped her check the new wire Elena's tech team had provided. This one would be undetectable even by the most sophisticated scanning equipment. "Remember," he said quietly, his hands lingering on her shoulders, "you're Catherine Harrison, who just witnessed a federal agent being killed. You're shaken, maybe having second thoughts, but ultimately committed to proving your loyalty to Rothmore."

"I know my role." Shea's stomach churned. This meeting would determine whether Rothmore bought their deception or saw through it.

At 3:55 PM, Shea knocked on the door to Rothmore's private office. A luxurious space on the Lucky Dragon's top deck that overlooked the river. Marcus Wade opened the door, his expression unreadable as he conducted a security scan. The device he used passed over her body, over her jewelry, detecting nothing.

"She's clean," Wade reported to Rothmore, who sat

behind a massive desk that screamed both wealth and power.

"Mrs. Harrison. Or should I say, Sheriff Callahan?" Rothmore's smile didn't reach his eyes. "Please, sit. We have much to discuss."

Shea took the offered chair, forcing herself to maintain eye contact despite wanting to look away from his calculating gaze. "I prefer Catherine, if you don't mind. Sheriff Callahan feels like someone from a life I'm leaving behind."

"Interesting choice of words." Rothmore steepled his fingers. "Tell me about last night. I understand you witnessed something rather dramatic in a warehouse district."

"I followed the woman. Elena Reyes." Shea let her voice shake slightly. "After you revealed she was DEA, I wanted to see who she was meeting, what she was planning. I thought if I could provide you with intelligence about her investigation, it would prove my commitment."

"And what did you witness?"

"Men waiting for her. An ambush. They shot her, dragged her body into a building, then set everything on fire." Shea wrapped her arms around herself in a gesture of self-comfort that looked entirely natural. "I've seen violence before in my work as sheriff, but nothing like that. Nothing so... calculated."

Rothmore studied her for a long moment. "You understand that you've now crossed a line that can't be uncrossed? You witnessed the elimination of a federal agent and said nothing to law enforcement. That makes you complicit, Sheriff. That makes you one of us."

"I understand." Shea met his eyes steadily. "And I'm okay with that. My career in law enforcement was going nowhere. Small-town politics, limited resources, no real power. You're offering something more."

"Power and wealth," Rothmore agreed. "But also risk. The life I offer isn't for everyone. It requires a certain flexibility of morality, a willingness to operate outside the law when necessary."

"I think I've demonstrated that willingness."

Rothmore smiled, and this time it held genuine warmth, or as close to warmth as a man like him could manage. "Yes, you have. Which is why I'm prepared to show you what you're joining."

He stood and moved to a hidden panel in the wall to reveal a large touchscreen display. With a few taps, a map of the United States appeared, dotted with glowing points of light.

"What you see here represents my organization's gambling operations," Rothmore's voice carried the pride of someone showing off a successful business empire. "Twelve states, operating both legally and in grey areas of the law. Each location is carefully positioned to maximize profit while minimizing law enforcement interference."

Shea leaned forward, genuinely fascinated despite herself. The scope was staggering. Far larger than any of their intelligence had suggested. "How much revenue are we talking about?"

"Last year? Five hundred and twelve million dollars." Rothmore let that number sink in. "That's just from the gambling operations. When you add money laundering services, loan operations, and our specialized project facilitation, the total revenue exceeds eight hundred million annually."

"Project facilitation?" Shea asked, playing the role of someone eager to understand the business.

"Exactly what it sounds like. Wealthy clients come to me with projects they can't accomplish through legitimate means. I facilitate those projects using a network of coerced experts. People with valuable skills who can be controlled through strategic leverage."

He pulled up another screen showing a list of "projects" completed over the past three years. Shea's blood ran cold as she read. Bank vault penetrations, corporate espionage, blackmail operations, and there, third from the bottom: "Military protocol breach for weapons acquisition."

"This Friday's operation," Rothmore continued, pulling up detailed plans, "has been in development for eighteen months. Most people believe we're targeting a Federal Reserve transfer. That's the story we've let leak through carefully controlled channels. The reality is far more valuable."

He zoomed in on logistics documents that showed convoy routes, security details, and classified information that should never have been accessible to civilians. "We're not robbing an armored car, Sheriff. We're intercepting a military transport carrying next-generation encryption keys and security protocols. Technology worth billions on the black market, particularly to foreign governments and corporate competitors."

"And that's where Bill Miller comes in," Shea said, connecting the pieces. "You need his software expertise to hack the military security systems."

"Precisely. The man is brilliant, even if his gambling addiction made him vulnerable to recruitment." Rothmore's expression hardened. "Though I'm beginning to suspect he's been less cooperative than he's pretended. His code has errors, subtle ones that might cause the operation to fail at critical moments."

Shea's pulse spiked, but she kept her face neutral. Bill's deliberate sabotage was working, making The Banker nervous. "What will you do with him after the operation?"

"The same thing I do with all temporary assets once their usefulness expires." Rothmore's tone was matter-of-fact, discussing murder with the casual indifference of someone discussing quarterly earnings. "Though first, I'll need him to verify his code is actually functional. Which is why we moved him this morning to a more secure facility where he can be properly motivated."

"The children," Shea said, playing her role. "You're using them as motivation."

"Of course. Ryan Miller is currently at a secondary holding facility along with several other children whose parents are working on various projects. It's remarkable how compliant people become when their children's lives hang in the balance."

Rothmore moved closer, his voice dropping to something almost intimate. "You seem disturbed by this, Sheriff. Does it trouble your conscience?"

"I'm adjusting my perspective," Shea replied carefully. "In law enforcement, we're taught that protecting children is the highest priority. But I'm beginning to understand that in your world, leverage is simply leverage. Sentiment doesn't enter into it."

"Exactly right. Sentiment is a weakness I eliminated a long time ago." He returned to his desk, pulling up another document. "The secondary facility is located here—" he indicated a location on a map "—approximately forty miles outside Memphis. Six children in total, guarded by a rotating team of eight operatives. Security is significant because the children represent leverage over assets, completing projects worth hundreds of millions."

Shea memorized every detail he revealed, knowing this intelligence was worth the risk of this entire deception. The location of the children. The scope of the operation. The true target of Friday's "heist." Her wire was recording all of it, all of it would be evidence to bring down not just Rothmore but his entire network.

"I'm impressed by the scale of your operation," Shea said honestly. "And I understand why you need people you can trust in key positions."

"Which brings me to your role moving forward." Rothmore pulled out a contract, an actual physical document, and slid it across his desk. "You'll continue operating as sheriff of Misty Hollow, but you'll also serve as a regional coordinator for my operations in Arkansas and Southern Missouri. You'll identify potential assets. People with gambling problems, people with valuable skills, people who can be recruited through financial pressure or coerced through leverage."

He tapped the contract. "The compensation is listed here. Base salary of five hundred thousand annually, plus bonuses based on successful project completions. In exchange, you provide intelligence on law enforcement activities, protection for my operations in your jurisdiction, and assistance in recruiting and controlling assets."

Shea pretended to read the contract, though she was actually calculating how much evidence they now had. Everything Rothmore had revealed, the organizational structure, the Friday operation's true target, the location of the remaining children, was being transmitted to Elena's team in real-time.

"And if I sign this," Shea asked, "what happens to Bill Miller and his son after Friday?"

"I'll be generous. Suppose Bill's code works perfectly and the operation succeeds. In that case, I'll release Ryan unharmed and give Bill a choice to continue working for me on future projects, or disappear with a substantial payment to ensure his silence." Rothmore's smile was cold. "Of course, if the code fails or I discover he's been sabotaging my operation, neither of them will leave Memphis alive."

"I understand." Shea picked up the pen Rothmore offered. "Where do I sign?"

"Not yet." Rothmore held up a hand. "First, I need you to prove one more time that you've truly crossed over to my side. Tomorrow morning, Bill Miller will be moved to a testing facility where we'll verify his code's functionality. I want you there, Sheriff. Please watch as we motivate him to ensure his complete cooperation. And if his son's life isn't sufficient motivation, I want you to be the one who escalates the pressure."

The request landed like a punch to Shea's gut. Rothmore wanted her to participate in torturing Bill and potentially threatening Ryan. To become directly complicit in crimes against the very people she'd sworn to protect.

"And if I refuse?" she asked quietly.

"Then you leave this office, and I never see you again. But Sheriff, if you leave, you should know that everyone you've told about my operation—your deputy, any federal agents you've contacted, anyone who knows what you've learned—will be identified and eliminated.

I have resources you can't imagine and reach that extend into agencies you think are untouchable."

The threat was clear. Walk away, and everyone she cared about would be hunted down and killed.

"What time tomorrow?" Shea accepted the devil's bargain even as her mind raced through options.

"Seven AM. I'll have Marcus pick you up from your cabin." Rothmore extended his hand. "Welcome to the organization, Sheriff Callahan. I have a feeling you're going to be a valuable asset."

Shea shook his hand, feeling ice in her veins as she sealed this terrible agreement. But beneath her fear and revulsion, determination burned. She'd gotten what she needed. The location of the children, the truth about Friday's operation, and evidence of Rothmore's entire criminal empire.

Now she just needed to survive until Elena's team could move, until they could extract Bill and raid both the primary facility and the secondary location holding the children. Survive until Friday, when Rothmore's entire operation would be in motion and vulnerable to being shut down permanently.

As she left Rothmore's office, Trevor's voice came through her earpiece, barely audible. "Did you get it? The locations?"

"Everything," Shea whispered. "He gave me everything. But Trevor, we don't have a lot of time before he expects me to hurt Bill and Ryan. We need to move now."

"Elena's already coordinating with DEA tactical teams. Multiple simultaneous raids are scheduled for Friday morning, right before the weapons transport attempt. We're going to take down every location at once—the casino boat, the facility where they're holding Bill, the secondary location with the children, even Rothmore's legitimate business fronts."

"What about me?" Shea asked. "Rothmore expects me at that facility tomorrow morning at seven."

"Then you'll be there," Trevor replied. "But this time, you won't be alone. This time, we'll be ready for whatever happens."

Shea returned to her cabin and immediately began transmitting everything she'd learned to Elena's encrypted server. Locations, names, organizational structure, the true target of the Friday operation. All of it went into the case file that would bring down The Banker's empire.

Her phone buzzed with a text from an unknown number: "Watched your performance today. Very convincing. But remember—I'll be watching tomorrow too. Don't disappoint me. —JR"

James Rothmore was keeping tabs on her, probably had been since the moment she left his office. Every move she made, every person she contacted, every decision...all of it would be monitored by someone who specialized in detecting deception.

Tomorrow would be the most dangerous day of her career. Tomorrow she'd have to stand beside evil men and pretend to be one of them while secretly working to destroy everything they'd built.

Tomorrow would determine whether justice prevailed or whether The Banker's criminal empire would continue destroying lives for years to come.

But tonight, she'd gathered the intelligence needed to bring him down. Tonight, Elena, Trevor, and an army of federal agents were preparing the operation that would end this nightmare.

Tonight, hope remained alive.

Chapter Fifteen

Pixel's voice crackled through Shea's phone at three in the morning, yanking her from the restless sleep she'd finally managed. "I found something. You need to see this now."

Twenty minutes later, Shea and Trevor were back in Pixel's loft, staring at screens filled with data that made Shea's exhausted brain struggle to process. Elena joined them via video call, her face grainy on the monitor.

"Bill's been leaving breadcrumbs everywhere." Pixel pulled up file after file. "Not just in the obvious places, but buried in metadata, hidden in image files, encoded in timestamps. The man's been documenting his entire captivity in ways his captors would never think to look."

He opened a series of photographs that appeared to be innocent surveillance camera stills. "These look like standard security footage, right? But watch what happens when I run them through a steganography decoder."

The images shifted, revealing text embedded within the digital files themselves. Coordinates. Dates. Names. A whole secondary layer of information invisible to casual observation.

"He's been creating a map." Trevor leaned forward. "Every location they've moved him, every person he's encountered, every piece of intelligence he could gather are all hidden in plain sight."

"Exactly." Pixel pulled up a geographical overlay showing multiple locations across three states. "Most of these we've already identified—the warehouse, the compound, the testing facility. But there's one location that keeps appearing in his files that we haven't accounted for yet."

He zoomed in on rural Oklahoma, about two hundred miles from the Texas border. "A ranch. Privately owned through another one of The Banker's shell corporations. And look at what Bill embedded in the security camera footage from this location."

The decoded text made Shea's stomach drop: "Secondary holding—children ages 4-11—minimal guard presence—isolated—extraction possible."

"There are more children," Shea breathed. "Not just the ones at the Memphis location. He's been holding kids at multiple sites to prevent a single raid from freeing them all."

Elena's voice came through the speakers, tight with controlled anger. "How many are we talking about?"

Pixel pulled up more decoded files. "Bill documented at least six children at the Oklahoma ranch. Combined with the four we already extracted and Ryan, that's eleven kids total whose parents are being coerced through kidnapping."

"Eleven families destroyed by this monster," Trevor said, his voice hard. "How long has this been going on?"

"Based on Bill's documentation? At least three years. Some of these children have been held for over eighteen months." Pixel's fingers flew across his keyboard. "He's also identified the guards, the rotation schedules, even the layout of the ranch buildings. Bill's been planning an escape attempt or documenting everything for whoever might eventually find his files."

Shea studied the ranch location on the map. "It's remote. Nearest town is forty miles away, and that's barely a town. Maybe two hundred people. Perfect place to hide kidnapped children where no one would hear them scream."

"It's also a five-hour drive from Memphis," Trevor pointed out. "If we're going to extract these kids before Rothmore's Friday operation, we need to move now."

Elena's face filled the main screen. "I can coordinate federal resources, but it'll take time to get DEA tactical teams positioned. The ranch is in FBI jurisdiction, and with the mole situation, I don't know who to trust in the Oklahoma field office."

"Then we don't wait for federal backup," Shea

decided. "Trevor and I go to Oklahoma now, scout the location, and extract those children ourselves if we have to."

"That's insane," Elena protested. "You're two people against however many guards they have stationed. Even with Bill's intelligence, you'll be outgunned and outnumbered."

"So, we even the odds." Shea was already planning logistics in her head. "We bring local law enforcement in at the last moment. County sheriff, state police, people who aren't connected to federal agencies where the mole might have influence. We hit the ranch, get the kids out, and by the time Rothmore realizes what's happened, they're already in protective custody."

Trevor was nodding, his tactical mind working through the details. "It could work. Small team, quick extraction, overwhelming local backup if things go wrong. We'd need to move fast though. Leave within the hour, arrive at the ranch by mid-morning, conduct reconnaissance, and execute tonight while it's still dark."

"I'm coming with you," a voice said from the loft's entrance.

Everyone turned to see Becky standing in the doorway, her expression set with determination that Shea recognized from their college days. "Before you argue, I've already arranged for my parents to keep Ryan for a few more days. I'm going to Oklahoma."

"Becky, this is a tactical operation," Shea

protested. "It's dangerous, potentially deadly. You're not trained for—"

"Those children have parents who are going through exactly what I went through," Becky interrupted. "Terrified, helpless, probably blaming themselves for the situations that led to their kids being taken. When we rescue those children, their parents are going to need someone who understands what they've been through. Someone who can help them process the trauma and guilt."

She moved further into the loft, her voice steady. "Plus, you're going to need someone in the vehicle coordinating communications while you two are conducting the actual rescue. I can do that. I've been doing dispatch work for a volunteer search and rescue organization for two years. I know how to manage multiple radio channels and keep track of moving assets."

Shea exchanged glances with Trevor, who shrugged slightly. "She's not wrong about needing someone to handle comms. And having a civilian presence might help when we're trying to explain to local law enforcement why two Arkansas officers are conducting an operation in Oklahoma."

"Fine," Shea conceded, though worry gnawed at her. "But you follow orders, stay in the vehicle, and if I tell you to run, you run. Understood?" Her friend had been a fierce adversary during their time during a girls' weekend when they'd been hunted by a group of men.

She could be a help now, too.

"Understood." Becky's relief was evident. "When do we leave?"

"Thirty minutes." Trevor was already gathering equipment. "Pixel, send us everything Bill documented about the ranch—guard schedules, building layouts, security systems. And keep monitoring for any indication that Rothmore knows we're onto this location."

As they prepared to leave, Elena's voice stopped them. "Shea, Trevor...be careful. If Rothmore discovers you've left Memphis before tomorrow's meeting, he'll know something's wrong. And if he realizes we've found his ranch..."

"Then he accelerates his timeline, and we lose any advantage we have," Shea finished. "I know. We'll be back by dawn, with or without those children. Either way, we show up tomorrow morning like nothing's changed."

~

The drive to Oklahoma stretched through the pre-dawn darkness, Interstate 40 carrying them west through Arkansas and into territory that grew increasingly rural as they left Memphis behind. Trevor drove while Shea reviewed Bill's files on her laptop, memorizing every detail of the ranch layout.

Becky sat in the back seat, quiet for the first hour before finally speaking. "I should have seen it. The signs were all there."

Shea looked up from her laptop. "Seen what?"

"Bill's gambling problem. His desperation." Becky's voice was thick with guilt. "I was his wife. I should have known how bad things had gotten before he was in so deep that these people could exploit him."

"Addiction is incredibly good at hiding itself," Shea said gently. "Gamblers, especially, become expert liars. They have to be to maintain the addiction while keeping family and friends from realizing how much they're losing. Besides, the two of you separated."

"But there were signs. Phone calls he'd take privately. Money that went missing from our accounts. Times when he said he was working late but came home smelling like cigarette smoke from casinos." Becky's reflection in the window showed tears on her cheeks. "I told myself I was imagining things, that I was being paranoid. But really, I didn't want to face the truth that the man I married was falling apart and I couldn't stop it."

Trevor glanced in the rearview mirror. "My uncle was a gambling addict. Lost everything—house, marriage, relationship with his kids. My aunt blamed herself for years, thinking she should have seen it coming, should have been able to fix him. But here's the truth: addiction is a disease, not a choice. Once it has its hooks in someone, they need professional help, not just willpower or family support."

"Bill went to Gamblers Anonymous," Becky said. "Or at least, he told me he was going. I found out later he'd been lying about that too, just using it as cover to go to more casinos."

"Which shows how powerful the disease is," Shea said. "Bill loved you and Ryan. That was obvious from everything we've learned about him. But the addiction was stronger than love, stronger than fear, stronger than logic. That's not your failure. That's the nature of what he was fighting."

Becky was quiet for a long moment. "When this is over, when Bill is safe and those other children are free, what happens to him? Does he go to prison for what he did while being coerced?"

"That depends," Shea replied honestly. "Federal prosecutors will have to decide how much of his cooperation was voluntary versus under duress. The evidence Bill gathered, the sabotage he attempted, the clues he left...That all demonstrates he tried to fight back even while being forced to commit crimes."

"He'll probably face charges," Trevor added. "But with a good lawyer and the evidence of coercion, he might get a suspended sentence or probation. The goal isn't to punish victims. It's to punish the people who exploited them."

"I don't know if I can forgive him," Becky admitted quietly. "For the gambling, for the lies, for putting Ryan in danger. But I also don't want to spend the rest of my life hating him. That's not healthy for any of us."

"Forgiveness isn't something you have to figure

out today," Shea said. "Right now, focus on getting through this. Save those kids, reunite them with their families, and help Bill testify against the people who destroyed so many lives. The rest can wait."

They drove through the sunrise, watching as the landscape transformed from the rolling hills of Arkansas to the flatter, more open terrain of eastern Oklahoma. Small towns passed by, each one looking like time had forgotten them—grain elevators, shuttered businesses, populations measured in hundreds rather than thousands.

"I've been thinking," Becky said as they approached their destination. "About what you said— that those parents will need someone who understands. After this is done, after Bill's legal situation is resolved, I want to start a support group. For families affected by gambling addiction, yes, but specifically for families who've been victimized by criminal organizations that exploit addiction."

"That's a good idea." Trevor glanced in the rearview mirror. "There's probably more need for that kind of support than anyone realizes."

"And maybe," Becky continued, "maybe sharing my story, being honest about the warning signs I missed and the choices I made, will help other families catch problems earlier. Before they end up with their children held hostage by criminals."

Shea reached back to squeeze her friend's hand. "Bill's not the only one who's going to help build a case against Rothmore. Your testimony, your perspective as a family member, that humanizes the victims in ways court documents can't."

The ranch appeared on the horizon exactly where Bill's coordinates indicated. A collection of weathered buildings surrounded by barbed wire fencing, isolated enough that the nearest neighbor was miles away. Trevor pulled off the highway onto a dirt road, parking behind a stand of trees that provided concealment.

"Reconnaissance first." Shea pulled binoculars from the glove compartment. "We need to confirm the children are there, count guards, and identify the best approach route."

Through the binoculars, she spotted a main house, a large barn, and several outbuildings. A guard stood near the main entrance, smoking a cigarette and looking bored. As she watched, a woman emerged from one of the buildings with a laundry basket, probably not a guard, maybe a cook or caretaker.

"Two visible guards, possibly more inside," Shea reported. "The building on the east side—see how it has bars on the windows? That's probably where they're keeping the kids."

Trevor peered through his own binoculars. "Camera on the main gate, another on the barn. We'll need to disable those before we approach. And look at that vehicle near the house. A black SUV with Oklahoma plates. I'll run them through the database, see if they're registered to one of Rothmore's shell companies."

"How are we going to get in?" Becky asked.

"We wait for dark," Shea replied. "Then we cut the power, disable the cameras, and go in fast. With luck, we'll have the children out before the guards can mount a coordinated response."

"And without luck?" Becky pressed.

Trevor answered, his voice grim. "Without luck, this turns into a firefight, and we have to hope the local sheriff's deputies we've called for backup arrive in time to tip the scales in our favor."

Chapter Sixteen

"Three guards," Trevor murmured beside Shea, his breath warm against the cold air. "Two on rotation, one stationary at the back entrance."

She nodded, tracking the movement of a man in tactical gear as he walked the perimeter. These weren't casual muscle. They moved with military precision, rifles held at ready positions, eyes constantly scanning. The kind of men who'd shoot first and never bother with questions.

"Where are the children?" Becky's voice trembled as she whispered from Shea's other side.

"Basement?" Shea said. "Underground, soundproofed. Less chance of anyone stumbling across something they shouldn't see."

They'd driven through the night to reach this place, following the digital breadcrumbs Bill had left in the code Shea had accessed at Rothmore's estate. The man was clever at hiding coordinates in metadata, encoding messages in what looked like random error logs. Each clue had been a risk, a tiny rebellion against the people who'd taken his son.

Trevor shifted, his shoulder pressing against hers. The contact was brief, probably unintentional, but Shea felt it like an anchor. They'd barely spoken during the drive, both of them processing what awaited them here. Becky had filled the silence with worried questions about Ryan, about Bill, about everything. Shea had answered when she could, but mostly she'd been trying to figure out how they'd pull this off without getting anyone killed.

"There," Trevor said, pointing. "Vehicle approaching."

Headlights cut through the darkness, an old pickup truck kicking up dust on the dirt road. Shea watched it pull up to the main house. A man got out—tall, thin, stooped shoulders. Even from this distance, even in the dim light, she recognized him.

"That's Bill," Becky breathed.

He looked worse than his mugshot. His clothes hung loose, his movements were jerky with exhaustion or fear or both. One of the guards met him at the door, exchanged a few words, and then let him inside. The whole interaction lasted maybe thirty seconds, but Shea saw everything she needed to see in Bill's body language. He was a prisoner pretending to be an employee.

"We need to contact him," Shea said. "Trevor, you remember the signal?"

"Baseball reference. Something about the Cardinals' 1987 season." Trevor pulled out his phone, fingers moving across the screen. "Bill's got to have his phone on him if he's been leaving us clues."

They'd found the communication protocol in Bill's last message. A convoluted system using a fantasy baseball forum that nobody in their right mind would monitor. Shea had thought it was paranoid when she'd first decoded it. Now she understood. When your child's life depends on staying undetected, paranoid is just another word for careful.

Trevor typed for a minute, then showed her the screen. *Remember that Cardinals-Giants game in '87? Crazy ending. What inning was that again?*

"Generic enough," Shea said. "Send it."

The waiting was the worst part. Shea watched the house, counting the seconds, wondering if Bill would even see the message. Wondering if they'd already lost him, if Rothmore had figured out what he'd been doing.

Five minutes passed. Then ten.

"Shea." Trevor showed her the phone.

The response had come through: *Bottom of the ninth. Game ended at 9:42 PM. Never forget.*

"Nine forty-two," Shea repeated. "Tomorrow night. That's when the weapons deal goes down."

"What about the rest?" Becky asked. "What does it mean?"

Shea studied the message again, looking for the layers beneath the surface. Bill was smart. Everything he wrote had multiple meanings. "Never forget" could be a reference to the game, but it could also be something else. A reminder. A promise.

Trevor caught it first. "He's telling us he hasn't forgotten why he's doing this. The kids. His son. He's still fighting."

Another message appeared: *Stadium security was a joke back then. Real easy to sneak in through the employee entrance. They never changed the master codes.*

Shea felt something click into place. "He built a backdoor. Into whatever security system he's set up here. He's giving us a way in."

"How do we get the codes?" Becky asked.

Shea was already typing. *Need ticket info. Where do I pick them up?*

The response came faster this time: *Check the dugout. Third base side. Look under the bench.*

"He's hidden something," Trevor said. "Probably in the house. We need to get closer."

Shea lowered the binoculars. The guards were good, but they were also bored. She'd watched them for a while now, noticed the way their attention drifted during the quiet moments between patrols. They weren't expecting trouble out here in the middle of nowhere. That overconfidence was an opening.

"We wait until full light," she said. "The morning shift change. That's when they'll be least alert."

"And then what?" Becky asked. "How do we get

six children out of there without those men noticing?"

"We don't hide it," Shea said. "We make them look the other way."

She outlined the plan, keeping her voice low. Trevor would create a distraction. Something loud, something that would pull the guards toward the front of the property. While they were occupied, Shea would go in through the back, find Bill, and get the security codes. Becky would wait in their vehicle, ready to move the moment they had the children.

"What about Bill?" Becky asked. "We're not leaving him there."

"We're not leaving anyone." Shea met her friend's eyes, saw the raw fear there, the guilt that had been eating at her since this started. "But Bill's our asset inside. He stays until we're ready to move on Rothmore. If we pull him out now, they'll know something's wrong."

"You're asking him to stay in that place." Becky's voice cracked. "With those men. After everything—"

"I'm asking him to finish what he started." Shea kept her tone gentle but firm. "Bill's been leaving us clues for weeks. He's been sabotaging their operation from the inside. He's been fighting for Ryan, for all those kids. Taking him out now would make all of that meaningless."

Becky looked away, blinking hard against tears. Trevor reached over, squeezed her shoulder. "Your ex-husband is braver than he probably ever thought he could be," he said quietly. "Let him see this through."

The sky was starting to lighten, stars fading into the gray promise of morning. Shea checked her watch. Five-thirty. The guards would change shift at six, like clockwork. They'd maintained the same pattern for three days, according to the surveillance logs the FBI had shared. Creatures of habit, even the dangerous ones.

"One more thing." Shea pulled out her phone and sent a text to the number Elena Reyes had given her. The DEA agent was coordinating with the FBI, setting up the raid on Rothmore's estate. Everything had to happen simultaneously. The rescue here, the takedown there. If either operation failed, the other was compromised.

The response came immediately: *FBI ready. Give the signal, and we move.*

Shea showed the message to Trevor. He nodded, his jaw set in that way she'd come to recognize. She trusted that mind, trusted him. Which was good, because what they were about to do was insane on every practical level.

"Becky," Shea said, "I need you to understand something. When we go in there, things might get violent. If they do, if shooting starts, you stay in the vehicle. You don't try to help, you don't try to be a hero. You wait for us to bring those children to you, and then you drive. You drive like hell, and you don't stop until you're at the FBI checkpoint twenty miles east. Are we clear?"

"I'm not leaving you—"

"You're protecting six children," Shea interrupted. "That's your job. That's the only job that matters. Trevor and I can handle ourselves."

Becky stared at her for a long moment, then nodded slowly. "Okay, I understand."

They waited as the darkness lifted, watching the ranch come into focus with dawn. Shea could see details now. The rust on the corrugated metal roof of the largest barn, the broken window on the second floor of the house, the cigarette butts scattered near the back door where the stationary guard stood smoking, his rifle slung over his shoulder.

At five fifty-eight, movement. A vehicle approached from the east, another pickup truck. The morning shift, arriving early. Shea watched the guards at the house step forward to greet the newcomers, saw the familiar dance of shift change—the brief conversations, the casual body language of men who did this every day and expected nothing unusual.

"Now," Shea said.

Trevor moved first, slipping away through the scrub oak. Shea gave him a three-minute head start, then turned to Becky. "Remember what I said. Stay safe. Those children are counting on you."

"Just bring them out," Becky whispered. "Please."

Shea circled wide, using the terrain and the growing light to her advantage. The guards were focused on their shift change, distracted by routine. She made it to the back of the property, pressed herself against the wall of the barn, listening. Voices carried on the morning air. Casual talk about the weather, about breakfast, about nothing that mattered.

Then Trevor's distraction hit.

The explosion wasn't huge, but it was loud enough. Somewhere on the far side of the property, a fireball climbed into the sky—one of the old propane tanks Trevor had spotted during surveillance, rigged with a timer. The guards reacted instantly, military training taking over, shouting orders as they moved toward the blast site.

Shea was already moving, sprinting across the open ground to the back door. The stationary guard had abandoned his post, drawn by the explosion. She tried the handle—locked, of course. She pulled out the lock picks she'd brought, hands steady despite the adrenaline singing through her veins.

The lock clicked. She was inside.

The house smelled like stale coffee and unwashed men. Shea moved through the kitchen, weapon drawn, clearing corners the way she'd been trained. The interior was sparse—cheap furniture, bare walls, the kind of place meant for function rather than comfort. Stairs led down to a heavy door with a keypad lock.

This was it. The basement where they kept the children. It had to be.

She tried the code Bill had hidden in his message.

1987, the year of the Cardinals game. The keypad beeped red. Wrong. Shea's heart hammered. She tried variations—8719, 1789, 8791. Nothing.

Footsteps above her. Someone was coming.

She pressed herself against the wall, gun raised. A figure appeared at the top of the stairs. Bill Miller, his face pale, his eyes wide with recognition.

"Sheriff," he breathed. "You found it."

"The code," Shea said urgently. "I need the code."

Bill descended quickly, his hands shaking as he punched in a sequence…nine, four, two, one, nine, eight, seven. The date and time of that Cardinals game, reversed. The lock clicked green.

"Six children," Bill said. "They're scared. They've been down there for weeks, some of them. There's a woman, Maria, who's been taking care of them. Tell her Bill sent you."

"Come with us," Shea said.

"I can't." Bill's voice was steady despite the fear in his eyes. "If I disappear now, Rothmore will know. He'll call off the weapons deal, scatter his people. You'll never catch them all. But if I stay, if I keep playing my part..." He swallowed hard. "Ryan's safe. That's what matters. I can do this. I can finish it."

Shea wanted to argue, wanted to drag him out of there by force. But she saw something in Bill Miller's face that stopped her. Determination, yes, but also redemption. He'd spent months as a prisoner, doing terrible things to protect his son. Now he had a chance to do something good, something that mattered beyond his own family.

"The raid happens tomorrow night," Shea said. "Nine forty-two. FBI's hitting Rothmore's estate. When they do, you get out. You run, you hide, whatever you need to do. But you survive this. You hear me?"

"I hear you." Bill managed a weak smile. "Tell Ryan... tell him his dad did the right thing. Finally."

Footsteps pounded overhead—the guards, returning from investigating the explosion. Bill's eyes widened. "Go. Now. I'll buy you time."

He turned and headed back up the stairs, his movements deliberate, loud enough to cover the sound of Shea opening the basement door. She slipped through, pulling it closed behind her as she heard Bill's voice above, saying something about checking the security monitors, his tone casual like nothing was wrong.

The basement was exactly what she'd feared. A converted prison, concrete walls, minimal light, and the smell of fear. Six children looked up at her from makeshift beds, their faces ranging from maybe four years old to early teens. A Hispanic woman in her forties stood protectively in front of them, her expression fierce despite the terror in her eyes.

"Maria?" Shea asked quietly. "Bill sent me. We're getting you out."

The woman's shoulders sagged with relief. "You're real. I thought... we've been praying, but I thought..."

"I'm real," Shea said. "And we don't have much time. Can the children walk?"

"Yes. They're weak, but they can move." Maria helped the youngest child to her feet, whispering reassurances in Spanish. The other children rose, clinging to each other, eyes wide with desperate hope.

Shea activated her radio, kept her voice low. "Trevor. Status."

"Guards are contained on the east side. You've got maybe three minutes."

"Heading out now."

She led them up the stairs, moving as quietly as possible with six children and one adult. The house was empty. Bill had drawn the remaining guard away somehow, buying them precious seconds. They emerged into the morning light, and Shea saw Becky's vehicle already pulled up near the barn, driver's door open, engine running.

"Go." Shea helped Maria load the children into the back. They piled in, small bodies pressed together, faces turned toward a freedom they'd almost stopped believing in. The youngest was crying, tears streaming down dirty cheeks. The oldest, a girl, maybe thirteen, kept looking back at the house like she expected someone to stop them.

"Everyone in?" Becky called from the driver's seat.

"Go, go!" Shea slammed the door and slapped the side of the vehicle. Becky hit the gas, tires kicking up gravel as she accelerated down the dirt road.

Shouting from the house. The guards had figured it out.

Trevor appeared beside her, breathing hard. "Time to leave."

They ran for a vehicle, hidden in the scrub oak. Behind them, gunfire erupted—wild shots, angry and desperate. A bullet pinged off metal somewhere close. Shea dove into the passenger seat as Trevor gunned the engine, their SUV lurching forward over rough terrain.

"They're following." Trevor kept his eyes on the rearview mirror.

"Let them." Shea pulled out her phone and sent the signal to Elena. *Go now. We have the children.*

The response was immediate: *FBI is moving. Rothmore's estate under siege. Good hunting.*

They hit the main road, Trevor pushing the vehicle to its limits. Behind them, the guards' truck was falling back. They'd realized too late that this wasn't a fight they could win, not out in the open, not with law enforcement likely on the way.

"We did it," Trevor said quietly.

Shea nodded, but she was thinking about Bill Miller, still back at that ranch, still playing his part. Still fighting his private war. They'd gotten the children out, they'd coordinated with the FBI, they'd set everything in motion for tomorrow night's raid.

But it wasn't over. Not yet.

Tomorrow night, nine forty-two PM. That's when they'd end this.

That's when James Rothmore would finally answer for everything he'd done.

Chapter Seventeen

The Rothmore estate looked like a war zone.

Shea joined the take-down on The Banker. She'd started the job and wanted to finish.

Shea counted at least forty FBI vehicles blocking every access point. Agents swarmed the property like ants on a disturbed hill. Helicopters circled overhead, spotlights cutting through the dusk even though full dark was still twenty minutes away. She'd left Trevor at the FBI checkpoint with Becky and the rescued children, ignoring his protests that she should stay back, let the feds handle it.

But Bill Miller was in there somewhere. And Elena Reyes had been undercover so long she'd become a ghost. Shea wasn't about to sit safely on the sidelines while people who'd risked everything were still in danger.

She badged her way through the outer perimeter, flashing her sheriff's credentials at agents who looked at her like she was crazy for wanting to get closer. The estate sprawled across twenty acres of manicured grounds. The main house was a three-story colonial monstrosity, white columns and wrap-around porches that screamed old money. Outbuildings dotted the landscape: a pool house, a separate garage structure that probably cost more than Shea's annual salary, guest cottages tucked among ornamental gardens.

"Sheriff Callahan?" An agent materialized beside her, FBI vest strapped over his suit. Late thirties, sharp eyes, the kind of focus that came from running point on a major operation. "Special Agent Lincoln. I've been coordinating with Agent Reyes."

"Where is she?" Shea asked.

"Last contact was seventeen minutes ago. She confirmed Rothmore was in the main house, second-floor office. We've got teams moving in from four different entry points." Lincoln's radio crackled with position reports, agents calling out cleared rooms. "We've already made fifteen arrests. Accountants, lawyers, muscle. Everyone on the property when we hit."

Gunfire erupted from somewhere inside the hous. Sharp cracks followed by the deeper boom of tactical shotguns. Chen's expression tightened. "That's west wing, second floor. Where Rothmore should be."

They moved toward the house, Shea keeping pace with Lincoln as more agents converged. The front doors hung open, splintered from the battering ram. Inside was pure chaos. Overturned furniture, scattered papers, the acrid smell of flashbang residue. Agents drug people out in zip-tie cuffs, reading them rights in rapid-fire monotone.

Shea recognized some faces from the files she'd studied. Vincent Caruso, Rothmore's head of security—a former Marine who'd been dishonorably discharged for black market weapons trading. Paula Santos, the accountant who'd been laundering money through a network of shell corporations. Derek Hunt, one of the enforcers who'd probably personally delivered threats to the families of kidnapped children.

But no Rothmore. And no Elena or Bill.

"Second floor." Lincoln headed for the stairs.

The gunfire had stopped, replaced by shouting of commands to get down, get on the ground, show your hands. Shea took the stairs two at a time, her weapon drawn. The second-floor hallway was wide and ornate, with oil paintings on silk wallpaper and crown molding that probably cost more per foot than most people made in a month.

An FBI agent emerged from a room at the end of the hall, his face grim. "Wade is gone. Window's open, rope hanging down to the south lawn."

"Seal the perimeter," Lincoln barked into his radio. "Suspect is mobile on the grounds, possibly armed—"

The sound cut through everything else—rotor blades, close and getting closer. Shea darted to the window, looked out, and felt her stomach drop.

A helicopter landed on the south lawn, a sleek black machine that had probably been waiting just beyond the property line. And sprinting toward it, two bodyguards flanking him like Secret Service, was James Rothmore and Marcus Wade.

"He's got an extraction plan," Shea said. "Lincoln—"

But the FBI agent was already moving, shouting into his radio for agents to intercept, for the surveillance helicopters to cut off the escape route. Shea followed Lincoln back down the stairs, out a side entrance that led toward the south lawn.

They weren't going to make it in time. Rothmore was fifty yards from the helicopter, forty, thirty. The bodyguards were lying down, suppressing fire, keeping FBI agents pinned behind vehicles and decorative stone walls. Professional work. These weren't thugs, these were trained operators.

Rothmore reached the helicopter. One of the bodyguards grabbed the door handle.

And then Elena Reyes stepped out from behind the pool house, directly into Rothmore's path.

Shea's breath caught. Elena looked like she'd been through hell. Her dark hair was matted, her face was bruised, and her clothes were torn. But the gun in her hand was steady, aimed directly at Rothmore's center mass.

"It's over, James," Elena's voice carried across the

lawn, clear despite the rotor noise. "FBI has your estate, your records, your people. There's nowhere left to run."

Rothmore froze. His bodyguards swung their weapons toward Elena, but she didn't flinch. Around the perimeter, FBI agents were closing in, creating a tightening circle. The helicopter pilot looked uncertain, his hand hovering near the controls as Wade made a dash for the thick stand of trees opposite the house.

"Agent Reyes." Rothmore's voice was surprisingly calm, the smooth baritone of a man used to being in control. "I heard you were dead. Tragic accident in Little Rock, wasn't it?"

"Disappointing that you believed it," Elena said. "I thought you were smarter than that."

Shea was moving before she consciously decided to, angling through the gardens to get a better position. Lincoln hissed at her to stay back, but she ignored him. Something was wrong about this. Rothmore was too calm, too focused on Elena. A man cornered should show panic, rage, desperation. But Rothmore looked almost pleased.

"You've been very clever," Rothmore said. "Playing dead, feeding information to the FBI. I assume you're responsible for this impressive show of force?"

"Among other things." Elena took a step closer. "But mostly I just wanted to see your face when it all came apart."

That's when Rothmore moved.

He was fast for a man in his fifties, faster than he

had any right to be. One of his bodyguards had been standing just behind Elena's right shoulder. Shea hadn't even registered him there; he had been focused on the two men by the helicopter. But Rothmore must have signaled him somehow, because the man lunged forward and grabbed Elena from behind, yanking her back against his chest.

Elena's gun discharged. A wild shot that went into the ground. The bodyguard's hand came up with a pistol, pressed it against Elena's temple.

"Nobody moves," Rothmore said pleasantly. "Or Agent Reyes won't have to fake her death a second time."

The FBI agents froze. Shea counted at least twenty of them now, all with clear shots, but none were willing to risk it. Elena's face was tight with fury and fear, her hands raised in surrender.

"Here's what's going to happen." Rothmore backed toward the helicopter like he was discussing weather. "My associate here is going to escort Agent Reyes onto that aircraft. We're going to leave. And if anyone tries to stop us, he puts a bullet in her brain. Simple enough?"

Lincoln was on his radio, voice urgent and low, probably coordinating sniper positions. But the bodyguard holding Elena was using her as a human shield, and he was moving—backing toward the helicopter, dragging Elena with him. Rothmore climbed aboard, settled into a seat, and looked out at the assembled law enforcement with something like amusement.

"You can't run forever, James," Elena said through gritted teeth. "We have everything. Your records, your servers, your people. They're already talking."

"People always talk," Rothmore said. "That's why you have lawyers. Good ones. The kind I can afford." He gestured to his bodyguard. "Bring her."

The man started dragging Elena toward the helicopter. She resisted, but he outweighed her by eighty pounds and had leverage. In thirty seconds, she'd be on that aircraft. In sixty seconds, they'd be airborne. And despite all the FBI helicopters circling overhead, despite the agents and the warrants and the evidence, Rothmore would vanish.

Shea had been moving during all of this, circling through the gardens, using ornamental bushes and decorative walls for cover. Nobody was watching her. All eyes were on Elena, on Rothmore, on the standoff playing out on the south lawn. She reached a position twenty yards from the helicopter, slightly elevated on a terraced garden level.

The bodyguard's back was to her. Elena's face was visible in profile. Rothmore watched his man work, confident and relaxed, already thinking he'd won.

Shea dropped to one knee, brought her weapon up, and controlled her breathing the way her father had taught her when she was sixteen and learning to shoot.

You don't aim, he'd said. You become part of the gun. You and the target are already connected. You're just completing what's already true.

The bodyguard was eight inches taller than Elena. His head was exposed above hers, but barely—maybe three inches of clearance. If Shea missed even slightly, if the man moved at the wrong instant, if Elena shifted position...

She pushed the thoughts away. There was only this moment, only this shot, only the space between intention and action.

Shea fired.

The suppressed round caught the bodyguard in the left temple, exactly where she'd aimed. He dropped like someone had cut his strings, dead before he hit the ground. Elena stumbled forward, free, spinning to look at where the shot had come from.

Rothmore lunged for the helicopter controls. "Go, go!"

But FBI agents were already rushing the aircraft, multiple angles converging. Rothmore grabbed for something in his jacket. Another weapon, maybe. Shea couldn't see clearly from her position, couldn't tell if he was armed or desperate or both.

She fired again.

This shot took Rothmore in the right shoulder, spinning him away from the controls. He screamed. The first genuine emotion she'd heard from him and collapsed against the helicopter's interior. The pilot threw his hands up in surrender, cutting the engine as agents swarmed the aircraft.

Shea lowered her weapon, her hands perfectly steady despite the adrenaline crash she knew was coming. Around her, chaos erupted in a different key. Agents secured Rothmore, some checking Elena, clearing the helicopter, establishing a perimeter. The professional machinery of law enforcement grinded forward now that the immediate danger had passed.

Lincoln appeared beside her, breathing hard. "Great shot, Sheriff."

"Two shots," Shea corrected. She ejected her magazine, checked the rounds by instinct even though she knew exactly how many she'd fired. "The first one mattered. The second was just insurance."

"You saved her life." Lincoln's radio went crazy with status reports of more arrests being made throughout the estate, suspects being transported, evidence being catalogued. "Rothmore's wounded but stable. He'll live to stand trial."

"Unfortunately, Wade escaped." Shea glanced at the tree line.

Elena strolled toward them, flanked by FBI agents who looked like they wanted to wrap her in bubble wrap. Her face was pale, her hands were shaking, but her eyes were clear. When she reached Shea, she stopped, opened her mouth like she was going to say something, then just shook her head.

"Thank you," Elena finally managed. "I

thought—when he grabbed me, I thought—"

"You're alive," Shea said. "That's what matters."

"The shot you made…wow." Elena's voice was shaky now. "Three inches of clearance, maybe less. If you'd been off by half an inch…"

"I wasn't." Shea holstered her weapon, suddenly exhausted. "Where's Bill Miller?"

"Upstairs. He's been shot." Elena pulled herself together with visible effort. "He's wounded but asking about his son and the other children."

Shea glanced at the main house, where agents were still leading people out in handcuffs. "How many arrests?"

"Thirty-three so far," Lincoln answered. "We've got accountants, lawyers, enforcers, tech specialists. Everyone who was here when we hit. Plus, we seized servers, files, and enough financial records to keep prosecutors busy for years." He paused. "But we missed some. Marcus Wade wasn't here. Neither were several other key lieutenants."

Shea shook her head. "No, I saw him dash for the woods when Rothmore grabbed Elena."

Lincoln's expression was grim. "We've got warrants out, APBs on every major airport and border crossing. They won't get far."

But Shea had seen enough of this operation to know better. Rothmore had built a syndicate with layers of authority and contingencies, with people in positions of power. Marcus Wade was his head of operations.

The man who'd coordinated kidnappings, who'd delivered threats, who'd probably killed anyone who became inconvenient. If Wade had escaped, he'd have resources. Money, connections, places to hide.

"We need to find him," Shea said. "Wade knows too much. He could rebuild."

"We will find him." Elena's voice was firm. "This is what we do, Sheriff. We don't give up. We don't stop. We run them down until there's nowhere left to run."

Agents loaded Rothmore into an ambulance, his hands cuffed to the gurney, a FBI escort on either side. He was conscious, his face twisted with pain and fury. As they passed, his eyes locked on Shea's.

"You're the one who infiltrated my organization. The sheriff."

Shea met his gaze without flinching. "And you're the one who kidnapped children. Guess we both had our roles to play."

"This isn't over." Rothmore's voice was tight with pain but still carried that unnerving calm. "You think you've won? You've disrupted one operation. There are others. There are always others."

"Then we'll shut those down too," Shea said. "However long it takes."

The ambulance doors closed, cutting off whatever else Rothmore wanted to say. Shea watched the vehicle pull away, flanked by FBI SUVs, headed toward a federal medical facility where he'd be treated and then immediately transferred to a maximum-security holding cell.

Medics rolled Bill Miller from the building, escorted by two agents. He looked like he'd aged ten years in the past few weeks. Gray in his hair that hadn't been there before, and lines around his eye. But when he saw Shea, his expression shifted to something almost like hope.

"Sheriff Callahan," he said. "They told me about Ryan, about the other children. You got them out."

"They're safe," Shea confirmed. "Your son is asking for you. We can arrange a reunion once the FBI finishes debriefing you and you've receive medical attention."

Bill's eyes welled up. "I thought when they took him, I thought I'd lost everything. My marriage was already gone, the gambling destroyed my career, and then Ryan—" He stopped, composed himself. "I did terrible things. Hacked into systems I had no business accessing. Helped them steal millions. But I also left you clues. I tried to fight back the only way I knew how."

"You did more than try." Shea patted his shoulder, taking note of the spreading circle of blood on the blanket covering his abdomen. "You gave us everything we needed. The digital trail, the security backdoors, and the coordination with the weapons deal. Without you, we don't pull this off."

"What happens to me now?" Bill asked quietly. "I'm going to prison, aren't I?"

Shea glanced at Lincoln, who nodded slightly. "That's for the prosecutors to decide," Shea said. "But I'll be writing a report about your cooperation. About the risks you took, the information you provided. That has to count for something."

Bill nodded, his eyes drifting closed. "Just make sure Ryan knows I tried to do the right thing. In the end. Make sure he knows that."

"I'll tell him," Shea promised.

More FBI vehicles arrived, mobile command units and evidence trucks, the full apparatus of a major federal operation. Shea watched it all, feeling strangely detached. They'd won. Rothmore was in custody, the children were safe, and the syndicate was dismantled. Thirty-three arrests, financial records seized, a criminal empire toppled.

But Marcus Wade was still out there. And others—lieutenants and operators who'd been smart enough or lucky enough not to be at the estate when the FBI came knocking. Rothmore's last words echoed in her mind: There are always others.

Elena appeared beside her again, holding two bottles of water. She offered one to Shea. "You look like you've been run over by a truck, Sheriff."

"Right back at you. Thanks." Shea accepted the water. "How long were you undercover?"

"Too long." Elena drank deeply, then lowered the bottle. "I watched terrible things happen. Had to participate in some of them to maintain my cover. I'm going to be seeing a therapist for a very long time."

"Was it worth it?"

Elena looked at the FBI agents loading evidence, at the arrested syndicate members being transported away, at the estate that had been a center of criminal power now reduced to a crime scene. "Thirty-three arrests. Six children saved. A pipeline of human misery shut down. Yeah. It was worth it."

Shea's phone buzzed. Trevor: *Children are secure. How are you?*

She typed back: *Alive. Rothmore in custody. Bill is wounded. Coming back soon.*

The response was immediate: *Thank God. We were worried.*

"You should go," Elena said, watching Shea's expression. "Your deputy. Trevor, right? He cares about you. More than just professionally, unless I'm completely misreading the situation."

Shea felt heat rise in her face. "We're partners. We work together."

"Sure, you are." Elena's smile was tired but genuine. "Go home, Sheriff. Let us handle the cleanup. You've done more than enough."

But leaving felt wrong somehow, like walking away from something unfinished. "Marcus Wade—"

"We'll find him," Elena interrupted. "But not tonight. Tonight, you go back to Misty Hollow. You write your reports. You take care of the people in your jurisdiction who need you. Let the FBI handle what we're good at. Grinding down criminals through institutional persistence and unlimited resources."

Shea wanted to argue, wanted to stay until every loose end was tied off. But exhaustion was catching up with her, adrenaline giving way to bone-deep weariness. And Trevor was waiting. The children were waiting. Ryan Miller was probably asking when he could see his father.

"Okay," Shea said. "But you keep me informed. Anything on Wade, anything on the lieutenants who got away, I want to know about it."

"You'll be the first call I make." She extended her hand. "Thank you, Sheriff. For everything. For the shot that saved my life. For not giving up on those children. For being exactly as stubborn and capable as they said you were."

Shea shook her hand, feeling the strength in Elena's grip despite everything she'd been through. "Who said I was stubborn?"

"Everyone." Elena's laugh was sudden and genuine. "Literally everyone I talked to when I started researching this case mentioned it. 'Sheriff Callahan doesn't quit.' 'Sheriff Callahan will run you into the ground.' 'Don't lie to Sheriff Callahan, she'll know.'"

"Sounds like I have a reputation."

"You do. And after tonight, it's going to be even bigger."

Shea marched back through the estate grounds, past FBI agents and evidence markers. The sun had fully set now, the estate lit by portable lights and emergency vehicles. It looked nothing like the carefully manicured grounds she'd seen in surveillance photos. It looked like what it was, a crime scene being dismantled by federal investigators.

At the outer perimeter, Trevor leaned against their SUV, arms crossed, face tight with worry that relaxed only slightly when he saw her approaching.

"You're okay," he said.

"I'm okay."

"You shot someone."

"I shot two people," Shea corrected. "One of them died. The other one is going to federal prison for the rest of his life."

Trevor studied her face. Whatever he searched for, he didn't seem to find it. "You saved Elena's life."

"I did my job."

"Your job doesn't include making impossible shots at twenty yards while a federal agent is being used as a human shield." Trevor's voice was quiet but intense. "Yeah, I heard about it. That was...Shea, that was incredible. And terrifying. And if you'd missed—"

"I didn't miss."

They stood there for a moment, the sounds of the FBI operation fading into background noise. Then Trevor did something unexpected. He pulled her into a hug, quick and fierce and over before she could really process it.

"Don't do that again," he said against her hair.

"Don't put yourself in that kind of danger. I feel like a broken record."

Shea pulled back, looked up at him. "This is the job, Trevor. This is what we signed up for."

"I know. Doesn't mean I have to like it."

They drove back to the FBI checkpoint in silence. When they arrived, Becky Miller rushed over, her face desperate with hope.

"Is it true? Did you get him? Is it really over?"

"Rothmore's in custody," Shea confirmed. "Thirty-three arrests total. The syndicate is dismantled."

"And Bill?"

"Safe, but wounded. The FBI will eventually debrief him, but he's asking to see Ryan. I imagine they'll arrange something soon."

Becky sagged with relief, tears streaming down her face. "Thank you. Thank you so much. I don't know how to—I can't even—"

"You don't have to thank me," Shea said gently. "Just take care of your son. That's all that matters now."

The children were being tended to by FBI victim specialists and medical personnel, receiving food and water and blankets, and the first kindness they'd experienced in weeks. Ryan Miller sat apart from the others, his eyes scanning for threats that no longer existed. He'd have nightmares for months.

Shea walked over and crouched down beside him. "Hey, Ryan. Remember me?"

The boy nodded slowly. "You're the sheriff. You

got me out."

"I did. And I just want you to know that your dad is safe. He's with the FBI right now, answering questions. But he's going to see you soon. He fought really hard to protect you. He never stopped fighting."

"Is he in trouble?" Ryan's voice was small, scared.

"Maybe a little," Shea admitted. "But he did the right things in the end. And that matters a lot."

"Can I see him? My dad, I mean. Can I see him tonight?"

"I'll make sure of it," Shea promised.

As she stood, Trevor offered her coffee from somewhere, steam rising in the cool night air. "You should drink this. You look like you're about to collapse."

"I feel like I'm about to collapse."

"Then let's go home. Back to Misty Hollow."

Shea laughed despite everything. "You know it won't be that simple. Wade is still out there. And Rothmore's operation had tentacles everywhere. This isn't over."

"Maybe not," Trevor agreed. "But tonight, it can be. For tonight, we can just breathe."

Shea looked at the children being cared for, at Becky Miller crying tears of relief, at the FBI agents coordinating what would be months of investigation and prosecution. They'd won. Not completely, not perfectly, but they'd won.

And sometimes, that was enough.

Chapter Eighteen

The hospital waiting room smelled like industrial cleaner and bad coffee. Shea had been sitting in the same plastic chair for three hours, watching CNN replay footage of the FBI raid on a muted television mounted in the corner. The chyron kept cycling through variations of the same headline: MASSIVE FBI OPERATION DISMANTLES CHILD TRAFFICKING RING. DOZENS ARRESTED.

They weren't calling it a gambling syndicate anymore. The media had latched onto the kidnapping angle, the children, the horror of it all. Which was accurate, Shea supposed, but it flattened the complexity into something digestible for the twenty-four-hour news cycle.

Trevor appeared with two fresh cups of coffee and settled into the chair beside her. Their shoulders touched—not quite deliberate, not quite accidental. He'd been doing that more often since the raid, finding reasons to stand close, to make contact. Shea didn't pull away. Each case they worked together brought them closer together. Had them realizing how precious life was and those who cared for you.

"Still no word?" he asked.

"Nothing. They've been in there for almost six hours now." Shea wrapped her hands around the coffee cup, grateful for the warmth. "The doctor said it was exploratory surgery. Internal bleeding from injuries we didn't know about."

Bill Miller had collapsed during his FBI debriefing, just keeled over mid-sentence while describing Rothmore's weapons storage protocols. The syndicate had been rougher on him than anyone realized. Broken ribs that had punctured his spleen, internal bruising, stress fractures in his left arm that suggested someone had twisted it behind his back with extreme prejudice. He'd been running on adrenaline and desperation, and when those finally gave out, his body had surrendered.

"Ryan?" Trevor asked.

"Becky took him to the cafeteria. Kid hasn't eaten properly in days. FBI specialists say he's handling it better than expected, but..." Shea trailed off, thinking about the look in Ryan Miller's eyes. That flat, thousand-yard stare she'd seen in soldiers, in abuse victims, in people who'd learned that the world wasn't safe. "He's ten years old. Nobody handles this well at ten. No one should go through this at his age."

Trevor's hand found hers on the armrest between their chairs. His fingers threaded through hers, callused and warm and solid. Shea glanced around, but the waiting room was empty except for an elderly man three rows away, absorbed in a worn paperback.

"We should probably talk about this," Trevor said quietly.

"About what?"

"About the fact that I'm holding your hand and you're letting me."

Heat rose in her face. "We're tired. It's been a long week. People do things when they're exhausted."

"People do things when they stop lying to themselves." Trevor's thumb traced patterns on the back of her hand. "I'm not good at pretending, Shea. Never have been. And I'm definitely not good at pretending I don't have feelings for you."

"Trevor—"

"I know all the reasons it's complicated," he interrupted gently. "You're the sheriff. I'm your deputy. There are professional boundaries and power dynamics, and what if it doesn't work out and we still have to work together?" He paused. "But I also watched you take an impossible shot to save someone's life. I watched you infiltrate a criminal organization, rescue kidnapped children, and dismantle a trafficking ring. And all I could think was that I didn't want to waste any more time pretending we're just colleagues."

Shea opened her mouth, closed it, tried to

organize thoughts that felt scattered and overwhelming. She'd been aware of the tension between them for months. The way Trevor's eyes lingered, the way her pulse quickened when he stood too close, the careful distance they both maintained like it was part of their job description.

"I don't know how to do this," she finally said. "The job is everything. It's what I am. And if we—if this goes wrong—"

"Then we figure it out like adults," Trevor said. "But we don't have to decide everything right now. We don't have to make grand declarations or change how we work together. We just have to stop pretending there's nothing here…between us."

Before Shea could respond, Becky appeared in the waiting room doorway, one hand on Ryan's shoulder. The boy looked slightly better after food. Some color had returned to his face.

Shea gently extracted her hand from Trevor's, stood up. "Any news?"

"They just called me," Becky said, her voice tight. "Bill's out of surgery. He's stable but critical. They said—" She stopped, composed herself. "They said the next twenty-four hours will determine whether he makes it."

Ryan made a sound somewhere between a whimper and a gasp. Becky pulled him closer, her own expression torn between concern and something harder to define. Shea recognized the complicated tangle of emotions that came with caring about someone who'd hurt you, who'd failed you, who'd also fought desperately to protect what mattered most.

"Can I see him?" Ryan asked. "Please. I need to see my dad."

"Soon," Becky promised. "When the doctors say it's okay. Right now, Daddy needs to rest, to heal."

"But what if—" Ryan's voice cracked. "What if he dies before I can talk to him?"

Shea crouched down to Ryan's level, meeting his eyes. "Your dad is tough. Tougher than he probably ever thought he could be. He survived weeks with those people. He left us clues and fought back in every way he could. He's not going to give up now."

"How do you know?"

"Because he has you," Shea said simply. "Because you're his reason for everything. People don't survive what your dad survived and then just quit."

Ryan absorbed this, his small frame trembling with the effort of holding himself together. Then he nodded, once, accepting her words like a lifeline.

A doctor emerged from the surgical wing—late fifties, surgical scrubs, the kind of exhaustion that spoke to hours of delicate work. "Miller family?"

Becky stepped forward, one hand still on Ryan's shoulder. "I'm his ex-wife. This is his son."

The doctor's expression was professionally neutral. "Mr. Miller came through the surgery. We repaired the damage to his spleen, addressed the internal bleeding, and set the fractures. But he's experienced significant trauma—both physical and psychological. His recovery will be lengthy and complicated."

"But he'll recover?" Becky's voice was barely audible.

"If infection doesn't set in, if his vitals remain stable, if he responds well to treatment... yes, he should recover. But we're talking about months of rehabilitation. Physical therapy, psychological counseling, and ongoing medical monitoring."

"Can I see him?" Ryan asked, his voice small but determined.

The doctor hesitated, clearly weighing protocols against compassion. "He's in the ICU. Normally we don't allow children, but given the circumstances..." He glanced at Becky. "Five minutes. And he won't be conscious yet. The anesthesia will take hours to wear off."

"I don't care," Ryan said. "I just need to see him. I need to know he's real."

They were led through sterile corridors, past monitoring stations and other patients' rooms, to a small ICU bay where Bill lay motionless among tubes and monitors. He looked even worse than Shea remembered. Pale as hospital sheets, face gaunt, breathing assisted by oxygen. But his chest rose and fell with a steady rhythm, and the monitors beeped their reassuring confirmation of continued life.

Ryan approached the bed as if he were afraid Bill might disappear if he moved too fast. When he reached his father's side, he carefully took Bill's hand, holding it between both of his own.

"I'm here, Daddy," Ryan whispered. "I'm safe. You did it. You saved me."

Bill didn't respond—couldn't respond, lost somewhere in medicated unconsciousness. But Shea noticed Ryan's shoulders relax slightly, saw some of the tension drain from his small frame. Sometimes just being present was enough.

Becky stood at the foot of the bed, her expression unreadable. Shea gave her space, stepping back into the hallway with Trevor. They watched through the window as Becky finally moved closer and placed one hand on Bill's shoulder. Not quite affectionate, not quite forgiveness, but acknowledgment. Recognition of shared history and complicated feelings, and the fact that, despite everything, this man had fought for their son.

"She still loves him," Trevor observed quietly.

"I think she wishes she didn't," Shea said. "Loving someone who destroyed your trust, who gambled away your stability, who lied about everything... that's its own kind of prison."

"But he also did everything he could to save their son. Including risking his own life." Trevor leaned against the wall, arms crossed. "People are complicated. We're capable of terrible things and heroic things, sometimes in the same day."

The five minutes stretched to ten, then fifteen. When Becky finally emerged with Ryan, her eyes were red but dry. "Thank you," she said to Shea. "For giving us this. For everything."

"We're not done yet," Shea said gently. "The FBI is going to want more statements. The prosecution will be building its case. And Bill is going to face charges."

"I know." Becky's jaw tightened. "His lawyer called while you were at the estate. Federal charges for computer fraud, unauthorized access to classified systems, and conspiracy. They're talking about twenty years."

Ryan made a distressed sound. Becky quickly added, "But his lawyer also said there might be a deal because of his cooperation. Because he helped bring down the syndicate."

"There will be a deal," Trevor said with certainty. "The FBI doesn't get a case like this without informants. Bill handed them everything they needed. Financial records, security protocols, and personnel information. Prosecutors know what that's worth."

They returned to the waiting room, settling into another stretch of limbo. Ryan curled up on two chairs pushed together, his head on his mother's lap. Within minutes, he was asleep. The first real sleep he'd probably gotten since his kidnapping.

Trevor's phone buzzed. He checked it, frowned, and showed Shea the screen.

The message was from FBI Special Agent Chen: *Need statements from you both. Tomorrow, 10 AM, Little Rock field office. Also...Arkansas State Police are asking questions about jurisdiction.*

Shea felt something cold settle in her stomach. "Jurisdiction."

"You operated in Oklahoma and Mississippi," Trevor said quietly. "Technically outside your authority as an Arkansas county sheriff."

"I rescued six kidnapped children."

"I know. But the law doesn't always care about outcomes. It cares about procedures." Trevor's expression was troubled. "The state police are going to want to know why you didn't coordinate with them, why you went into another state without authorization. Why you took a shot that could have killed a federal agent if you'd missed."

"Elena would be dead if I hadn't taken that shot."

"I know that. But that's not how the review board will see it. They'll see a county sheriff who exceeded her authority, operated without oversight, and discharged her weapon in a federal operation she had no official role in."

Shea closed her eyes, suddenly exhausted beyond measure. She'd known this was coming. Had felt it hovering at the edges of her awareness since the moment she'd pulled that trigger. You couldn't do what she'd done and expect there to be no consequences. Even when you did everything right, even when lives were saved, the machinery of institutional authority still ground forward.

"They're going to suspend me," she said.

"Probably. Pending review." Trevor moved closer, his presence solid and reassuring. "But it's temporary, Shea. Once the FBI confirms your role, once the evidence is processed, once everyone understands what actually happened, they'll reinstate you. This is just bureaucracy doing what bureaucracy does."

"And if they don't reinstate me?"

Trevor was quiet for a moment. Then: "Then we figure out what comes next. Together."

That word—together—carried weight beyond its simple syllables. Shea opened her eyes, found Trevor watching her with an expression that made her chest ache. Partnership. Support. Something deeper that neither of them had quite named yet.

"You should go home," she said. "Get some sleep. Tomorrow's going to be a long day."

"I'm not leaving you here alone."

"Trevor—"

"I'm not leaving," he repeated firmly. "We're partners, remember? Which means when you're sitting in a hospital waiting room at two in the morning, worried about bureaucratic consequences and whether a federal informant is going to survive surgery, I'm sitting here too."

Shea wanted to argue, wanted to maintain some

pretense of professional distance. But she was tired, and scared, and the warmth of Trevor beside her felt like the only solid thing in a world that had suddenly become uncertain.

"Okay," she said quietly.

They sat in silence for a while, watching CNN cycle through the same footage. Shea recognized herself in one clip, just a glimpse, walking across the Rothmore estate grounds with her weapon drawn. Someone had leaked body camera footage to the media. Great. That would make the jurisdiction review even more complicated.

Around 3 AM, another doctor appeared—this one younger, less exhausted. "Bill Miller's vitals have stabilized. He's responding well to treatment. Barring complications, we're cautiously optimistic about his recovery."

Becky sagged with relief so profound she nearly collapsed. The doctor continued, "He'll remain in the ICU for at least forty-eight hours. After that, if everything goes well, we'll move him to a regular room. But I want to be clear…his recovery will be lengthy. Months of physical therapy. Psychological support. This isn't something he walks away from."

"But he will walk away from it," Becky said. "Eventually."

"Eventually," the doctor confirmed.

After he left, Becky turned to Shea. "I don't know how to feel. About Bill, about everything. I'm so angry at him. For gambling, for the lies, for putting us in danger. But I'm also—" She stopped, struggling. "I'm also grateful because he saved Ryan. Because when it mattered most, he fought back. How am I supposed to reconcile those things?"

"You don't have to reconcile them right now," Shea said. "You're allowed to have complicated feelings about complicated situations. That's not weakness. That's just being human."

Becky nodded slowly, processing this. "The lawyer said there might be a deal. Minimal jail time, probation, in exchange for testimony. Do you think that's fair? After everything he did?"

"I think justice is rarely simple," Shea said. "Bill committed crimes. Real crimes with real consequences. But he also cooperated, provided evidence, and risked his life to help us shut down a trafficking ring. The question isn't whether he deserves punishment. It's what kind of punishment serves society's interests. And sometimes, a cooperating witness serves those interests better than another body in prison."

"You sound like a lawyer."

"I sound like someone who's seen too many cases end badly because we prioritized punishment over pragmatism." Shea stood, stretching muscles stiff from hours of sitting. "Bill will have to live with what he did. That's its own kind of punishment. But if he serves minimal time, gets probation and counseling, and a chance to rebuild his relationship with his son—that might actually produce something positive. Redemption, maybe. Or at least the possibility of it."

Trevor's phone buzzed again. He checked it, his expression darkening. "State police confirmed. They're launching a formal investigation into your actions. Suspended pending review, effective immediately."

Shea had expected it, but hearing the confirmation still felt like a physical blow. "How long?"

"Four to six weeks, typically. Could be longer depending on what they find."

"And what will they find?"

"That you saved six children," Trevor said firmly. "That you dismantled a criminal syndicate. That you took a shot that saved a federal agent's life. They'll find a sheriff who did her job, even when that job took her outside the comfortable boundaries of standard procedure."

"You're optimistic."

"I'm realistic. And I know you, Shea. You don't do things halfway. You don't take shortcuts or make reckless decisions. Everything you did, you did for the right reasons. The review board will see that."

Shea wanted to believe him. But she'd been in law enforcement long enough to know that right reasons didn't always matter. Procedures mattered. Jurisdiction mattered. The appearance of propriety mattered, sometimes more than actual results.

Ryan stirred in his sleep, mumbled something indistinct, then settled again. Becky stroked his hair, her movements gentle and protective.

"I should get him home," Becky said quietly. "But I don't want to leave. What if Bill wakes up? What if he needs to see us?"

"He's not waking up for hours yet," Trevor said. "Take Ryan home. Get some real sleep in a real bed. We'll call you the moment anything changes."

Becky hesitated, then nodded. She carefully woke Ryan, who protested sleepily but allowed himself to be guided toward the exit. At the doorway, Becky turned back.

"Shea, thank you. I know you're facing consequences because of what you did. Because you helped us, that's not fair."

"Fairness is overrated," Shea said. "Getting the job done matters more."

After they left, the waiting room felt emptier, quieter. Shea sank back into her chair, suddenly aware of just how exhausted she was. Days of surveillance, hours of infiltration, the raid, the shooting, the endless debriefings and statements, and now this—the consequences she'd known were coming but had pushed to the back of her mind.

Trevor moved his chair closer, eliminating the polite distance they'd maintained for the benefit of the Miller family. His arm went around her shoulders, pulling her against his side.

"We should talk about what happens next," he said.

"Next?"

"If you're suspended for six weeks, someone has to run the sheriff's office. That'll probably be me, as senior deputy. Which means I'll be your boss, technically, which makes this—" He gestured between them. "—even more complicated."

Shea laughed despite everything. "You think our relationship is defined by organizational hierarchy?"

"No. But HR departments do." Trevor's tone was dry. "We're going to have paperwork. Disclosure forms. Probably mandatory counseling about workplace relationships and power dynamics."

"Sounds romantic."

"Doesn't it?" Trevor's hand found hers again, fingers interlacing. "But I meant what I said earlier. About not wasting time pretending. If we're going to do this, whatever this is, we do it honestly. No hiding, no sneaking around, no pretending we're just colleagues when we're clearly something else."

"And if the review board decides I exceeded my authority? If they decide not to reinstate me?"

Trevor was quiet for a moment, considering. "Then you'll figure out what comes next. Maybe you run for sheriff again in the next election. Maybe you do something else entirely. But whatever happens, you don't face it alone. That's what partners do. They face things together."

There was that word again. Together. It sounded less frightening each time Shea heard it.

She leaned into Trevor's warmth, allowing herself this moment of vulnerability. Outside, dawn was beginning to break. She could see it through the waiting room windows, the sky shifting from black to deep blue to the first hints of pink and gold.

"The other children," Shea said. "The ones we rescued. What happened to them?"

"FBI reunited them with their families last night," Trevor said. "All six. There were a lot of tears, a lot of trauma counseling appointments scheduled, but they're home. They're safe."

"That's something."

"That's everything," Trevor corrected. "Six families who get their children back. Six kids who don't have to live in fear anymore. Whatever else happens, whatever the review board decides, whatever charges Bill faces, that's real. That matters."

Shea closed her eyes, breathing in the smell of hospital antiseptic and Trevor's familiar cologne. She thought about Ryan sleeping peacefully beside his mother for the first time in weeks. About Bill fighting for his life in the ICU, having finally done something heroic after months of failure and fear. About Elena Reyes, alive because Shea had taken an impossible shot and trusted her training.

"I'd do it again," she said quietly. "Everything. Even knowing the consequences. I'd still take that shot. I'd still operate outside my jurisdiction."

"I know," Trevor said. "That's why you're a good

sheriff. That's why people trust you. That's why I—" He stopped, seemed to reconsider his words. "That's why I believe in what we do."

But Shea had heard what he almost said. *That's why I love you.* The words hung unspoken between them, acknowledged but not yet claimed.

Not yet. But soon.

Her phone buzzed with a text from Elena Reyes: *Heard about the suspension. Bullshit. I'm writing a letter to the review board. So is Lincoln. So is every FBI agent who was there. You saved my life, Sheriff. We don't forget that.*

Shea showed Trevor the message. He smiled. "See? You've got allies. People who know what you did."

"That doesn't always matter to bureaucrats."

"Then we make it matter." Trevor's tone was firm, determined. "We fight this. We document everything. We get statements from everyone who was there. We show the review board exactly what happened and why you made the choices you made. And we trust that the truth matters more than technicalities."

Shea wanted to believe him. Wanted to trust that doing the right thing would be recognized, that saving lives mattered more than jurisdictional boundaries. But she'd been in this business long enough to know better.

Still, sitting here in Trevor's arms, watching dawn break over Little Rock, feeling the solid warmth of his presence beside her—maybe belief was enough. Maybe trust was its own kind of courage.

"We should get some sleep," she said. "Real sleep, in an actual bed. Before the FBI debriefing."

"Your place or mine?"

The question was casual, but Shea heard the layers beneath it. An invitation. A step forward. A acknowledgment that they were moving past professional boundaries into something else entirely.

"Yours," she decided. "Mine is probably being watched by state police investigators looking for evidence of misconduct."

"You're paranoid."

"I'm realistic." Shea stood, offered Trevor her hand. He took it, let her pull him to his feet. "Besides, your place has better coffee."

"My place has instant coffee and questionable milk."

"Still better than mine."

They left the hospital as dawn spread across the city, painting everything in shades of gold and pink. In a few hours, they'd be at the FBI field office, giving statements, defending decisions, and navigating the bureaucratic aftermath of dismantling a criminal syndicate. But for now, for this moment, they were just two people driving through an awakening city, hands clasped between them, moving forward into whatever came next.

Together.

Chapter Nineteen

The Misty Hollow Community Center hadn't been this packed since the vote to allow alcohol sales three years ago. Shea stood at the back of the room, watching residents file in. Farmers in clean flannel shirts, shop owners still wearing name tags, and retirees who normally spent Tuesday evenings at bingo. They kept glancing at her, some offering supportive nods, others with expressions she couldn't quite read.

Trevor appeared at her elbow, two Styrofoam cups of terrible coffee in hand. "Standing room only. Guess this town takes your actions seriously."

"That's comforting." Shea accepted the coffee.

The town council sat at a long table on the raised platform commonly used for school plays and community theater. Five members, each representing a different district of the county. Shea knew them all— had worked with them, attended their fundraisers, town halls, and endless budget meetings. But tonight, they looked different, formal and distant, hiding behind the armor of official procedure.

Mayor Ferguson called the meeting to order with three sharp raps of his gavel. He'd been one of Shea's earliest supporters when she'd first arrived as sheriff in Misty Hollow.

"This emergency hearing has been called to address recent events involving Sheriff Shea Callahan." Ferguson's voice carried the practiced authority of decades of wrangling with town councils and county commissioners. "Specifically, her actions during a multi-state investigation into organized crime and child trafficking."

Council member Donald Priest leaned forward, his jowls quivering with barely contained indignation. Priest owned the largest car dealership in three counties and had opinions about everything, most of them wrong. "Multi-state is exactly the problem. Sheriff Callahan operated in Oklahoma and Mississippi, both outside her jurisdiction, without coordinating with state police or obtaining proper authorization. That's not law enforcement. That's vigilantism."

Murmurs rippled through the crowd. Shea couldn't tell if they agreed or protested.

Council member Jennifer Torres raised her hand. Late thirties, former public defender, generally reasonable. "With respect to Donald, Sheriff Callahan was participating in an FBI operation. She rescued six kidnapped children and helped dismantle a criminal syndicate. Those aren't the actions of a vigilante. Those are the actions of a dedicated law enforcement officer."

"Who exceeded her authority," Priest shot back. "Who discharged her weapon during a federal raid she had no official role in. Who took a shot that could have killed a DEA agent if she'd missed by half an inch."

"But she didn't miss," Torres countered. "She saved that agent's life."

"That's not the point—"

"That's exactly the point," Torres interrupted. "Results matter. Outcomes matter. Six families have their children back because of Sheriff Callahan's actions."

The third council member, Robert Wilson, cleared his throat. Robert ran the county's only hardware store and had a reputation for careful, measured thinking. "I think we need to hear from Sheriff Callahan herself. Let her explain her decisions, walk us through her reasoning. Then we can make an informed judgment."

Patricia nodded. "Sheriff Callahan, please come forward."

Shea walked down the center aisle, aware of every eye tracking her movement. She'd worn her dress uniform—figured if she was going down, she might as well look professional doing it. When she reached the podium facing the council, she set down her coffee and met the mayor's eyes.

"Sheriff Callahan," Ferguson said, his tone formal but not unkind, "please explain to this council and to the community you serve why you felt it necessary to operate outside your jurisdiction during the investigation into the Rothmore syndicate."

Shea took a breath, organizing her thoughts. "Three weeks ago, I was approached by DEA Agent Elena Reyes, who was working undercover in James Rothmore's organization. She had intelligence about a gambling syndicate that was kidnapping children to coerce parents into committing crimes. One of those parents, Bill Miller, was from our state. His son Ryan, ten years old, had been held hostage for weeks."

She saw faces in the crowd soften at the mention of Ryan's age. The details mattered. Made it real.

"I coordinated with the FBI and DEA throughout the investigation," Shea continued. "But when we located the ranch in Oklahoma where six children were being held, we faced a time-critical situation. The syndicate planned to move the children within 48 hours. If we waited for proper jurisdictional protocols, for state police coordination, for all the bureaucratic machinery to grind through proper channels—those children would have disappeared."

"So, you took matters into your own hands," Priest said accusingly.

"I made a judgment call," Shea corrected. "The same kind of judgment call I make every day as sheriff. When someone's life is in immediate danger, you don't wait for permission. You act."

Council member Michael Webb spoke for the first

time. African American, early fifties, retired Army colonel who ran a small construction company. He had a son Ryan's age. "What about the shooting? Reports say you killed one man and wounded another during the FBI raid on Rothmore's estate."

"I did." Shea met his eyes directly. "James Rothmore was attempting to escape via helicopter. One of his bodyguards was using DEA Agent Reyes as a human shield, holding a gun to her head. I had a clear shot at the bodyguard and took it. He died instantly. Then Rothmore reached for what appeared to be a weapon, and I fired again, wounding him in the shoulder. He survived and is currently in federal custody awaiting trial."

"You took a shot while a federal agent was being used as a human shield," Priest said, his voice dripping with disbelief. "Do you understand how reckless that was? How easily that could have gone wrong?"

"I understand the risk," Shea said evenly. "I also understood the alternative. If I didn't take the shot, Rothmore would have escaped. Elena Reyes would likely have been killed. And dozens of criminals would have scattered, taking their operation underground where we'd never find them again."

"You're not a sniper," Priest pressed. "You're a county sheriff. What made you think you were qualified to make that shot?"

"My years of law enforcement experience." Shea's voice hardened. "Four hundred hours of firearms training. Expert marksman certification. And the knowledge that if I didn't act, someone was going to die. Those qualifications seemed sufficient at the time."

Jennifer Torres was taking notes, nodding occasionally. Robert Wilson looked thoughtful. Michael Webb's expression was unreadable. And Pries looked like he'd already made up his mind and was waiting for his chance to speak.

"I'd like to call a witness," Ferguson said. "Deputy Trevor Bolton, please come forward."

Trevor had been sitting in the front row. He stood, walked to the podium beside Shea. Their shoulders almost touched. Not quite contact, but close enough that everyone in the room could see the connection between them.

"Deputy Bolton," the mayor began, "you accompanied Sheriff Callahan throughout this investigation. Can you speak to her decision-making process?"

Trevor's jaw was set, his posture military-straight. "Sheriff Callahan made every decision based on the best available intelligence and the immediate safety of victims. She coordinated with federal authorities at every stage. She followed proper tactical protocols. And when faced with a time-critical situation where children's lives were at stake, she acted with courage and precision."

"You're biased," Priest said flatly. "Everyone in this room has seen how you two look at each other.

You're standing so close right now you might as well be holding hands. Your testimony is worthless."

Angry murmurs erupted from the crowd. Someone in the back shouted, "Let him speak!"

Ferguson gaveled for order. "Council member Priest, you will show respect for witnesses."

"I'm showing respect for facts," Priest shot back. "Deputy Bolton is romantically involved with Sheriff Callahan. That's not speculation. That's obvious to anyone with eyes. Which means his testimony about her decision-making is compromised by personal feelings rather than professional judgment."

Trevor's hand found Shea's. A deliberate gesture, public and unmistakable. "You're right," he said calmly. "I am romantically involved with Sheriff Callahan. Over the past few months, our feelings have developed into something more than a partnership "

He squeezed Shea's hand once, then released it, turning to face the council directly.

"But my personal feelings don't change the facts of what happened. Six children were rescued. A criminal syndicate was dismantled. Thirty-three arrests were made. And a federal agent is alive because Sheriff Callahan took an impossible shot and trusted her training. Those are measurable outcomes. Those are results. And if you think my relationship with Shea compromises my ability to recognize good law enforcement when I see it, then you don't understand what professional judgment actually means."

The room erupted—some applauding, others shouting objections, everyone suddenly having an opinion. Ferguson hammered the gavel repeatedly, calling for order with increasing volume.

When the noise finally subsided, Webb spoke. "I served twenty-six years in the Army. I've seen combat. I've made decisions under pressure that cost lives and saved lives. And I can tell you that what Sheriff Callahan did, coordinating with federal authorities, extracting hostages under fire, taking a precision shot to save an agent's life, that's not vigilantism. That's courage. That's the kind of leadership we should celebrate, not condemn."

"It's also outside her jurisdiction," Priest insisted. "Outside her authority. Setting a precedent that sheriffs can operate wherever they want, whenever they want, without coordination or oversight. That's dangerous. That undermines the entire structure of law enforcement."

"What's your solution?" Jennifer Torres asked. "We suspend her? Fire her? We punish her for saving children's lives because she didn't follow proper bureaucratic procedures?"

"I'm saying there need to be consequences," Priest said. "I'm saying that even when outcomes are good, process matters. Rules matter. If we let this slide, what's next? Does she go to Texas? Does she go to California? Where does her jurisdiction end if we don't enforce boundaries?"

Robert Wilson spoke up. "I think we're missing something important here. The FBI invited Sheriff Callahan's participation. They coordinated with her throughout. She wasn't operating as a lone wolf. She was assisting federal authorities in a major investigation. That's fundamentally different from a sheriff deciding unilaterally to operate in another state."

"The FBI can't grant jurisdiction," Priest argued. "Only the state can do that. And Arkansas State Police weren't consulted, weren't involved, weren't given any opportunity to coordinate. That's the problem."

Shea listened to the back-and-forth, feeling as if her career was being dissected like a biology lab specimen. But now she spoke up.

"Council member Priest is right about one thing. Process matters. Structure matters. If every law enforcement officer made unilateral decisions about where and when to operate, we'd have chaos." She paused, choosing her words carefully. "But process isn't an end in itself. It's a tool for achieving justice, protecting people, and maintaining order. And when process becomes an obstacle to those goals, when following proper channels means children remain in danger, then we have to ask what we're actually serving. Are we serving the law? Or are we serving the bureaucracy that's supposed to implement the law?"

"That's a dangerous philosophy," Priest said.

"Maybe," Shea agreed. "But so is rigid adherence to procedure when lives are at stake. I'm not saying rules don't matter. I'm saying they have to be balanced against circumstances, against urgency, against the fundamental purpose of law enforcement, which is protecting people. If this council decides that the balance was wrong, that I crossed a line that can't be forgiven, then I'll accept whatever consequences you impose. But I won't apologize for saving six children."

The room was silent now, as everyone processed her words. Ferguson glanced at his fellow council members and seemed to read something in their expressions.

"I'd like to hear from community members," Patricia said. "This is an open hearing. Anyone who wishes to speak, please come forward."

Old Tom Henderson was first. Eighty-three years old, walked with a cane, and had lived in Misty Hollow his entire life. "I've known four sheriffs in my time. Three of them were politicians who cared more about getting reelected than doing the job. Shea Callahan is different. She gives a damn. She shows up. And when my grandson got mixed up with meth dealers last year, she didn't arrest him. Instead, she got him into treatment. Saved his life. So maybe she bent some rules going to Oklahoma. Maybe she didn't file all the right paperwork. But she got results. And in my book, that counts for something."

More people came forward. The high school principal. The pastor of First Baptist. The librarian. Each with their own story, their own reason for supporting Shea. It wasn't unanimous. Some expressed concern about procedures, precedent, and jurisdictional issues. But the overwhelming sentiment was clear: Misty Hollow stood behind their sheriff.

After the fourteenth speaker, the mayor called for a vote. "We have several options before us. Full suspension pending investigation. Termination for exceeding authority. Official reprimand with conditions. Or no action taken. I'd like to hear proposals from council members."

Jennifer Torres spoke first. "I move that Sheriff Callahan receive an official reprimand for operating outside established jurisdictional protocols, with the condition that any future multi-jurisdictional operations must be coordinated through proper state channels. But I also move that we recognize her service, her courage, and the lives she saved."

"I second that motion," Webb said.

"I oppose," Priest said immediately. "A reprimand isn't enough. There needs to be consequences that actually matter. Suspension, demotion, something that sends a clear message about boundaries and authority."

Wilson raised his hand. "I agree with Jennifer's motion, but I'd add one additional condition. Sheriff Callahan should be required to submit quarterly reports to this council detailing any multi-jurisdictional cooperation or federal assistance. Not for approval. Just for transparency. We're kept informed of operations that extend beyond county lines."

"That's reasonable," Torres said. "I'll amend my motion to include quarterly reporting."

Ferguson looked at each council member. "We have a motion for official reprimand with conditions: future multi-jurisdictional operations must be properly coordinated, and quarterly reports will be submitted to this council. All in favor?"

Torres, Wilson, and Webb raised their hands.

"Opposed?"

Priest's hand shot up. The fifth council member, Sarah Vickers, who'd been silent throughout the hearing, hesitated, then slowly raised her hand as well.

"Motion carries, three to two," Ferguson announced. "Sheriff Callahan, you are hereby officially reprimanded for operating outside established jurisdictional protocols. However, this council recognizes your service and the lives you saved. You will retain your position as sheriff, subject to the conditions outlined. Do you accept these terms?"

Something unknotted in Shea's chest. Not quite relief—relief would come later, when the adrenaline faded, and she could process what had just happened. But something close to it.

"I accept," she said.

"Then this hearing is adjourned." Ferguson gaveled once, final and definitive.

The room erupted in applause. People surged forward, wanting to shake Shea's hand, offer congratulations, and share their own thoughts about what had transpired. Trevor stayed close, his presence steady and grounding as Shea navigated the crowd.

Rebecca Santos hugged her fiercely. "Thank you. Just—thank you."

Old Tom Henderson clapped her on the shoulder. "You did good, Sheriff. Don't let those bureaucrats tell you different."

Eventually, the crowd thinned, people heading home to their regular Tuesday evening routines. The council members filed out, Priest pointedly avoiding eye contact, Torres offering an encouraging nod. Ferguson was the last to leave.

"That was closer than I would have liked," the mayor said quietly. "Priest is going to make noise about this for months. Maybe years. And Sarah Vickers is up for reelection. She can't afford to look soft on accountability, not with Priest breathing down her neck."

"I understand," Shea said.

"I don't think you do." The mayor's expression was serious. "You have to be more careful from now on. The quarterly reports aren't optional. They're a political cover for the council members who supported you and me. If anything like this happens again, if you operate outside your jurisdiction without an ironclad justification, they will come after you. And next time, I might not be able to protect you."

"I'll be careful," Shea promised.

"See that you are." He softened slightly. "But for

what it's worth…I'm glad those children are home. And I'm glad we have a sheriff who dares to do what's necessary, even when it's complicated."

After the mayor left, only Trevor and Shea remained in the community center. The janitor was starting to stack chairs, giving them pointed looks that suggested he'd like to lock up and go home.

"Official reprimand," Trevor said. "Could have been worse."

"Could have been better."

"Could have been unemployed." Trevor pulled her close, his arms wrapping around her waist. "You keep your job. You keep your badge. And you only have to submit quarterly reports, which you were probably going to do anyway to keep people informed."

"The relationship is public now," Shea said. "People are going to have opinions."

"People always have opinions. That's what people do." Trevor kissed her forehead, gentle and reassuring. "But we knew this was coming. We knew that once we stopped pretending, there would be scrutiny. So, we deal with it. We maintain professional boundaries at work. And we ignore anyone who thinks two adults being in a relationship somehow undermines our ability to do our jobs."

Shea leaned into him, allowing herself this moment of vulnerability. "Priest was right about one thing. You're biased. When it comes to me, you're not objective."

"Of course, I'm not objective." Trevor's voice was warm with affection. "I'm biased toward the woman who took an impossible shot to save a federal agent. I'm biased toward the sheriff who rescued six children. I'm biased toward someone who cares more about getting justice than following procedures. If that makes me unprofessional, I'll live with it."

The janitor cleared his throat meaningfully. Trevor and Shea separated, headed toward the exit.

Outside, Misty Hollow was settling into the evening. Streetlights were coming on, shops closing, the comfortable rhythm of a small town at rest. Shea's truck sat parked in front of the sheriff's office, Trevor's beside it.

"Your place or mine?" Trevor asked.

"Mine," Shea decided. "I need to see my own space, sleep in my own bed. Process everything that just happened. Hug Heidi."

"Want company?"

"Always."

They drove separately to maintain some appearance of propriety, even now. But when Shea pulled into her driveway, Trevor's truck was right behind her. They went inside together, and for the first time in weeks, Shea felt like she could breathe.

At home, she let Heidi into the backyard she hadn't been in since Shea left. The dog bounded out with a bark and chased a squirrel up a tree.

Trevor settled onto the couch while Shea made

real coffee. The good stuff, not the sludge they survived on at work. When she returned with two mugs, he'd kicked off his boots and was reading something on his phone.

"FBI released a statement." He showed her the screen. "Praising your cooperation, emphasizing that you were operating with their knowledge and coordination. Chen really went to bat for you."

"Won't matter to Priest," Shea said. "Or to state police investigators who are still reviewing the case."

"No," Trevor agreed. "But it matters to everyone else. It matters to the community. It matters to the people who voted to keep you as sheriff."

Shea sat beside him, close enough that their thighs touched. She sipped her coffee, letting the warmth and caffeine work their restorative magic.

"I was scared tonight," she admitted. "Standing there while they debated my career, my choices, everything I've worked for. I was scared they'd take it all away."

"But they didn't."

"But they didn't," she echoed. "Official reprimand. Quarterly reports. Could have been so much worse."

"Could have been so much better," Trevor said, mirroring her earlier words. "But we take what we get, and we keep moving forward. That's the job."

They sat in comfortable silence, drinking coffee, processing the evening. Eventually, Trevor's arm came around her shoulders, pulling her closer. Shea set down her mug and turned to face him.

"Thank you," she said. "For testifying. For being public about us. For standing beside me even when it complicated things."

"Where else would I be?" Trevor's hand cupped her face, thumb brushing across her cheekbone. "We're partners. In everything. That doesn't change because some council member disapproves."

"Priest called your testimony worthless."

"Priest is an idiot." Trevor leaned forward, his forehead resting against hers. "My testimony was worth exactly as much as anyone else's. Maybe more, because I've worked with you every day. I know how you think, how you make decisions, how you handle pressure. If anyone's qualified to speak to your character and judgment, it's me."

"Biased testimony," Shea murmured.

"Informed testimony," Trevor corrected. Then he kissed her. Slow, deep, and full of everything they'd been holding back during the hearing, during the weeks of investigation and danger and uncertainty.

When they finally separated, Shea was breathing hard, her heart racing. "We should probably talk about boundaries. Professional behavior at work. How we navigate this going forward."

"We should," Trevor agreed. "But not tonight. Tonight, we just exist in this moment. We survived. We kept our jobs. We're together. Everything else can wait until tomorrow."

Shea nodded, settling back against him.

Official reprimand. Quarterly reports. Public scrutiny of her relationship with Trevor. Jurisdiction restrictions that would make future investigations more complicated.

She could live with all of that. Because six children were home. Because a criminal syndicate was dismantled. Because she'd done the right thing, even when the right thing came with consequences.

And because Trevor was here beside her, solid and steady and unshakeable in his support.

Tomorrow would bring new challenges. But tonight, for this moment, she allowed herself to simply be.

Sheriff Shea Callahan. Officially reprimanded. Officially in a relationship. Officially still fighting for justice in Misty Hollow, Arkansas.

Chapter Twenty

The envelope was on Shea's desk when she arrived at the office Thursday morning, propped against her coffee mug as if someone had deliberately staged it. Plain manila, no postage, no return address. Her name was written in block capitals with a black marker.

Shea set down her keys and stared at it for a long moment before calling out, "Trevor? Did you put this here?"

Trevor emerged from the evidence room, carrying a box of files. "Put what where?"

"This envelope." She gestured without touching it. "On my desk."

His expression shifted immediately from casual to alert. "No. I got here twenty minutes ago. It was already there. I figured Doris put it there. It says important on the outside, so she would've wanted to make sure you saw it first thing."

They both looked at the envelope like it might detonate.

"Back door was locked when I arrived." Trevor set down the box. "Front door too. The security system was armed. Whoever left this either had a key or—"

"Or they're better at breaking and entering than our security system is at detecting it." Shea pulled latex gloves from her desk drawer and snapped them on. "Could be nothing, but it could be someone dropping off information."

"Could be a threat."

"Could be that too."

Shea carefully picked up the envelope and felt its weight. Something solid inside, small and flat. Not a bomb. Wrong shape and weight. She slit it open with a letter opener and then tilted the contents onto her desk blotter.

A playing card fell out. King of Spades. And beneath it, a folded piece of paper.

Trevor moved closer as Shea unfolded the note. The handwriting was neat, almost architectural in its precision:

Sheriff Callahan,

Congratulations on your recent victory. Thirty-three arrests, considerable assets seized, headlines proclaiming justice served. Quite impressive.

But you and I both know the game isn't over. The house always wins in the end. It's simply a matter of time and odds.

I propose a conversation. Just you and me. No

federal agents, no backup, no wire. There's a matter we need to discuss regarding our mutual acquaintances in custody.

Tonight, 10 PM. The old Morrison grain mill, Highway 49 near the county line. Come alone, or don't come at all.

I promise you, Sheriff—this meeting will be worth your while.

—MW

"Marcus Wade." Trevor read over her shoulder. "He's calling you out."

Shea studied the card. King of Spades, the death card in some traditions. A threat or a message or both. "He wants to negotiate. Probably trying to leverage information about Rothmore's operation in exchange for immunity. Or he wants to negotiate a release."

"Or he wants to kill you." Trevor picked up the card with his own gloved hand, examining it. "This is classic intimidation. The dramatic note, the symbolic card, the isolated location. He's trying to control the situation, put you on the defensive."

"It's working." Shea pulled out her phone and photographed the note and card. "I need to call the FBI. Lincoln needs to know Wade's made contact."

She dialed, put the phone on speaker. Lincoln answered on the second ring, his voice carrying that permanent edge of someone managing too many cases simultaneously.

"Sheriff Callahan. Please tell me you have good news."

"Mixed news. Marcus Wade just invited me to a meeting. Tonight, ten PM, Morrison grain mill."

Silence on the other end. Then: "He sent you a written invitation to meet at an isolated location?"

"Playing card and everything. Very theatrical."

"It's a trap," Lincoln said flatly. "He wants you alone so he can eliminate the person who dismantled his boss's operation. You're not going."

"I'm absolutely going," Shea corrected. "This is our chance to bring him in. He's been underground for three weeks. We don't know where he's hiding, who's helping him, or what resources he has left. If he's reaching out—"

"Then he's desperate," the agent interrupted. "Which makes him unpredictable and dangerous. Sheriff, I appreciate your courage, but I cannot authorize a civilian law enforcement officer to walk into what is obviously an ambush."

"Good thing I'm not asking for authorization." Shea kept her tone professional but firm. "This is my jurisdiction. My case. My decision."

"Your funeral," he muttered. Then, louder: "Fine. But we do this properly. Full tactical support. Surveillance teams, sharpshooters, SWAT on standby. We turn that grain mill into a fortress before Wade shows up."

"He'll spot federal presence from a mile away,"

Shea argued. "The note said to come alone. If I bring an army, he disappears, and we're back to square one."

"If you go alone, you die. Those are your options. Pick the one that keeps you breathing."

Trevor was already shaking his head. Shea could read his expression: *No way in hell are you doing this alone.*

"Compromise," Shea said. "Trevor comes with me. We approach carefully, maintain a position where we can see Wade, but he can't trap us. You have federal teams staged two miles out, ready to move on my signal. But invisible until I need them."

Lincoln was quiet for a moment. "This is against every procedure in the book."

"Procedures didn't bring down Rothmore's syndicate."

"No, but almost getting yourself killed multiple times did." The agent sighed, the sound of a man accepting reality he didn't like. "Okay. Trevor goes with you. You wear vests, you maintain cover, you do not—I repeat, do not—let Wade close the distance. First sign of trouble, you signal, and we come in hard. Clear?"

"Crystal."

"And Sheriff? Wade was Rothmore's head of operations. He's killed people. Probably dozens. He's not going to politely surrender because you show up with a badge and good intentions."

"I know what he is," Shea said quietly. "That's

exactly why I need to be there."

After she hung up, Trevor leaned against her desk, arms crossed. "You know this is insane."

"Completely."

"He's going to try to kill you."

"Probably."

"And you're going anyway."

"Wouldn't be the first time." Shea met his eyes. "I need you to trust me on this. Wade wants something—information, leverage, maybe just the satisfaction of looking me in the eye. Whatever it is, it's an opportunity. We can't let it slip away."

"I trust you," Trevor said. "I don't trust him. There's a difference."

The mill had been abandoned for fifteen years, a slowly collapsing structure of rusted metal and rotting wood on twenty acres of overgrown industrial wasteland. Three main buildings connected by elevated walkways, surrounded by empty grain silos that looked like massive concrete tombstones. Multiple entry points, endless hiding spots, sight lines that favored defenders over approaching targets.

"Perfect ambush location." Trevor studied satellite imagery on Shea's computer. "High ground positions here, here, and here." He pointed to the silos. "These drainage ditches limit our approach. If Wade has backup, they could pin us down from multiple angles."

"Then we don't let ourselves get pinned." Shea traced a route with her finger. "We approach from the east, use this access road. Park a quarter mile out, move in on foot. Stay in cover, maintain distance, keep our backs to clear terrain so we can retreat if necessary."

"And if he's inside one of the buildings?"

"We don't go inside. We make him come to us, meet in the open where we can see threats coming."

Trevor didn't look convinced, but he nodded. "I'll take point. You stay behind me, use me as cover."

"We go together," Shea corrected. "Side by side. Partners."

"Partners don't let partners walk into obvious deathtraps."

"Sure, they do. They make sure they're both wearing body armor when they do it."

Evening crept toward night with agonizing slowness. Shea tried to do paperwork, tried to focus on normal sheriff business—a domestic disturbance complaint, budget requests, a stolen tractor report. But her mind kept circling back to the grain mill, to Marcus Wade, to the playing card sitting in an evidence bag on her desk.

The house always wins.

At eight PM, Lincoln called with final tactical arrangements. FBI teams were positioned in a perimeter two miles out. Far enough to remain invisible, close enough to respond within three minutes of Shea's signal. Local state police had been notified but told to stay clear unless specifically requested. This was a federal operation now, which meant if things went sideways, at least Shea wouldn't face another jurisdictional review.

Small mercies.

At nine-fifteen, Shea and Trevor geared up in the sheriff's office. Body armor over civilian clothes. No uniforms. Nothing that screamed law enforcement. Pistols in hip holsters, backup weapons at ankle and small of the back. Tactical lights, extra magazines, and first aid kits. They looked like they were preparing for war, which wasn't far from the truth.

"Last chance to call this off." Trevor checked his Glock's action for the third time.

"Not a chance."

"Didn't think so. Had to try."

They took Trevor's truck, which was newer, more reliable, and had better sight lines than Shea's aging F-150. The drive to the grain mill took twenty-three minutes, Highway 49 cutting through darkness broken only by occasional farmhouse lights and the distant glow of Fayetteville on the horizon.

The access road was gravel, with potholes nearly invisible behind overgrown bushes. Trevor killed the headlights half a mile out, navigating by moonlight and memory. When they reached the quarter-mile mark, he pulled off into a clearing and killed the engine.

Silence settled like a physical weight. No traffic sounds, no animal calls, just wind through dead grass and the distant creak of rusting metal.

"Radio check," Trevor said quietly.

Shea activated her comm unit. "Lincoln, you reading me?"

"Loud and clear, Sheriff. We're in position. Say the word, and we're moving."

"Stand by. We're going in."

They moved through the darkness with weapons drawn, using the terrain for cover—drainage ditches, abandoned equipment, piles of rotting lumber. The grain mill emerged from the shadows like something from a nightmare, its broken windows and sagging roofline silhouetted against the night sky.

No lights. No visible movement. Just stillness and decay and the feeling of being watched.

Trevor touched Shea's arm and pointed. A black SUV was maybe thirty yards from the main building. Recent model, clean despite the dirt road. Someone was here.

They circled wide, approaching from an angle that kept the building between them and the SUV. Shea's heart hammered against her ribs, adrenaline singing through her bloodstream. Every shadow could hide a threat. Every sound could be movement.

"Sheriff Callahan!" The voice echoed from inside the main building. Male, confident, and carrying the smooth quality of someone used to being in control. "I appreciate punctuality. Please, come inside. We have much to discuss."

Trevor immediately shook his head. Shea activated her comm. "Lincoln, target has verbally confirmed presence. Requesting we engage inside the structure."

"Negative," the agent's voice crackled back. "Do not enter the building. Repeat, do not enter. Too many variables, too many ambush points."

Shea raised her voice. "We talk out here, Wade. In the open. Where I can see you."

Silence. Then laughter, genuine and unsettling. "You're smarter than I gave you credit for, Sheriff. Very well. Open-air negotiation, it is." Wade stepped from the building.

But Shea noticed the bulge under his jacket. Armed. Definitely armed.

He stopped twenty feet from the building entrance, far enough to maintain distance but close enough to be clearly visible in the moonlight. "Deputy Bolton. I wasn't expecting company."

"Disappointed?" Trevor steadied his weapon on Wade's center mass.

"Merely noting your presence. I did ask the sheriff to come alone." Wade's eyes fixed on Shea. "You're causing me considerable inconvenience, Sheriff. Rothmore's arrest, the asset seizures, thirty-three of my colleagues in federal custody. That's going to take years to rebuild."

"You're not rebuilding anything," Shea said. "You're going to join them in custody. This is over."

"Is it?" Wade smiled, and there was nothing warm in the expression. "I still have resources. Connections. Money hidden in places your FBI friends will never find. I could disappear—South America, Eastern Europe, Southeast Asia. Start over, build a new operation. Hell, I've done it twice before."

"Then why reach out?" Shea kept her weapon trained on him. "Why risk meeting if you can just disappear?"

"Because you interest me." Wade took a step forward.

"Stay where you are," Trevor barked.

Wade stopped, his hands still visible. "I've been in this business twenty-three years, Sheriff. I've dealt with federal agents, state police, cartel enforcers, military contractors. But you are different. You infiltrated our organization. You extracted hostages. You took a shot that should have been impossible and made it look easy. That's rare. That's valuable."

"Get to the point," Shea said.

"The point is simple. I want to hire you."

The words hung in the night air, absurd and surreal.

"You're out of your mind," Trevor said.

"I'm practical," Wade corrected. "Rothmore's operation is finished, yes. But there are others. Networks that need security, operations that need someone with your particular skillset. I'm offering you a position with excellent pay, complete autonomy, the chance to actually make a difference rather than fighting bureaucracy in a nothing county in Arkansas."

"You're offering me a chance to become a

criminal," Shea said flatly. The man had nerve trying to buy her.

"I'm offering you a chance to stop pretending the system works." Wade's voice took on an evangelical quality. "You saved six children, Sheriff. Heroic work. And what did you get for it? An official reprimand. Jurisdiction restrictions. Political pressure. The system you serve punished you for doing the right thing. How long before you realize it's broken? How long before you understand that people like us, people who get results, we're wasted working within rules designed by cowards?"

"I'm not like you," Shea said.

"Aren't you? You operated outside your jurisdiction. You shot two men. You made tactical decisions that saved lives and couldn't care less about the procedures. That's exactly what I do, Sheriff. The only difference is I get paid better, and I don't answer to politicians who think justice means paperwork."

Something cold settled in her gut. Because underneath the recruitment pitch, she heard the truth: he was desperate. He'd lost his boss, lost his organization, lost his power. And now he was trying to rebuild by converting the person who'd destroyed everything.

"I'm not interested," Shea said. "Last chance, Wade. Surrender. Get on the ground, hands behind your head. This doesn't have to end badly."

Wade's smile faded. "Actually, Sheriff, it does."

He moved fast, impossibly fast for someone his

size. His hand went to his jacket, emerging with a pistol already clearing leather.

Shea fired.

The shot caught Wade in the right shoulder, spinning him backwards. But he didn't go down. He didn't even slow. His gun came up, muzzle flash lighting the darkness as he returned fire.

Shea dove left behind a rusted fuel tank as rounds sparked off metal where she'd been standing. Trevor fired three times, controlled bursts, forcing Wade to shift his aim.

"Lincoln, we're engaged!" Shea shouted into her comm. "Target is armed and hostile, need immediate support."

"Three minutes out."

Three minutes. An eternity in a firefight.

Wade retreated toward the building, firing suppressing shots that kept Shea and Trevor pinned. Blood darkened his jacket shoulder, but his gun hand was steady.

"You made the wrong choice, Sheriff!" Wade's voice echoed off metal and concrete. "We could have built something together."

More gunfire. This time from the silos. Multiple shooters, high ground positions, exactly what Trevor had predicted. Rounds kicked up dirt around the fuel tank, punched through rusted metal, and forced Shea to press herself flat against the ground.

"He's got backup." Trevor returned fire with three-round bursts toward the silos. "At least two shooters, maybe three."

Shea's mind raced through options. They were pinned down, outnumbered, and taking fire from multiple angles. The FBI was three minutes away—might as well be three hours. If they stayed here, they'd be overwhelmed. If they retreated, Wade would escape.

Neither option was acceptable.

"Trevor, suppressing fire on the silos. I'm flanking left, going for Wade."

"Shea, no—"

But she already moved low and fast, using abandoned equipment for cover. Rounds tracked her movement, close enough that she felt the supersonic crack of near misses. Her body armor would stop center mass shots, but head hits, leg hits, anything outside the protective zone…those would kill her just fine.

Wade was at the building entrance, reloading. He saw Shea coming and brought his weapon up.

She fired twice, both rounds hitting his center mass. The armor he was wearing absorbed the impacts. But the force staggered him backward and bought her precious seconds.

Shea closed the distance, her weapon trained on Wade's head. "On the ground. Now."

Wade's eyes met hers, and she saw the calculation there, the split-second decision tree of a man weighing odds. Then his hand moved, not bringing up his weapon but reaching for something at his belt.

A grenade.

"Shea!" Trevor's voice sounded distant and desperate.

Time slowed. Wade's thumb was on the pin. If he pulled it, if he dropped it between them, they were both dead. The building would collapse, federal backup would find bodies in the rubble, and Wade's backup would disappear into the darkness.

Shea made her choice.

She dove forward, inside Wade's guard, her left hand grabbing his wrist as her right hand brought her pistol up under his jaw. They collided, the grenade clattering away still pinned, both of them going down hard on concrete and gravel.

Wade was stronger, bigger, heavier, and trained in close combat. His fist caught her temple. Stars exploded across her vision. He grabbed for her weapon and tried to wrench it away.

But Shea had years of taking down drunk farmers and meth-addicted drifters twice her size. She knew how to fight dirty, to use leverage rather than strength. Her knee came up hard into Wade's injured shoulder. He screamed, grip loosening.

She rolled, came up on top, pistol pressed against his chest.

"Don't move."

Wade froze, breathing hard, blood soaking his shoulder.

The gunfire from the silos had stopped. Shea

risked a glance. Trevor stood with his weapon trained toward the structures. The backup shooters were either down or retreating.

"Clear!" Trevor shouted. Then, moving toward them: "Shea, you okay?"

"Yeah. I've got Wade."

But Wade still stared at her with those calculating eyes. Still thinking, still planning. His hand twitched toward his belt. Not the grenade, something else.

"Don't," Shea warned.

He smiled. "You won't shoot an unarmed man."

"Try me."

His hand moved.

The gunshot echoed across the grain mill. Not from Shea's weapon, but from somewhere behind her. Wade's head snapped back, a neat hole appearing in his forehead. He collapsed, instantly dead, his expression frozen in surprise.

Shea spun, weapon raised—

Trevor stood fifteen feet away, his pistol still aimed where Wade had been, his face grim and certain.

"He was reaching for a backup weapon," Trevor said quietly. "Behind his belt. I saw it."

Shea looked back at Wade's body. Sure enough, partially visible behind his belt buckle, a small pistol in an ankle holster that he'd been shifting his hand toward.

"Good shot," she said, her voice steadier than she felt.

"He was going to kill you."

"I know."

Headlights cut through the darkness, multiple vehicles, moving fast. The FBI had arrived, three minutes turning into two and change. Agents swarmed the grain mill, securing the perimeter, calling out clearances as they swept the silos.

Lincoln marched to Shea, his gaze taking in the scene: Wade's body, the scattered shell casings, the blood on Shea's face where Wade had hit her.

"You okay?"

"Better than him." She holstered her weapon, suddenly exhausted beyond measure. "His backup—the shooters in the silos—"

"We got two of them," an FBI agent reported, approaching. "One dead, one wounded, and in custody. Third one got away on foot, but we have helicopters searching."

Lincoln examined Wade's body. "He came prepared. This wasn't a negotiation. This was an execution attempt."

"Except he tried to recruit me first," Shea said. "Wanted me to join whatever operation he was planning to rebuild. When I refused, he decided I was too dangerous to leave alive."

"Good thing you're hard to kill." He stood and gestured to the FBI agents. "Bag everything. Document everything. This is going to be reviewed six ways from Sunday. Officer-involved shooting, federal operation, jurisdiction questions. Again."

Trevor's placed a hand on her shoulder, steady and grounding. "Let them handle it. You need medical attention."

"I'm fine."

"You're bleeding from your temple, and you just went hand-to-hand with a trained killer. You're going to the hospital."

Shea wanted to argue, wanted to stay and manage the scene, and maintain control. But her head was pounding, her body was starting to register the impacts and bruises, and frankly, she was tired of fighting.

"Okay," she said. "Hospital. But you're driving."

They walked back toward Trevor's truck, leaving the FBI to their documentation and evidence collection. Behind them, the grain mill blazed with portable lights, agents swarming like ants on a disturbed hill.

"You killed him," Shea said quietly.

"I did." Trevor's voice held no hesitation, no doubt. "He was reaching for a weapon. He would have shot you. I made the call."

"Thank you."

"That's what partners do." Trevor opened the truck door for her. "They keep each other alive."

Shea climbed in, leaning back against the seat. Through the windshield, she stared at the grain mill, the lights, the organized chaos of federal agents doing their work. Marcus Wade was dead. The syndicate was truly dismantled now, its leadership in custody or killed.

It was over.

Except it wasn't, not really. There would be investigations, reviews, and more reports to file. Questions about why she'd agreed to meet Wade, whether proper protocols were followed, and if the shooting was justified. The machinery of institutional authority would grind forward, examining, judging, and second-guessing.

But that was tomorrow's problem. Tonight, she was alive. Trevor was alive. Wade was dead, and six families still had their children, and sometimes that was enough.

Trevor started the engine and navigated carefully back toward the highway. His hand found hers in the darkness, fingers interlacing.

"We make a good team"

"The best," Shea agreed.

And as they drove toward Misty Hollow, toward the hospital and paperwork and whatever came next, Shea allowed herself to believe it.

Together, they could handle anything.

Even the house didn't always win.

Sometimes, if you were smart enough and brave enough and had the right partner beside you…Sometimes you beat the odds.

Chapter Twenty-One

Three months later, Misty Hollow looked like itself again.

Shea stood on the courthouse steps, coffee in hand, watching Main Street come alive with morning routines. Normal. Comfortable. Home.

"You're thinking too loud." Trevor stepped beside her with his own coffee. He'd taken to meeting her here before the shift. Not arriving together, maintaining that professional boundary, but finding these moments before the workday demanded they be sheriff and deputy rather than whatever they were becoming.

"Just watching the town," Shea said. "Remembering how it looked three months ago."

"Scared. Angry. Fractured." Trevor sipped his coffee. "Now look at it. People feel safe again. That's your doing."

"Our doing," Shea corrected.

They'd filed the HR paperwork two months ago.

Disclosure of romantic relationship, acknowledgment of potential conflicts of interest, and agreement to maintain professional boundaries during work hours. The county administrator had reviewed it with the enthusiasm of someone doing an audit, asked pointed questions about command structure and decision-making protocols, then stamped it approved with a reminder that any perceived favoritism would be grounds for review.

So far, so good. Trevor still called her "Sheriff" at work, still followed the chain of command, still maintained the professional distance they'd always had. But after hours, when they weren't wearing badges, it was different. There were dinners at Shea's house, Saturday mornings spent at Trevor's place, conversations that stretched into the early hours about everything and nothing.

It was complicated. It was also the best relationship Shea had ever had.

"Bill Miller's being released today." Trevor checked his phone. "Hospital discharge scheduled for ten AM. Becky's picking him up."

"I heard. He called yesterday, wanted to thank me again." Shea had stopped counting how many times Bill had expressed gratitude for her rescuing Ryan, for helping dismantle the syndicate, for not treating him like just another criminal. "Prosecution finalized his deal. Two years probation, five hundred hours of community service, and mandatory counseling."

"Could have been twenty years," Trevor observed.

"Could have been. But he cooperated, testified against everyone in Rothmore's organization, and provided evidence that led to seventeen additional arrests. Federal prosecutors got what they needed."

They walked toward the sheriff's office, falling into a comfortable rhythm. Inside, Deputy Butler manned the front desk, fielding a call about someone's cow getting loose again.

"Morning, Sheriff. Deputy Bolton." Butler covered the phone receiver. "Henderson's Angus is in the Johnsons' corn again. Third time this month."

"Tell Johnson we'll send someone out," Shea said. "And tell Henderson if it happens again, we're citing him for negligent livestock management."

"Yes, ma'am."

The office felt different now—busier, more professional. They'd hired two additional deputies after the syndicate case, upgrading from a skeleton crew to something approaching adequate staffing. The county council had approved the budget increase without much argument, still riding the goodwill from Shea's official reprimand that everyone understood was really recognition.

Shea settled at her desk and started working through the morning reports. Domestic disturbance— resolved without arrest. Traffic accident on Highway 49—minor injuries, no citations issued. Suspicious person reported near the old Morrison grain mill—

She paused, reading that one twice. The grain mill. Where Marcus Wade had died. Where she'd nearly died.

"Trevor, look at this."

He came over and read the report. "Kids, probably. Teenagers exploring the abandoned building, looking for thrills. Want me to check it out?"

"I'll go with you. After we handle Henderson's cow situation."

The day unfolded with the mundane rhythm of rural law enforcement. Loose livestock, property disputes, a shoplifting complaint at the hardware store that turned out to be a misunderstanding about store credit. Normal problems. Solvable problems. The kind of work that had drawn Shea to this job in the first place.

Around noon, her phone rang. Becky.

"Shea? I'm sorry to bother you, I know you're working, but I wanted you to know that Bill's home. He's settled. He's..." Her voice caught. "He's asking to see Ryan. I told him Ryan's therapist says it needs to be gradual, supervised, but Bill's ready. He wants to start rebuilding."

"That's good, Becky. That's a positive step."

"Is it?" Becky sounded uncertain. "I keep wondering if I'm doing the right thing. Letting Bill back into Ryan's life. He put us in danger. He lied for months. How do I forgive that?"

Shea chose her words carefully. "You don't forgive it by forgetting it happened. You forgive it by acknowledging what he did. Both the mistakes and the redemption. Bill made terrible choices. But when it mattered most, he fought back. He saved his son. That has to count for something."

"Ryan has nightmares," Becky said quietly. "He wakes up screaming that bad men are taking him again. The therapist says it's normal and that trauma takes time to process. But I look at my son, and I think Bill's gambling caused this. Bill's addiction put Ryan in that basement."

"And Bill's courage got him out." Shea paused. "I'm not saying you have to trust him again. I'm not saying the relationship can go back to what it was. But maybe, just maybe, you can build something new. Something based on honest acknowledgment of what happened and who Bill is now, not who he was."

Becky was quiet for a moment. "The support group I started, for families affected by gambling addiction, Bill asked if he could speak at one of the meetings. Share his story, talk about what he went through. I don't know if I'm ready for that."

"Then tell him you're not ready. Set boundaries. Take it slow." Shea softened her tone. "But Becky? The fact that Bill's asking, that he wants to help other families avoid what you went through? That says something about where he is in his recovery."

After they hung up, Shea sat at her desk, thinking

about second chances. About redemption. About whether people could truly change or if they just became better at managing their worst impulses.

Trevor knocked on the door frame of her office. "Ready to check out that suspicious person report at the grain mill?"

"Yeah. Let's go."

They drove out to the mill in Trevor's truck, the same route they'd taken three months ago. The building looked the same. Rusted metal, broken windows, decay, and abandonment. But the FBI had removed all the crime scene tape weeks ago, declared the structure safe enough to leave standing, even if it should probably be demolished.

No signs of trespassers. No teenagers exploring. Just wind through broken glass and the creak of aging metal.

"False alarm." Trevor strolled the perimeter. "Or whoever was here already left."

Shea stood where Wade had died, looking at the concrete where Trevor's shot had ended the threat. They'd cleaned up the blood, removed the evidence, but she could still see it in her mind. Wade's calculating eyes, the reach for his backup weapon, Trevor's decisive action.

"You ever think about it?" she asked. "The shooting?"

"Every day." Trevor joined her, his shoulder brushing hers. "I think about what would have happened if I'd hesitated. If I'd second-guessed. You'd be dead. So yeah, I think about it. And every time, I know I made the right call."

"State police cleared you in two weeks. That's fast."

"That's evidence. Body camera footage showed him reaching for the weapon. FBI confirmed he had a backup pistol. The shooting was clean." Trevor turned to face her. "But the review board's determination doesn't really matter. What matters is that you're alive. That's the only outcome I care about."

Shea leaned into him briefly. Just a moment of contact. Then she stepped back, professional distance reasserting itself even though they were alone.

"We should head back. I've got that community meeting tonight."

~

The meeting was in the high school auditorium. Another full house, though this time the energy was different. Celebratory rather than tense. The mayor was presenting Shea with a commendation for her work on the syndicate case, despite the official reprimand that remained in her file.

Politics. Always politics.

Elena Reyes was in the audience, sitting near the back. She'd moved to Misty Hollow six weeks ago, opened a private investigation firm in a renovated storefront on Main Street. Business was good. Safe work, such as corporate background checks, insurance fraud investigations, and the occasional domestic case. She'd told Shea it felt good to do work where she didn't have to lie about who she was, where she could go home at night and actually sleep.

After the ceremony, complete with awkward handshakes and posed photos for the local paper, Elena caught up with Shea in the parking lot.

"Nice speech from the mayor," Elena said. "Very carefully worded to praise your results without endorsing your methods."

"That's his specialty. Political tightrope walking." Shea unlocked her truck. "How's the PI business?"

"Steady. Not exciting like federal operations, but also nobody's shooting at me. I call that a win." Elena glanced around and lowered her voice. "I heard about Wade. About the meeting at the grain mill. You okay?"

"I'm here. That's more than he can say."

"Trevor made the shot?"

"Clean kill. Wade was reaching for a backup weapon. State police cleared it without much fuss."

Elena nodded slowly. "Good. Wade was dangerous. One of those true believers who thought the rules didn't apply to him because he was smarter than everyone else. Better that he's gone."

They stood in comfortable silence for a moment, two women who'd faced violence and survived, who understood things most people never would.

"You should come to dinner," Shea said impulsively. "Tomorrow night. Nothing fancy, just barbecue and beer. Trevor will be there. Maybe bring a friend if you have one."

Elena smiled. "I'll bring potato salad. And I'm working on the friend situation. There's a librarian who keeps recommending mystery novels."

"She's a good person."

"I've noticed." Elena's smile widened. "Thanks for the invitation, Sheriff. It's nice to feel like part of a community instead of just observing from the outside."

After Elena left, Shea sat in her truck, watching the parking lot empty. Through the auditorium windows, she could see the maintenance staff starting cleanup, folding chairs, sweeping floors. Normal evening routines in a typical small town.

Her phone buzzed. Text from Trevor: *Your place or mine?*

She typed back: *Mine. I'll cook.*

You don't cook.

I order takeout very effectively.

That's my girl.

Shea started the engine, headed home through streets she knew by heart. Past the diner where she'd eaten breakfast more times than she could count. Past the hardware store where she bought supplies for her forever-unfinished home renovations. Past the park where kids were playing despite the late hour, parents were watching from benches, everything safe and ordinary.

Her house was dark when she arrived, but she'd

left the porch light on. A habit now, something that made coming home feel less empty. Inside, she loved on Heidi before changing out of her uniform, pulling on jeans and a comfortable sweater, and starting to tidy the living room, even though Trevor had seen it messy plenty of times.

He arrived twenty minutes later with Chinese takeout and a six-pack of beer.

"I know you said you were cooking, but I picked this up on the way." He kissed her hello.

"I'll reheat in the microwave. "

They settled on her couch with food and beer, the TV playing something neither of them was really watching. Trevor's arm came around her shoulders, pulling her close.

"Becky called," Shea said. "Bill's home. He wants to start rebuilding with Ryan."

"That's good, isn't it?"

"I think so. But it's going to be hard. For all of them." Shea picked at her lo mein. "Ryan's in therapy. Bill's in therapy. Becky's running a support group. Everyone's trying to heal from what happened." She tossed a noodle to Heidi, who caught it mid-air.

"That's what people do," Trevor said. "They survive trauma, then they do the hard work of recovering from it. Doesn't mean they forget. Doesn't mean it doesn't leave scars. But they move forward."

"You speaking from experience?"

Trevor was quiet for a moment. "You can't tell

me you forgot about Troy."

"No, I can't." How could she forget how close Trevor came to being killed by his serial killer twin? "Bill Miller's got a long road ahead. But if he's willing to walk it, if he's genuinely committed to being better, then maybe Ryan gets to have a father who shows him what redemption looks like."

"And if he's not? If Bill relapses, starts gambling again, puts them in danger?"

"Then Becky protects Ryan. Sets boundaries. Does what's necessary."

Trevor pulled Shea closer. "But you can't live your life expecting the worst from people. Sometimes you have to give them room to be better than they were."

Shea leaned against him. "I'm glad you're here."

"Where else would I be?"

They finished dinner, cleaned up together, and then returned to the couch. Outside, Misty Hollow settled into the night as porch lights came on, cars pulled into driveways, and families gathered in warm houses.

"Elena's coming to dinner tomorrow," Shea said. "I invited her. Hope that's okay."

"Your house, your invitations." Trevor smiled. "Though if she's bringing potato salad, I'm making ribs. Can't have sad store-bought sides at a proper barbecue."

"You're very particular about barbecue."

"Texas upbringing. It's basically religion."

Shea laughed, feeling tension she hadn't realized she was carrying drain away. This was good. This thing they were building—relationship, partnership, whatever label applied. It felt solid. Real. Like something that could last beyond the crisis that had sparked it.

"The quarterly report is due next week," she said, grimacing. "Town council wants updates on any multi-jurisdictional coordination."

"We haven't had any. Unless you count that time we helped state police with the highway chase that crossed county lines."

"That barely counts. They asked for assistance, we provided backup, and everyone stayed in their lane." Shea sighed. "I hate the paperwork part of this job."

"Everyone hates paperwork. That's why it's an effective punishment for exceeding your authority." Trevor's tone was teasing. "Though technically you're just providing transparency, not being punished."

"Feels the same from where I'm sitting."

Her phone buzzed with a text from an unknown number. Shea frowned and opened it.

Sheriff Callahan, this is Bill Miller. I got your number from Becky. I hope it's okay to reach out. I wanted to thank you again for everything you did. For Ryan, for me, for giving me a chance when you had every reason not to. I know I can't undo the past. But I'm trying to build something better. Wanted you to know that. —Bill

Shea showed Trevor the message. "What do I say

to that?"

"The truth. That you're glad he's doing the work. That you hope he succeeds. That you'll be watching." Trevor paused. "But also that you believe in second chances when people earn them."

Shea typed carefully: *Bill, I'm glad you're home. I'm glad you're committed to recovery and rebuilding with Ryan. The road ahead won't be easy, but nothing worth doing ever is. Keep doing the work. Keep being honest. Keep showing up. That's all anyone can ask. — Sheriff Callahan*

She sent it, then set down her phone. "Think that was okay?"

"Perfect." Trevor kissed her temple. "You're good at this—the balance between accountability and compassion. It's one of the things I love about you."

Shea froze. Trevor realized what he'd said, his expression shifting from casual to careful.

"Sorry," he said. "Too soon? I know we haven't really talked about—"

"It's not too soon," Shea interrupted. "It's just...are you sure? We've been navigating this for three months. We work together. We're under institutional scrutiny. There's paperwork and policies and people watching to see if we're compromising professional judgment. And you're saying—"

"I'm saying I love you," Trevor said firmly. "Yes, it's complicated. Yes, we have to navigate policies, paperwork, and people's opinions. But none of that changes how I feel. None of that changes the fact that I want to be with you, in whatever form works for us."

Shea's chest tightened with emotions she'd been carefully managing. "I don't know how to do this. The relationship part. I've spent so long being in law enforcement, defining myself by the job, that I don't know how to be someone who also has this. Who also has you."

"Then we figure it out together," Trevor said. "Same way we figure out everything else. We communicate. We set boundaries. We make mistakes and learn from them. We show up for each other, even when it's hard. Especially when it's hard."

"You make it sound simple."

"It's not simple. But it's worth it." Trevor cupped her face, his thumb brushing across her cheekbone. "You're worth it. This is worth navigating the complications."

Shea kissed him, slow and deep and full of everything she didn't quite have words for yet. When they separated, she pressed her forehead against his.

"I love you too," she said quietly. "In case that wasn't clear."

"It's clear now." Trevor smiled, that rare full smile that transformed his usually serious face. "So, what do we do with this information?"

"We keep doing what we've been doing. We work together professionally. We come home to each other. We figure out the rest as we go." Shea settled back against him. "And maybe, eventually, we stop feeling like we have to justify this to anyone but ourselves."

They sat in comfortable silence, the TV still playing unwatched, the evening settling around them like a familiar blanket. Heidi curled up at their feet.

Outside, Misty Hollow slept, safe and ordinary, the kind of place where the biggest problems were loose cattle and teenagers at abandoned grain mills.

Shea's phone buzzed again. Another text from Bill Miller: *Thank you, Sheriff. That means more than you know. I won't let you down.*

She hoped he meant it. That was all anyone could ask.

"What are you thinking?" Trevor asked.

"About second chances. About whether people can really change or if they just become better at managing who they've always been."

"Both, probably." Trevor's hand found hers, fingers interlacing. "We're all managing who we've always been while trying to become something better. That's just being human."

"Very philosophical for a Tuesday night."

"I have my moments."

Shea laughed, feeling the last of her tension dissolve. This was good. This life they were building—professional partnership, romantic relationship, shared commitment to protecting their community. It was messy and complicated, and sometimes felt impossible to balance.

But it was theirs.

And in the end, that was enough.

Three months after dismantling a criminal syndicate. Three months after nearly dying at an abandoned grain mill. Three months after making choices that had cost her an official reprimand, but saved six children's lives.

And tomorrow she'd wake up, put on her uniform, and do it all again. Handle loose cattle, property disputes, and the mundane challenges of rural law enforcement. Come home to Trevor. Navigate the complications of their relationship with honesty and intention.

Live a life that mattered, measured not in headlines or commendations but in small moments of connection and community and choosing to show up even when it was hard.

Later, sleep came easily, dreamless and deep. And when morning arrived, when Shea's alarm went off, and she had to face another day of being sheriff, she'd be ready.

Because she wasn't facing it alone.

Because Trevor would be there, solid and steady and certain.

Because Misty Hollow was home, and worth fighting for, and sometimes the best you could do was show up and do the work and trust that it mattered.

And in the darkness of her bedroom, Shea knew it did matter.

All of it.

Every choice, every risk, every moment of courage and doubt and determination.

It mattered.

And tomorrow, she'd prove it again.

www.cynthiahickey.com
Cynthia Hickey is a multi-published and best-selling author of cozy mysteries and romantic suspense/thrillers. She has taught writing at many conferences and small writing retreats. She and her husband run the publishing press, Winged Publications. They live in Arizona and Arkansas, becoming snowbirds with three dogs. They have ten grandchildren who keep them busy and tell everyone they know that "Nana is a writer."

Connect with me on FaceBook
Twitter
Sign up for my newsletter and receive a free short story
www.cynthiahickey.com

Follow me on Amazon
And Bookbub
Shop my bookstore on my website for better prices and autographed books.

Enjoy other books by Cynthia Hickey

Romantic Suspense and Thrillers

The Sheriff of Misty Hollow
Girls' Weekend Survival

Stay in Misty Hollow for a while. Get the entire series here!

Secrets of the South
The Lovers' Lane Murders
The Prom Night Hitchhiker
Up in Smoke

The Seven Deadly Sins series
Deadly Pride
Deadly Covet
Deadly Lust
Deadly Glutton
Deadly Envy
Deadly Sloth
Deadly Anger
Get the whole set here

Brothers Steele
Sharp as Steele
Carved in Steele
Forged in Steele
Brothers Steele (All three in one)

The Brothers of Copper Pass
Wyatt's Warrant
Dirk's Defense
Stetson's Secret
Houston's Hope
Dallas's Dare
Seth's Sacrifice
Malcolm's Misunderstanding

HIGH STAKES

The Game
Suspicious Minds
After the Storm
Local Betrayal
Hearts of Courage Boxed Set

Overcoming Evil series
Mistaken Assassin
Captured Innocence
Mountain of Fear
Exposure at Sea
A Secret to Die for
Collision Course
Romantic Suspense of 5 books in 1

Wife for Hire – Private Investigators
Saving Sarah
Lesson for Lacey
Mission for Meghan
Long Way for Lainie
Aimed at Amy
Wife for Hire (all five in one)

One Hour (A short story thriller)
One Night (a short story thriller)

COZY MYSTERIES

The Tail Waggin' Mysteries
Cat-Eyed Witness
The Dog Who Found a Body

Troublesome Twosome
Four-Legged Suspect
Unwanted Christmas Guest
Wedding Day Cat Burglar
The entire Tail Waggin' Series

Tiny House Mysteries
No Small Caper
Caper Goes Missing
Caper Finds a Clue
Caper's Dark Adventure
A Strange Game for Caper
Caper Steals Christmas
Caper Finds a Treasure
Tiny House Mysteries boxed set

A Hollywood Murder
Killer Pose, book 1
Killer Snapshot, book 2
Shoot to Kill, book 3
Kodak Kill Shot, book 4
To Snap a Killer
Hollywood Murder Mysteries

Shady Acres Mysteries
Beware the Orchids
Path to Nowhere
Poison Foliage
Poinsettia Madness
Deadly Greenhouse Gases

Vine Entrapment
Shady Acres Boxed Set

Nosy Neighbor Series
Anything For A Mystery
A Killer Plot
Skin Care Can Be Murder
Death By Baking
Jogging Is Bad For Your Health
Poison Bubbles
A Good Party Can Kill You
Nosy Neighbor collection

Christmas with Stormi Nelson

The Summer Meadows Series
Fudge-Laced Felonies
Candy-Coated Secrets
Chocolate-Covered Crime
Maui Macadamia Madness
All four novels in one collection

The River Valley Mystery Series
Deadly Neighbors
Advance Notice
The Librarian's Last Chapter
All three novels in one collection

Cozies not part of a series
Coffee, Tea, or Murder
Scones to Die For

Mischief and Mayhem

Time Travel
The Portal

Historical cozy
Hazel's Quest

Historical Romances
Novellas
Runaway Sue
Taming the Sheriff
Sweet Apple Blossom
A Doctor's Agreement
A Lady Maid's Honor
A Touch of Sugar
Love Over Par
Heart of the Emerald
A Sketch of Gold
Her Lonely Heart
Abigail's Proposal
Sophia's Hope
Moira's Quest
Savannah's Trial
Josephine's Dream
A Most Reluctant Bride
Competing Hearts
A Teacher's Heart
Lesson of Love

SERIES
Finding Love the Harvey Girl Way
Cooking With Love
Guiding With Love
Serving With Love
Warring With Love
All 4 in 1

Finding Love in Disaster
The Rancher's Dilemma
The Teacher's Rescue
The Soldier's Redemption

Woman of courage Series

A Love For Delicious
Ruth's Redemption
Charity's Gold Rush
Mountain Redemption
They Call Her Mrs. Sheriff
Woman of Courage series

Short Story Westerns
Flowers of the Desert

Contemporary

Romance in Paradise
Maui Magic
Sunset Kisses

CYNTHIA HICKEY

Deep Sea Love
3 in 1

The Red Hat's Club (Contemporary novellas)

Finally
Suddenly
Surprisingly
The Red Hat's Club 3 – in 1

STANDALONES
Finding a Way Home
Service of Love
Hillbilly Cinderella
Unraveling Love
I'd Rather Kiss My Horse

Whisper Sweet Nothings (a Valentine short romance)

Christmas Romances (Contemporary and Historical)
Dear Jillian
Romancing the Fabulous Cooper Brothers
Handcarved Christmas
The Payback Bride
Curtain Calls and Christmas Wishes
Chrithmas Gold
A Christmas Stamp
Snowflake Kisses
Merry's Secret Santa
Holly's Hope

A Christmas Deception
A Christmas Castle

317